I0779698

WINNER TAKES ALL

AMANDA BRYK

Winner Takes All
Copyright © May 2025 by Amanda Bryk

First Edition

All Rights reserved.
No portion of this book may be reproduced,
stored in a retrieval system, or transmitted in any form by any
means-electronic, mechanical, photocopy, recording, or other-
except for brief quotations in print reviews, without prior
permission of the author.

Paperback: 978-1-962608-06-0
ebook: 978-1-962608-07-7

Cover Design: Ashley Morgan

WINNER TAKES ALL

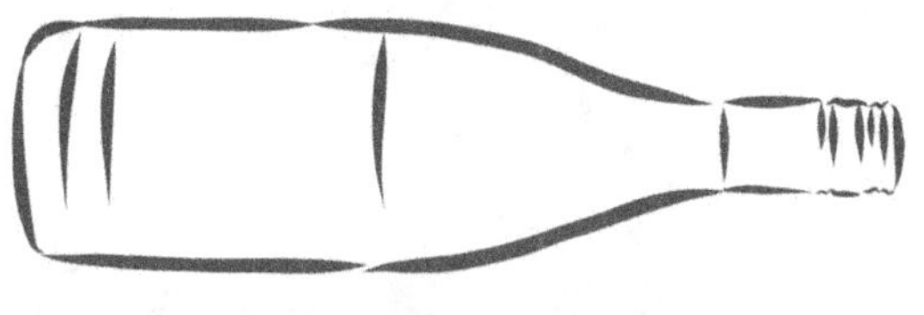

AMANDA BRYK

To the person who loves me,

on my best days and my worst.

May our years be filled with shared memories,

book shopping, and brunch.

CHAPTER 1
ALEXIS

I restart the tutorial from the beginning and watch the video for a third time, pausing when she gets to the eyes. "I have to get this right," I say the words aloud as if I need verbal confirmation.

The art of applying a full face of flawless makeup exists so far outside my wheelhouse that it might as well reside on another planet. But what I lack in talent, I make up for in *natural beauty*, or so I've been told. When I look at the mirror, I feel like I've been lied to, but there's no room for self-doubt in the plans for this evening.

The perfect wing-tipped black eyeliner is my current obsession, New Year's resolution, and ultimate life goal. I press the silicone stencil firmly in place and channel my best impression of a girl who knows what she's doing.

"Okay, that's not terrible. Now for the easy part." The sarcasm in my tone is evident even though I'm the only one listening. Muttering a silent prayer, I resign myself to the truth. Divine intervention might be my only hope for matching results on the other side.

I exhale deeply to steady my shaking hand.

My left eye looks pretty good, leaving the dominant side still to be done. According to the advice given by the twenty-something-year-old in the video, this should yield the best chances for a symmetrical outcome.

I can't cross my fingers for luck and draw the perfect line. So, for the first of many times tonight, I'll need to believe in myself and go for it.

Since when do I care so much about color-correcting foundation, lip stains, coordinating palettes, liquid eyeliner, and non-clumping mascara? Since Friday, around lunchtime, when a particularly handsome gentleman asked me to be his date for this evening.

...

When I signed up for Mid-thirties Mingle, I assumed it would be like every other dating app out there, promising the world topped off with a bow while delivering the same old broken-down bullshit. It wouldn't have surprised me in the least if all I'd received were thinly veiled requests for sex and poorly crafted dick pics. After all, I'd tried nearly every app the internet offered and had yet to be impressed. I started to think maybe I was too picky.

If I'm being honest, I was one rejection away from lowering my standards, dropping the height requirement, and eliminating any mention of higher education. But, when I added my honest wish list for a potential partner into the lengthy questionnaire, seven profiles appeared on my screen.

As I flipped through every photo and read over each profile, my dating pool dried like a shallow puddle on a suffocatingly hot summer day, narrowing my selection to one. Riley Sinclair. Thirty-four years old, six-foot-two, athletic, light brown hair, enchanting green eyes, never married, no kids, works as a financial consultant in the city.

Somehow, the man had me giddy, even in digital photo form.

It took me a moment to gather my courage, but eventually, I typed out a text and convinced myself the right man would appreciate a confident woman. Or rather, that was the persona I hoped to convey with my introductory message. But I never had the opportunity to hit send. As I sat behind my computer, working up the nerve, an alert chimed, and a private chat box opened at the bottom of my screen.

Riley would like to send you a message. Do you accept? Please respond Yes or No to continue.

Without warning, my heart lodged into my throat, leaving me thankful my fingers would be responsible for talking. The response was an immediate YES, and so began one of the best online exchanges I'd had in ages. We spent the rest of the day deep in conversation, toiling over the details. It was impressive how much we had in common, and by that evening, he no longer felt like a stranger. The next day, when he asked me on a date, my stomach did a series of cartwheels while I read over his lengthy invitation.

Sunday night, I have a table reserved at Seventy-Two South. A group of us are planning to watch game seven of the championship, and you mentioned being a fan of local sports. I thought it might be a fun first date. Two of the guys are bringing their wives, so I can assure you everyone will be on their best behavior. Not sure if my roommate is inviting anyone. Fair warning: you might be the rose between two thorns. Does a group date make things more or less awkward? What do you think? If you aren't enjoying yourself, you can kick me under the table, and we can make our escape. I want to watch the game, but I'd rather spend time with you.

Could I risk saying no? Not a chance.

Despite my persistent overthinking, I'd never had an issue connecting with strangers in social situations and often made fast friends. If I used active listening skills instead of sitting there with glazed eyes, waiting for my turn to talk, there was always common ground to build on. A group date wouldn't have been my first choice, but I'd never been afraid to try new things.

Sounds like fun. I'd love to meet, if you don't think they'll mind you bringing a plus one. What time should I plan to be there?

The reservation is for 6:00 pm, but everyone's meeting at the house around 5:00. We rented a party bus to take us downtown. I promise we're not a pack of drunken ex-frat boy assholes out to relive our younger days. This option is cheaper and safer once you factor in parking and a possible DUI. You can leave your car at the house and ride with us if you'd like, or I could call in a favor and make sure you have a spot reserved at the restaurant. Whatever you feel more comfortable with.

He seemed to go out of his way to be accommodating, and I wondered if it was all an act for my benefit or a glimpse into his genuine nature. I assumed time would reveal all in short measure. Men were generally easy to read, and the façade tended to crumble quickly as the end of the date approached.

...

I critique the appearance of the woman staring back at me in the mirror and swallow any lingering apprehension. "It's only a first date, not till death do us part. What's the worst that can happen?"

I'm old enough to know better and smart enough to think ahead. I'm taking my car and meeting him in a public place. I shared his dating profile and our plans for the night with my best friend, who warned me to be careful. I thoroughly stalked his public profiles, including his LinkedIn account and his employer's website. I even looked into his friends who were included in the photos. I've done my due diligence, and now I'm ready to meet the man behind the messages that have had me smiling from ear to ear.

I unlock my phone and open the app to find our conversation where I left it. We've talked quite a bit since Friday, so it takes me a moment to scroll to the top, find the restaurant's name, and triple-check the time. Seventy-Two South is an upscale steak house with rave reviews. I know because I looked it up when Riley asked me out. And the time of our date, 6:00 pm, is seared into my memory. I'm not sure why I'm even looking at the message other than to calm my nerves and convince myself that all of this is real.

> I'm leaving the house now. If I get to the restaurant before you, should I wait at the bar? Do you think you'll be able to pick me out of a crowd?

His response comes almost instantly, despite its length, and I wonder if he said the words aloud or simply possesses impressive dexterity.

> Considering you're the most beautiful woman I've ever seen, and I've been looking at your pictures constantly for the last three days. Yeah, I'm pretty sure I'll recognize you. But I don't like the idea of you waiting at the bar alone, so when you get there, tell the hostess the reservation is under Kade. We'll see you soon. I'm looking forward to tonight, Alexis.

I smile and tuck the phone back into my pocket. My body is a jumble of emotions, but I'll need to get on the road if I plan to make it to the restaurant on time.

In high school, my choir teacher had a large wooden sign above her desk that read, *Early is on time, on time is late, and late is unacceptable.* I must have read those words a million times over my four years in the building because, eventually, that mantra became ingrained into my personality.

Slipping into my tennis shoes, I double-check my pockets for keys, wallet, and phone before walking out the door and locking it behind me. As cute as I may be, I've never been much of a girly girl. Purses, makeup, and pretty shoes have never held my interest. I grew up with older brothers, so I played sports and video games and spent weekends in the gym trying to hit a new max on my bench press.

I might have the face of a porcelain doll, but inside, I'm not nearly as hollow and fragile as men typically think.

Driving along the freeway with the city skyline in full view, I'm surprised by the number of cars on the road. It's a Sunday evening, but this feels more like Thanksgiving traffic.

"I should've left sooner," I scold myself for the oversight and open the music app on my phone. My usual first-date playlist won't cut it, so I hit shuffle on the collection of songs labeled Workout #5.

Something about late 1990s-early 2000s music hits differently, in a way that makes me want to fight someone. Not literally. It's just a vibe. But as I cruise along the freeway, blasting my newest playlist comprised mostly of heavy metal bands of old, I know I'm ready for whatever the night has in store.

Unfortunately, the closer I get to the city, the thicker the traffic becomes, and the frustration swelling within me makes the idea of punching someone all the more tempting. I'm annoyed and horny, and the combination has left me reeling. I'd give anything to take the edge off.

Why didn't I think to rub one out before leaving the house?

I don't *need* a man to get off, but the thought of sitting on Riley Sinclair's dick has been near the forefront of my brain for the better part of the last three days. And it doesn't help that the friends featured in his profile pictures are equally orgasm-inducing. More than once, I've imagined their hands, faces, and other unmentionable parts playing out the scenes already scripted in my head, courtesy of the books loaded onto my shelves.

The ache between my thighs surges as my focus drifts. I'm never going to make it through the night if I can't get myself under control. If I get caught with wandering, lustful eyes, I'm done for. Women have a sixth sense for these things, and I'm about to be in the company of ladies who have already staked a claim. I'm the outsider, so I'll need to tread carefully.

The more I tell myself *not* to think about sex, the harder my brain latches onto the topic, and by the time I pull into the reserved parking lot next to Seventy-Two South, I'm nearly undone at the edges. I'm later than I had intended, but still five minutes early, and the oversized SUVs I've parked between offer adequate cover for a girl seeking discretion.

Popping the sunshade into my front window, I recline my seat ever so slightly and pray for a moment of privacy. A few minutes is all I need. The lust-fueled ache building between my thighs has my body tingling, intensified by the promise of a release so close at hand.

My fingers graze over the top of my panties as the seam of my jeans presses into the back of my hand, willing me to go harder. Faster. Deeper. This isn't the time or the place for playful teasing. I need to get off quickly before I get caught. With the game set to start in an hour and the city bursting with pre-drunk spectators, there's practically a cop stationed on every corner.

I turn my head and glance out the back window, checking again to make sure the coast is clear, before squeezing my eyes shut. I circle my clit with a fevered pace, and it isn't long before I'm able to manifest Riley in the passenger seat and the largest member of his friend group over my shoulder in the back.

"You feel so good," I moan under my breath as my body begs for more. "Please, don't stop. You have no idea how badly I've needed this."

The two men take turns telling me, in graphic detail, exactly what they plan to do with me. Riley's well-tailored professionalism hints at his need to be in control, making him the perfect dominant. His friend, on the other hand, is a savage. Within the confines of my mind, he claims me, over and over again, until my body is shaking and my palm is soaked in the proof of his indulgence.

"You're too damn good at that." My head drops to the side, empty of its contents, and I lie puddled in my driver's seat.

If I'm not careful, I'm going to ruin myself. No man will ever live up to the pleasure my imaginary boyfriends are willing to dish out, whether in book form or figments of my own creation.

I suck in a deep breath, hold the air for a beat, and release it with steady control. I feel my diaphragm drop as I empty my lungs. Then, I repeat the process a second time, and once more for a third, recalling the benefits of the breathing exercise I learned in high school.

Now that I've gotten my fix and fueled my muscles with fresh oxygen, it's time to sober up and play it straight. Unfortunately, not *all* the evidence from my parking lot antics is so easily hidden, but I do my best to dry my fingers with a brown paper napkin from the glove box.

What I wouldn't give for one of those individually packaged wet wipes. The kind that BBQ restaurants include with your takeout. But I haven't treated myself to that level of comfort in ages. I'm half tempted to lick my fingers clean, but heaven forbid Riley goes in for a nice-to-meet-you kiss on the cheek. I don't need him thinking I have a girlfriend waiting for me at home.

I should stop overthinking everything and remember why I'm here. Tonight is meant to be fun. I'm not auditioning for a promotion or meeting my future husband.

Dates are easy to come by, and if history is any indicator, this will be the first and last time I hang out with the deliciously handsome Riley Sinclair and his wolfpack. Guys never call back when I want them to. They flirt and smile and say a whole lot of things I want to hear, but *I'll call you in the morning* typically means *I'll call you never*, and the laughs we shared remain with the night that is destined to become the basis of nothing.

Stepping out of the car, I slip further into a headspace that has me wishing I'd stayed home. My hand smells like foreplay, and for a split second, I'm reminded of my years in college and the cute indie girl who broke my heart. Or maybe I broke her heart. Or maybe hearts were never involved, and hindsight has me viewing the past through rose-colored glasses. All I know is I graduated and she moved across the northern border to a different country, and I couldn't have followed even if I wanted to.

I did want to.

So many times, I thought about the relationship and how much she meant to me. I still think about it. Every year on her birthday, when social media is kind enough to remind me of the girl who got away, I regret never saying the things I should have.

Eager to avoid the parking lot attendant's suspicious gaze, I sneak along the side of the brick building and step over the metal guardrail separating the vehicles from the sidewalk, where a team of nicely dressed valets are stationed. One of the men moves in front of me and opens the restaurant door before my reaching hand can grip the handle.

"Thank you," I smile reflexively as I slip past.

There's still a full hour until tip-off, and the city is buzzing with anxious excitement. Inside the restaurant, patrons are dressed to the nines or embellished from head to toe in team spirit. Visually, it's an interesting mix. As for myself, I opted for jeans and a low-cut sweater. My outfit is just the right amount of dressed-up-casual and first-date-sexy, which I hope Riley will appreciate.

"Good evening, hun." A hostess, no older than twenty-two, addresses me with a welcoming smile. Given her age, it's impressive she's been trusted to run the head of the house on a night that's sure to bring a fair bit of chaos. "Do you have a reservation with us tonight?"

"I do, yes. Um…" I blank for a moment, debate which name I should give, and second-guess myself. "I believe it's under Kade?"

My lack of confidence must seem adorable because she offers a reassuring touch to my arm and a smile as sweet as spun sugar.

"Oh my god, you're so freakin' cute. Jaxson is going to love you!" His name rolls off her tongue as though she's said it a million times, implying a nonprofessional level of familiarity.

The distinct prick of jealousy ripples beneath my skin as poisonous barbs shoot out in all directions. But why? It shouldn't affect me one way or another. What does it matter if he's slept with half the women in town? My date for the night isn't named Jaxson Kade, and I don't particularly care what he thinks of me.

Okay, that's a lie. I care. But only because I want this night to go off without a hitch.

And, well, I did just get myself off in the car thinking about him.

"Oh, I'm…" I know what I mean to say, that I'm here for someone else, but the words get caught in my throat.

Deep breathing isn't going to cut it. I need a refresh and a restart and about ten shots of this establishment's finest vodka. Thankfully, there's a panic room in sight. The sign for the restroom is to the right of the bar, and there's no time like the present to make my escape. "If you'll excuse me, I need to…"

"Well, speak of the devil." Her words wash over mine, snuffing out my timid attempts at politeness as she addresses the man behind me. "If it isn't my favorite brother."

"I'm your only brother, Smalls. But it's nice to hear I'm *someone's* favorite." The deep richness of his voice fills the space around me, replacing all other sounds. "We've got one more joining us tonight, so let me know when she gets here."

I watch the hostess as her eyes narrow.

She seems to stifle a laugh while glancing back and forth between us. "Did you two not exchange photos before planning this date?" Her hands lift in my direction, indicating I am, in fact, the prize behind door number one. "This exquisite beauty standing *right in front of you* is your plus-one, idiot."

The tacked-on jab at his intelligence makes me snicker, and for a moment, the suffocating tension shatters and falls to pieces around me. My brothers and I are notorious for this sort of sibling banter, and I find its sudden appearance soothing. I shift my gaze to the man over my shoulder and welcome my body to follow the same path.

Holy shit!

Jaxson Kade is even bigger than I expected, and the visual shock of this discovery jump-starts my racing heart. I knew from the photos and my ability to do simple math that Kade would be taller than Riley, but I wasn't expecting him to be a giant. I've always been attracted to taller men, but Kade's height would fall somewhere in the range of *beyond my wildest dreams.*

I want to climb him like a tree and sit on his branches.

"Ah, yes. I see it now." His blue eyes pierce my personal bubble, leaving me unprotected and in jeopardy of being consumed by his gravity. "You're the one." He takes my hand and presses it to his lips, kissing the divot between two knuckles. And then, he inhales.

Time stops as his nostrils flare and his lungs fill, pulling the corners of his lips into a smile.

He may be the devil, after all, because when his eyes open, there's a fire burning from within, scorching his blue eyes and turning them black. His voice rings in my ears, saying only one word, *MINE*, even though his lips never leave my skin.

I'm certain he's come to claim me, soul and all.

"I'm sorry. If you'll excuse me for a moment." My request is breathy.

If a person could die of embarrassment, the hostess would already be calling the coroner.

I slip my hand free from Kade's confident grip, spin on my heels, and retreat toward the restroom with hastened steps. This is what I get for being greedy within the confines of my fantasies. With one inhalation, he saw everything, leaving me exposed and naked and on full display in a restaurant full of people who weren't even looking. But their eyes are irrelevant in the grand scheme of things.

He saw me.

And I get the feeling he doesn't intend to look away.

CHAPTER 2
ALEXIS

Thank the heavens, I don't actually have to pee because the queue for the ladies' restroom is nearly as long as the line of people driving into the city. I offer a barrage of *I'm sorry, excuse me, I have to wash my hands* to the waiting women, painfully aware they all think I'm an asshole who's cutting the line. It takes some maneuvering and more fake smiles than I typically care to dole out, but eventually, I make it to the row of sinks fastened neatly to the wall.

I've done some questionable things in my life and have felt the sting of embarrassment on more than one occasion, but this has got to be a new low.

Holding my hand under the automatic dispenser, I fill my palm with a generous amount of foam and work my hands into a lather. I don't know what kind of soap this is, but unless it was blessed by a priest, I don't think it will do much to cleanse me of my sins. At the moment, however, it's all I've got.

Perhaps I can make myself small enough to blend in with the crowd and sneak out the back door. I could message Riley from the parking lot, apologize for my abrupt disappearance, and offer an excuse that doesn't so much as hint at the truth. Runaway dog. Dead grandma. Explosive diarrhea. Okay, maybe not that last one, but something equally urgent.

Anything would be better than, *I accidentally gave your intensely hot roommate a sneak preview of my pussy. Sorry. My bad.*

I purify my hands in the warm water before repeating the process for a second time. Lather. Rinse. Repeat. The shampoo bottle mantra plays in my head, and I wonder how many times I can wash my hands before onlookers begin to question my sanity. Some of these women probably assume the drugs are kicking in, and I'll be rollin' my way through the evening's festivities.

In truth, I haven't consumed drugs like that in ages.

The memories of sweaty nights dancing to thumping house beats with nameless boys and after-party showers that felt like a million fingertips make me smile beyond what perhaps they should. I lived more dangerously than a girl in her twenties ought to, not caring about the consequences. It's a wonder I'm still alive and relatively unscathed. Thankfully, I've matured in my thirties, although not enough to know better than to masturbate in a public parking lot before a first date. Hopefully, that level of wisdom awaits me in my forties.

I dry my hands with a paper towel and exit through the incoming traffic. My head and heart are caught between wanting to return home and itching to make the most of my night out. Fortunately, my decision is made for me, and my plans to shrink and disappear are quickly erased when I lock eyes with a man casually leaning against the corner of the bar. He's handsome in a way that would've made him unapproachable had this not been a pre-scheduled engagement.

Stepping forward with a clever grin and extended hand, Riley greets me with a predictable level of masculine confidence. "Turns out I was right."

I'm used to men online thinking they're right about everything, but despite that, it's an odd approach. Right about what? The question forms like a thought bubble above my head. Did his roommate say something the second I walked away? Of course, he did. Kade most likely told everyone I'm some nymphomaniac who can't keep her hand out of her pants. Who knows? It's been a few minutes. By now, I've undoubtedly graduated to full-blown whore offering back-alley blowjobs to anyone with a dollar in their wallet. I'm sure the group shared a hearty laugh at my expense because I'm an absolute idiot.

"About?" I ask, not certain I care to hear the answer, but when I look into his eyes, I find no trace of cocky indignation. Quite the opposite.

"You're the most beautiful woman I've ever seen," he says, maintaining his hold on my hand.

"Oh." Thrown off by his response, I'm convinced I've heard him incorrectly over the chattering crowd. My brain struggles to receive compliments on a good day, and right now, I'm sifting through a hodge-podge of contradicting emotions. My splintered consciousness attempts to rally by hopping onto the first detour and circling back, but when I open my mouth, someone else seems to be speaking. "In regards to physical appearance, you're not exactly difficult to look at."

What the hell am I saying? No one talks like that.

Riley and I have spent the last three days corresponding via the dating app's messenger feature, not quite comfortable enough to exchange phone numbers but interested enough to meet in person. For three days, I could edit my responses and lead with my best foot forward. And now, I'm standing here with my foot in my mouth, wondering how he continues to regard me with such unabashed interest.

"Alexis, if my roommate said something to upset you, I apologize. I was outside, tipping the driver, but that's no excuse. I should've made every effort to meet you first. If you'd like, I could challenge him to a fight in the parking lot. I know Kade looks like a big, tough guy, but..." Riley leans forward, and his tone takes on an even more intimate quality. "I'm willing to do whatever it takes."

"He didn't upset me." I release a delicate whisper of a laugh and offer my date a sheepish smile.

"There's no need to get killed defending my honor."

While I appreciate the chivalry on display, Kade would obliterate Riley in a fight. Of that, I have no doubt. I scan the room and locate the hulking beast of a man sitting against the far wall. His full attention seems focused on the conversation happening at the corner bar instead of the one taking place at the table. The man seated across from him snaps his fingers in an effort to steal Kade's attention, but collects little reaction.

"Well, in that case, are you ready to officially meet the group?" The warmth of Riley's hand as it gently squeezes my palm brings my focus back to where it belongs. "Or do we need a round of liquid courage?"

"I think we should be okay to order drinks at the table if I can borrow a bit of your bravery." Another subtle laugh brings with it an honest smile, and I feel the tightness in my shoulders begin to release. The last thing I want is for his friends to think I'm some uppity bitch who's too self-important to join them for a night out after accepting their generous invitation.

My horniness has created an unintended situation, and my overthinking has blown everything out of proportion. I need to take a chill pill with a mind-eraser chaser and pull my shit together. Quickly.

Riley is here, clearly none the wiser, so that means Kade never said anything. Chances are, he didn't even notice. Women tend to be more self-aware of their own scent, and men are typically oblivious to damn near everything.

"They're excited to meet you." Riley links his fingers to mine. "But I'm here to spend time with you, not my friends. I meant what I said…"

"You'll have to remind me." Riley's charm and good looks are turning my brain to mush, and I'm at risk of melting into a pool of girl goo and becoming a slip-and-fall hazard for the surrounding guests if he continues to use his bedroom voice every time he talks to me.

"We can leave anytime you want. I have a hot tub at home and a bottle of wine with your name on it. That was meant to be our second date, but I'm happy to be greedy and keep you all to myself tonight. Say the word, and we're out of here."

I smile playfully and suck in a ragged breath as he leans in closer. "The word."

We've barely spoken a handful of lines and know only as much as we've cared to unearth online, yet I want him to kiss me. I hunger for it. I want to feel his lips pressed against mine. I want him to take me home, bathe me in expensive wine, and bend me over the side of a hot tub that costs as much as my car. I want to discover if he's capable of everything he's done to me in my head.

"You're cute." Riley cups the side of my neck, and I catch myself leaning into his touch. "Let me make the customary introductions, and then we can get out of here."

"Okay."

Going home with a guy to hook up on a first date all but guarantees I'll never hear from him again. It's stupid and potentially dangerous, but that's what makes it exciting. If Riley Sinclair turns out to be the next American psycho, so be it. I can think of worse ways to go.

He maintains a hold of my hand as we weave a path across the overcrowded restaurant, making our way toward the table where his friends are seated. Riley is tall, with broad shoulders, and the path to our destination is narrow. Unable to peek around him, I follow blindly, like a lemming, blissfully unaware of the cliff that awaits me.

"This is about to be one hell of a night. Let's go!" A man adorned in burgundy and gold says to no one in particular.

"Game seven, baby! Winner takes all!" Riley calls back, and the surrounding tables erupt into a wave of hoots and cheers, fueling the excitement within the restaurant and drowning out any casual conversation that had previously existed.

Tonight feels like once in a lifetime for our city. I can't ask Riley to miss that, not when I know he's been looking forward to it. I appreciate his willingness to accommodate my needs and prioritize my comfort, but first-date sex is a dime a dozen, whereas this game is history in the making.

Before we reach the table, my mind is made up. Even though the lower half of my body is begging to make its way into the hot tub and onto Riley's cock, my head knows better. We're sticking around and having the date he initially planned. Whatever happens after that is fair game. There will be plenty of time to celebrate or go home and lick our wounds after the time on the clock ticks down to zero and the season's final buzzer sounds.

CHAPTER 3
ALEXIS

I wouldn't call myself the rose between two thorns. Positioned between Riley and Kade, I feel more like a lettuce sandwich handcrafted with the finest artisan bread. They are impressive, to say the least, and I find myself painfully aware of every one of my unremarkable features. Even with a full face of makeup and my favorite low-cut sweater, I'm not fancy enough to be mixed greens. I'm iceberg lettuce at best. And any false confidence I might have possessed while bigging myself up in the car, ran into the street and got run over by a truck the moment I took a seat at the table reserved for beautiful people.

"Alexis." The sound of my name passing his lips calls me home like a dinner bell. "This is Chuckie, the best wide receiver a guy could hope for and an even better friend. He met Elise last year in some small-town sports bar, and they were married two months later. We all flew to Vegas for the wedding, and I lost an absolute fortune in the casino. It was a good time." Riley motions to the smiling blonde beauty and her equally fair husband seated across from me at the table. If these two ever have kids together, they're at risk of being born transparent.

"Yeah, it was nice that you guys showed up. Chuckie still doesn't talk to his mom after she boycotted the wedding." Her smile fades as she's reminded of the painful memory, although Elise does her best to sound nonchalant.

I think it's important to be supportive, even if deep down you disagree with someone's choices.

Chuckie's parents lost a son, and for what? Their own stubbornness. What a waste. I know I'm only meeting the pair tonight for the first time, but they seem happy and in love. The way Elise leans against Chuckie's arm, knowing he'll be there to support her, is as clear a sign as any. These two are meant to be together, and no arbitrary amount of time dating would've altered the outcome.

"Jakob and I roomed together all four years of college after meeting during a recruitment visit. He played full back and could shotgun cheap beer faster than anyone else on the floor. Hailey was a cheerleader. They dated off and on during senior year. I'm pretty sure I've *heard* them have sex no less than a million times."

Hailey blushes as Jakob and Riley exchange a not-so-subtle look across the table, and I get the feeling there's a story buried under a thin layer of dirt she isn't interested in unearthing for the group. Most likely a drunken night or two that turned into a sweaty threesome. So long as all parties were consenting, I see no reason to be embarrassed, but I appreciate that some people are more private about their sex lives than others.

"The cheerleader and the football player. I think that's super cute. Sports romance is all the rage these days. If he'd been a hockey player, I'd encourage you to turn your story into a best-selling novel." I attempt to shift the focus off of Hailey's sex life and back onto the romance that's held them together after all these years.

Everyone at the table seems to be around the same age, so if we make eighteen our starting point for college and tack on the standard four years, that brings us to twenty-two. But they started dating senior year, so that'd be twenty-one. Thirty-four minus twenty-one is thirteen.

Thirteen years. Holy shit!

I've frequently dreamt of being in a committed relationship, but after years of turning over stones and kissing frogs, I realize that card might not be in my deck. My longest relationship lasted somewhere in the realm of thirteen months, and I found out later he'd been cheating on me for most of it.

As Riley continues making introductions, I can't help but wonder if he's secretly jealous of his friends. He labels them by their on-field position, even though college ended nearly a decade and a half ago, and they haven't played on a team together since. I can only assume he was the quarterback and sees himself as the head of his friend group, even though they've slowly moved on and left him behind.

"And, of course, you've already met this gigantic loser. My roommate, Kade." Riley nudges my shoulder, pushing me flush against the solid wall that is Jaxson Kade.

Less than half an hour in, and my date is already reminding me of lessons hard learned. Riley's cockiness is bordering on annoying, and the novelty of his classic good looks is wearing thin. It's not so much the words he's saying. Mostly, it's his tone. He holds himself in high regard, which is fine, but he speaks as though his friends exist somewhere beneath him, and I hate that.

"Yeah, Jax and I go way back," I smirk and roll my eyes while pushing back against him.

If Riley insists on giving people titles, breaking them into groups, and placing them into a hierarchy, I'll happily keep the company of anyone he shoves to the bottom.

"Oh my god, I knew it!" Elise squeals and rubs her hands together excitedly. "The second I saw you two together, I knew there was a story. You have to tell us. Please!"

I had been joking around, which I thought would be clear. But, no such luck. With one sentence, I painted myself into a corner, and now I'm freaking out. I should admit that I'm a liar and socially awkward, and pray the waitress comes around at some point to take our drink order, but I'm too much of a coward. My heart is beating out of my chest, and the ability to verbalize our shared language is suddenly lost. Between having my hand down my pants and my foot in my mouth, this night feels like a game of Twister where I'm the player and the mat.

"I was actually, um…" My left leg begins bouncing as I fidget with the hem of my pants and fumble for the words. I hate being called out. I know I'm the one who prompted the misunderstanding, and the question was meant with good intentions. Logically, I recognize this is my fault, but secretly, I'm cursing Elise and her future bloodline for picking up the ball and running with it.

"Come on, babe, I think we should tell 'em." Kade slips his giant bear paw of a hand onto my lap and comes up with my fingers braided into his. Lifting my hand into the space between, he bends to place a kiss on my finger. "After all, you and I both love a good story."

I'm not sure what he means. The individual words make sense, but when I string them together, I'm lost. I don't know him, but I wish I did. Kade casts such a light that all others fall into shadow, except for me, and the warmth of his radiance has me glowing.

"Well, they're your friends, so maybe you should be the one to tell them." I can't determine if he's playing along for my benefit or seeing how far I'll take things before exposing me to the group.

Luckily, the waitress arrives with a large tray of drinks, temporarily delaying my execution. I wish Riley and I had been here when they ordered because I could use some liquid courage right about now.

She starts with Kade, placing a large draft beer in front of him with a smile and a wink, but he doesn't seem to notice. Some men are so oblivious when it comes to women flirting. Does it happen so frequently that he fails to register the advances, or is she an ex he's purposely going out of his way to ignore?

I watch intently as she circles the table, matching the assortment of drinks with their new owners. The guys all ordered beer while the ladies opted for delicious-looking fruit-flavored cocktails. It doesn't surprise me that someone added Riley to this first round. The group has been friends since college, and I'm sure they've been drinking together since then. I expected them to include him. But when the waitress reaches over my shoulder to place the last three glasses in front of me, I'm stunned.

"You don't have to drink those if I got the order wrong." Kade squeezes ever so slightly, and I realize that while our hands have dropped out of sight, our palms and fingers have remained married.

I look to Riley to gauge his reaction, but he's singularly focused on the beer in front of him, as though it's the last bottle of ice water in hell. And now that we're all friends, I'm on my own.

I lift each glass in turn, taking a sip to reveal its contents. The first is filtered tap water, which I can deduce by simply using my eyes. The second is Diet Coke, which practically runs through my veins. I live on a steady intake of caffeine and croutons when I'm working, so this beverage is well-known to me. The third glass is smaller and contains a liquid that smells like vacation and bad decisions. Its refreshing sweetness mingles with my taste buds like an old friend.

"Grey Goose and pineapple." I set the glass on the

table and lick the whispered kiss of its flavor from my bottom lip. "Looks like you're three for three."

I'm not sure how he did it. Maybe Kade works as a bartender and has a knack for guessing this sort of thing. Or maybe he can read minds, which would be a terrifying revelation. I've already considered, more than once, the likelihood of his dick matching size with the rest of him, and I'm certain he would know plenty of entertaining ways to exploit my curiosity.

The possibility heats my cheeks as I lift the shortest glass and swallow the beverage in a series of quick gulps.

"I think we need a round of shots. Something with vodka." Kade flashes a smile, and the girl holding the empty tray glares daggers in my direction, as though I've stolen attention that belongs to her. "How about cherry bombs?"

The combination of cherry vodka and Red Bull is on my short list of favorites, so I'm not the least bit disappointed with his choice. I am, however, thirsty and require more than a sip.

"Could you make mine as a drink, please? Tall."

I'm not sure why she's mad at me, but I'm not trying to fan the flames.

"You haven't changed a bit," Kade says with a wink, reminding the party of our previous conversation.

"We want details, Kade. Quit stalling. How the hell did Riley wind up on a date with your ex?" Hailey jumps into the conversation, eager for the details neither Kade nor I possess.

The ladies in the group seem oddly invested in this fairy tale backstory, while Riley appears disinterested. If it were me in his shoes, I'd be the first one in line with questions, but he's acting like he can't be bothered. His lack of interest could be a display of annoyance, and if that's the case, I should own my truth and find a path back to a fresh start.

"You haven't taken your eyes off her since we walked in, and that drink order was oddly specific. Jakob and I have been married for years, and he couldn't order me a drink if his life depended on it." Hailey's observation causes my heart to skip a beat.

How did Kade know my drink order, and why does it feel like he can see into my soul? I guess the devil is gifted with many talents. I wonder how his forked tongue would feel between my thighs and what sort of tricks he might be able to accomplish with his tail.

"Because you order something different every place we go! Margaritas with Mexican food. Martinis when you only want appetizers and dessert. Rum and Coke with chicken wings. Sweet white wine when we're eating steak or feeling fancy. You're all over the board, but I'm confident I could narrow it down to a section of the menu. So, don't make me sound like one of those dickhead husbands who doesn't pay attention because I see you, baby." Jakob shares a kiss with his wife, who smiles happily at her mistake. "There's no one else I'd rather look at."

"Well, I stand corrected." Hailey beams at her husband's sudden romantic outburst as if she's seeing this side of him for the first time, and it's a welcome discovery.

"He's not my ex." I realize too late how that sounds and amend my statement. "I mean, Jax and I, we've never dated."

Both couples look on with suspicion, waiting for me to continue.

The first time I called him Jax, it was meant as a joke and a bit of a jab. The nickname was meant to add a level of realism to the claim that we'd previously been acquainted. It was meant to ruffle Riley's feathers. But this time, when I said it, I did so without thinking. The name hadn't had the desired effect on the first go around, but it rings a bit louder the second time.

At long last, Riley diverts his attention from the pregame coverage to enter the discussion and wax poetic. "We're all in our mid-thirties, and virginity is a long-forgotten keepsake we gave away to someone we didn't end up with. If you guys slept together at some point, I'm not overly worried about it." He pops an arm across the back of my chair, staking his claim. "Sounds like Kade had a chance, and he blew it. Not surprising."

CHAPTER 4
ALEXIS

The thorns beside me, while sharp, are beginning to feel more like a rock and a hard place. Or more like a dead end and a warm place. I'm torn between feeling like I shouldn't be here and really wanting to stay.

"Time to make things interesting. You know the drill. Ten a square. Let's set the payouts at one for the first and third, two for the half, and six for the final. With seven of us, that's fourteen each and two left over. We can flip for the extra." Riley pulls a folded sheet of paper and a pen from his pocket and tosses them in the center of the table before looking at me. "There's an ATM outside if you don't have cash."

He might as well be speaking in tongues.

"What are we doing?" I'm officially lost in the number sauce, and the ladle seems impossibly far away.

Elise offers to explain while the guys ante up. "He's talking about betting on the game. You write your name in however many boxes you want, and once the board is full, we use an app to draw two numbers between zero and nine. That determines the order along the top and side. Then, we flip a coin to decide which is home and away. At the end of each quarter, we use the score to find the winner. The payouts for the first and third quarters are a hundred bucks, two hundred at halftime, and if your name is in the box that matches the last two digits of the final score, you win six hundred dollars. It makes the game more interesting, but you don't have to play if you don't want to."

"Yeah," Hailey shoots Riley a glare that narrows her eyes to slits. "It's pretty shitty to point your date in the direction of an ATM because you feel the need to turn everything into a bet."

Chuckie splashes a wad of cash onto the table and hands his wife the pen before catching my eye.

"Alexis, we can spot you forty if you want to play. And then if you win, you can pay it back, and if you don't…no worries."

"I pulled three hundred out of the bank on the way here, so I've got an extra twenty you can have." Jakob places a stack of crisp bills in a neat pile on top of the cash already littering the table and holds the extra twenty out to me.

I wave them off and tuck my hands into my lap, attempting to conceal my discomfort. It's nice of the guys to offer, but it hardly seems fair. "You don't have to do that. Thank you, though. I think I might have some money in my car. You know, in case of an emergency."

Normally, this would be true, but the small drawer behind my steering wheel is currently empty. I left the house without my wallet yesterday and had to stop for gas and food. If Riley had told me to bring cash, I would have. With a simple heads-up, he could have saved me the embarrassment of looking like a broke-ass loser in front of his friends.

A stabbing pain stings my nose, and there's no denying tears are soon to follow. I try to convince myself it's not worth being upset over. Deep down, I know I should laugh it off. I should tell them to have fun without me and cheer for them when they win, but I don't want everyone else to feel uncomfortable if I'm the only one not participating.

"Let me see your keys. It's safer if I run out." Kade stands and holds out his hand. "Did you park next to the building? I told my sister to save a spot for you."

My swelling emotions evaporate and settle into calm. The chivalry on display from all three men may be unfamiliar, but it isn't lost on me.

"Yeah, it's between two black SUVs, but I can go." I drop my head and fish the keys from my pocket.

"Perfect. I'm sure I can find it. I need to make my rounds and say hello to a few people." Kade takes the keys and hands me three freshly minted one-hundred-dollar bills before plucking a twenty from the pool of cash on the table. "You pick us some winning squares, and I'll keep whatever money I find in your car. Deal?"

I shake my head, wanting to warn him I'm a bad bet, but he doesn't stick around long enough for me to object.

CHAPTER 5
KADE

I check my watch for the third time in ten minutes, swallow the last of my beer, and place the empty glass in the cup holder. Her car is cute and clean and way too small for a guy my size. I shouldn't be in here, but I couldn't resist.

I recline the passenger seat, close my eyes, and inhale. Pulling in the scent of her that lingers in the small space, I imagine her seated behind the steering wheel.

Did she touch herself while she was driving like some horny little daredevil racing full speed to chase down her orgasm? Or was she sensible enough to exercise restraint and wait until after she parked?

By the time she got through traffic, I bet her clit was throbbing with the need for a release.

I wonder who she was thinking about while she soaked her palm.

Standing in the restaurant, she looked so pretty with her pupils blown out and that post-orgasm flush in her cheeks. I knew this night was going to be torture the second I saw her, but then she had to go and tease me with a hint of that delicious pussy.

I tug at the leg of my jeans, attempting to create space.

It isn't normally within my character to disrespect a woman's personal space, but this girl's got me too far gone, and there isn't enough readjusting in the world that's going to accommodate my needs. I undo the front of my jeans and release my straining cock. "She's gonna kill me for this."

I cycle through snippets of prior sexual encounters and toss in a new fantasy for good measure. Every memory is rewritten as it crosses my mind. Each face and body is replaced with hers.

She's in the driver's seat with her back pressed against the door. Her jeans crumpled on the floor, and her panties pushed to the side. She circles her clit with two fingers. Taking her time. Making me watch as she teases herself.

I run my hand up her leg, pausing when I sense her heat. She's turned on for me. I can feel how warm and tight and wet she is as she pushes two of my fingers inside. Moaning my name as she grinds herself down on my hand.

Her lips playfully kiss the head of my cock as her fingers encircle the base. She uses her thumb and then her tongue to apply the perfect amount of pressure, stroking the length before taking me into her mouth.

I braid my fingers into her hair and slowly drive my hips forward, encouraging her to take a bit more. "You're so good at sucking my cock. I knew you would be. Look how well you take me."

She chokes as she swallows the base but doesn't pull back. "Such a good girl."

"You like sucking my cock, don't you, baby? I bet you'd like to swallow my cum like a good little whore. If you keep taking me deep like that, I'm gonna finish down your throat."

She moans and takes me further still, daring me to follow through with my threat.

I want to please her the way she's pleasing me, but she won't let go. She's so hungry for my cock. I massage the lips of her pussy. Taking my time to appreciate how wet she is for me.

"Do you want another man filling this tight pussy while I fuck your mouth?" I add another finger and push inside. Stretching her out. Getting her ready for all I have to offer. "You want to be used, don't you? You need it so badly. You were thinking about it while you were touching yourself. Weren't you, baby? Thinking about how good we'd feel inside you."

I shorten my strokes and quicken my pace.

She's straddling my legs. Her back arched as she springs up and down on top of me. She's so close to an orgasm. I can almost feel her pussy tighten around me. See her tits bounce as she rides my cock. Hear her voice as she begs for every last drop.

Please, Jax. I want to feel you cum inside me.

I grab the glass from the cupholder and blow my

load into the bottom. Stroking until there's nothing more to give.

"Oh fuck." The mental clarity accompanying my release hits like a ton of bricks as reality reconstructs around me. "What the hell did I just do?"

I check the glove box for a napkin and ensure I'm properly tucked away before exiting the car. The last thing I need is some line cook catching an eyeful of my flank steak when he pops out to the back alley for a smoke.

While I thoroughly enjoyed the much-needed quiet, it's time to return, find a way to win her over, apologize without actually admitting what I did, and offer to have her car professionally detailed first thing in the morning.

I toss the napkin into an open trash bin and dip through the back door next to the cooler, where a straining barback attempts to carry a pair of kegs that weigh more than he does. We exchange a knowing look. He doesn't have to ask, and I don't have to voice my offer. I take the full kegs, one in each hand, and deposit them behind the bar.

Being unconditionally helpful is my strong suit.

I make a show of pretending my hands were made dirty in the effort and wash them in the sink lined with empty glassware. On any other night, I would linger. I would tap the new kegs and carry out the empties. Haul trash to the dumpster. Wash glasses. Mix drinks. I've been a guest bartender on more than one occasion, and I'll admit the tips weren't bad. I do particularly well with bachelorette parties.

"I love you." A familiar voice materializes beside me. "But you need to go away. I'm busy, and you take up too much space."

While trying to craft the perfect retort, I hesitate, get distracted by the vibrating phone in my pocket, and come up empty. A quick "love you too" is all I manage to get out before my heart drops.

CHAPTER 6
KADE

From my seat at the empty side of the table, I read the text message again.

Riley: Congratulations! You're an asshole. Stop making my date uncomfortable. And you owe the table $20. Alexis won both coin flips and put your name on the extra squares. Hope you're happy.

I get the distinct impression that my roommate is not the least bit concerned with my happiness. Not now, and not ever. It reminds me of what he said earlier. *Sounds like he had his chance and blew it.* His backhanded response came across like wishful thinking at the time, but now it feels more like fore-shadowing.

Perhaps Riley was right to accuse me of scaring off his date. That was never my intention, but I have been told I'm intimidating. I thought my actions were playful, but now, looking back on it, it's possible I crossed the line. After all, she doesn't know me. We've never met. And yet I'm certain her touch felt familiar, as though her fingerprints linger on my skin like a new tattoo marking the occasion of our meeting.

"Let me see that sheet." I drop my phone on the table and look at the paper, finding my adopted name labeling nearly a third of the squares.

Jax

She wrote it thirty times.

That has to mean something.

"Can I borrow the pen?" My disappointment dissolves as my eyes trace over her delicate hand-writing.

I add her to a pair of boxes marked with my nick-name, liking the way we look together. Then, I use the pen to scratch a line through fourteen of my dedicated squares, adding my version of her name to the marred boxes in a bold, heavy-handed script. After all, she is their rightful owner. Irregardless of what she might think, I owe her that much.

I drop the pen and rub my hands together, joining the conversation already in progress while watching the front door with rapt attention. According to the group, Riley followed his date outside after she received an urgent call.

"You have to admit, the timing was suspect. You left with her keys and didn't come back. Then, all of a sudden, she got an *important phone call* and needed someplace *quiet* to talk. All I'm saying is…it seemed like a convenient excuse." Hailey does little to dull her suspicions.

"Yeah. Maybe." I imagine Lex finding me in the car, dick in hand, muttering about how well she takes my cock. The fantasy version of events concludes with her on top of me as we orgasm together, and the thought makes me grin. In reality, she most likely would've called the cops, and rightfully so.

"When Alexis won the last two squares, Riley was so pissed." Jakob collects the assortment of bills from the center of the table and begins sorting them into piles. "I figured *that's* why she took the phone call. To get away from him for a minute."

"How so?" This is new information I didn't hear the first time. Or perhaps they failed to mention it.

"He's such a baby. I bet he used to throw his plastic baseball bat when he'd strike out in tee ball." Hailey's spot-on description makes me chuckle, but my concern lingers.

Elise picks up where she left off. "This year's poor sportsmanship award goes to…Riley Sinclair."

I shake my head while the girls bust apart laughing. I want to circle back and press for further details, but decide against it. Better to let the group move on to a new topic since I'm pretty sure I already know the answer. Riley sent a text saying I was making his date uncomfortable, but it could be that he was doing that all on his own.

Fucking asshole.

She isn't even his type. I've known the guy since we were eighteen, and if you lined up his exes, you'd be hard-pressed to distinguish one from the next. Constantly the same. Five-foot-four, blonde, arm candy, looking for a guy with money to be her new *daddy*. I gag at the reminder of how often I've heard the term moaned from across the hall. Fortunately for Riley, he was born into privilege and landed a job that affords him the finer things life has to offer.

Finer by society's standards, but not better.

This girl is different. Her beauty lies in her intricacy. She takes up space in a way he'll never appreciate. And I want to protect her, mostly because I know she doesn't need me to.

"So, what'd you guys think about that buzzer-beater in game six? Shit had me leaping off the couch and cheering as if we'd already claimed the title. I'm not sure my heart can take another last-second decision like that." Chuckie clutches his chest as though phantom pains loiter beneath the surface. He's always been the excitable type. The guy wears his emotions on his sleeve, which is admirable.

Robot is the word most often used to describe me. Though once, an ex-girlfriend did say I had the emotional depth of a potato chip. Whatever that means. Perhaps I was being salty.

The discussion at the table fades into the background as I refocus on the conversation outside the front window. Riley leans in close and touches her arm, most likely rattling off his bloated list of accomplishments. My roommate is nothing if not predictable. And shallow. Don't get me wrong, he and I are friends, but his self-importance has always rubbed me the wrong way.

As a left tackle on the football field, my job was to protect him, but that was a long time ago. Tonight, he's on his own.

I wring my hands together again, trying to relieve the gnawing feeling chomping at my bones. Why am I so bothered by the sight of them together and the smile she gifts so freely? Everything I found in the course of my online digging tells me she's a good person. Strong and capable, but also creative and kind. She's wildly talented if the photos are to be believed, and exceptionally skilled with her hands. Although right now, it's her mouth that's got me distracted.

That smile is going to be the death of me.

"Kade!" Jakob waves his hands, disrupting my line of sight. He grabs my attention before passing the ball to his wife.

"Come on, Kade. Spill your guts." Hailey probes.

"You aren't exactly subtle. It's obvious you've slept with her at some point. Give us the details."

I raise an eyebrow and smirk before fake coughing a *Shhhh* into the back of my hand. There's no time for the truth and even less for a lie. The last thing I need is to get caught talking about her as she's walking through the front door. I'm not sure if she would slap me or turn tail and leave. Either way, I'm not interested in finding out.

The restaurant bursts into cheers as the game begins, and our team takes first possession of the ball. I use the distraction to quietly adjust the position of my chair, pretend to watch the game seven finale, and act the part of an interested sports fan. Normally, I wouldn't have to feign interest in local sports, but tonight, I couldn't care less. I wish the TVs would disappear, along with the crowd and my friends.

My attention is on the pair returning to the table, and all I want is to be alone.

Alone. With her.

Trying and failing, I do my best to hold still as the empty chair pulls back far enough for a certain brunette to drop onto the seat beside me.

Her elbow unintentionally brushes against my arm, eliciting another undeserved apology. "I'm sorry."

"It's my fault. Today was arm day, and my muscles are still swollen." I tighten my hand into a fist and flex my bicep in what has got to be the biggest meathead response I've ever given.

Did I seriously flex on a girl, hoping she'd be impressed?

"Those noodle arms?" She pokes a finger into my muscle. "Come on, bro. Do you even bench?" Her playful jab is capped off with a smirk and a wink. "I'm kidding. They're very nice."

My heartbeat quickens, threatening to crack my ribs as she bites back a smile.

As covertly as possible, I slip my hand onto her leg and squeeze her thigh as infinite conversations happen within the span of a glance. Her eyebrows pull together, and she nibbles her bottom lip. Slight hints that she questions my intentions, but remains willing to trust my motives.

She drops her voice to a nearly inaudible whisper as her fingers brush over the back of my hand. "You know what they say about hand tattoos."

I lean close enough to draw in the scent of her shampoo and brush a strand of hair behind her ear. "They make pretty necklaces for good girls."

When she turns her head, our lips are a breath apart. "That's the rumor."

Yet again, she floods my senses, and my arms aren't the only thing swollen. She's toying with me right here in front of everyone, but she's doing it in a way that's neither broadcasting nor hiding. She isn't ashamed of her interest, even though I may not be the only one catching her eye.

Without missing a beat, she turns to Riley and tags into the conversation happening at the other end of the table. Something about advancing technology destroying the purity of the game.

I feel like I was damn near murdered in a drive-by flirting, and she's moved on with no fucks given.

Is it confidence or cockiness? Neither seems to fit. She apologizes for the smallest infraction. And yet, I have zero doubt she took time to get herself off in the parking lot before walking into the restaurant to meet us. One second, she's a timid little mouse, and the next, she's a lion. I'm certain I've never met anyone like her, but somehow, she reminds me so much of myself.

When the waitress arrives with our second round of drinks, she dispenses them into the center of the table, leaving us to take our pick. "Would you like to start with a few small plates of food to share? Or were we all set to order?"

"We'll take one of each appetizer and order food later." I turn to the woman beside me, brushing her arm in hopes of regaining her undivided attention. "Do you eat muscles?"

She looks momentarily shocked and then laughs. "That's a strange way to ask for a blowjob."

Her words hit me like a convoy of armored trucks, and I'm dead.

"He's talking about the appetizer, sweetheart."

The tone in which Bethany says *sweetheart* brings me back to life and has me flashing her a look. I don't tolerate disrespect, which she's well aware of, and she's currently skating on thin ice. I've apologized more than once and been kind while rejecting her advances, but if she thinks being rude to the ladies in my party will get her somewhere with me, she's wrong.

"Well, that's not nearly as much fun, is it?" Lex's response is pure candy-coated razor blades, and I'm living for it. She leans into me, practically fusing herself to my arm, and places a hand on my chest. "Either way, the answer is yes."

This girl is fire. I'm going to enjoy playing with her.

The annoying waitress, the rowdy patrons filling the restaurant, my table of friends, and her forgotten date disappear into the haze at the fringe of my vision. I brush the hair back from her face to tuck it behind her ear, wanting to touch her. Needing desperately to kiss her. Craving a taste of the lips that demand my attention.

But when I hesitate, the moment is lost, and she pulls away with a forlorn expression.

"I'm sorry. I'm not sure why I said that." Alexis offers an apology to the table as she turns away from me. "That was rude."

"Oh my god, girl! Don't even apologize," Hailey jumps in. "That was amazing. I'm pretty sure I'm in love with you, and if one of these guys doesn't take you home tonight, I'm going to divorce Jake and snatch you up for myself."

"What's going on?" Riley takes a long swig of his beer before slipping his hand beneath the table. "Who's getting divorced?"

"I think you should schedule an appointment to get your hearing checked," Elise says with a laugh. "The competition for your girl is getting thick, and you're not even in the running."

"I'm not worried," he says dismissively before returning to the game.

Riley is the sort to make everything into a competition, and he's acting impartial. Is he so arrogant that he thinks he doesn't have to try, or does he still not view me as a worthy opponent? The guy lives for a good rivalry and places bets on the smallest odds and outcomes, yet appears unfazed by my obvious interest in his date. Even our living situation is a wager among friends with a hefty prize awaiting the winner.

It didn't make sense for the group of us to pay rent and utilities at four different places when we all intended to work in the same city after graduation, so Riley devised a plan that would be mutually beneficial to all parties while simultaneously turning our housing situation into a competition. The four of us pooled our resources and bought an impressive piece of real estate. Paying one-quarter of a mortgage and sharing utilities was a great deal cheaper for a guy starting out in his career.

The bet is ongoing, and the rules are simple.

- Expenses are divided evenly among the guys remaining in the house.
- No live-in girlfriends allowed.
- Shared ownership is forfeit upon marriage.
- The last man single wins the house.

Having never met a woman interesting enough to captivate my full attention, I set my sights on beating Riley and winning the ultimate prize. But as I sit here now, feeling entirely whole, the house is no longer my concern.

CHAPTER 7
ALEXIS

This date, if one could call it that, bears little resemblance to the evening I expected. On the plus side, the drinks are fantastic, the food is top-notch, and the conversation is engaging. Kade has shown a genuine interest in my hobbies and asked for details about my job. He hasn't so much as glanced at the television. Even when I spent fifteen minutes rambling about the ins and outs of designing custom special edition hardcover books and complaining about impatient authors who often call for updates outside of my posted scheduled work hours, he seemed to hang on my every word. Whereas, Riley's attention has remained glued to the game.

"Do you read all the books you design artwork and covers for, or does the author tell you what they want, and you go from there?" Elise asks between sips of her drink, pushing the empty glass to the side when only ice remains. "I don't think I'd be able to read a horror novel, even if it was for work. I'm such a baby when it comes to that stuff. I don't know how Kade does it."

"I mostly stick to romance since that's what I'm known for. I try to read all of the stories, but it depends on the turnaround time and the scale of the project. I've learned to put my foot down and stand up for myself. Everyone wants their books finished yesterday, but I'm not willing to sacrifice quality for quickness, and I've yet to miss a deadline." I retrieve the phone from my pocket and notice a series of missed calls and text alerts.

Bypassing the messages without reading them, I open the folder containing examples of my art and hold the phone out in front of me. A smile lights my features as the women scroll through the images with genuine fascination.

"It's cute that you've found a way to profit off of your passion, but I can't imagine there's much of a retirement package with your online store. Do you really make enough selling page markers and painted books to cover your monthly expenses?" Riley's question strikes a nerve, but he doesn't pause long enough for me to respond. "I looked at your page, and your work is good. You've got talent, but I think you'd benefit from an outside financial perspective. I'd be willing to sit down sometime and review the numbers."

Another incoming text buzzes the phone gripped tightly in my hand, and I pull my arm back across the table. Dropping my head to read the message, I lock my eyes to the screen to keep from forgetting my manners and remind myself to breathe. In my current mental state, my response to Riley's unsolicited fatherly advice would surely signal the end of our evening. Perhaps, no great loss to my distracted date, but I'd hate to leave the others on such a foul note.

> Look up! Nick and I are at the bar attempting to get a drink.

"Has anyone told you yet today that you're an asshole?" Elise and Hailey take turns shouting their disapproval. "It's no wonder you're still single. Have fun living alone in that big house once Kade gets married."

I ignore the conversation around me and scan the mass of people vying for the attention of several distracted bartenders. Finally, I find a familiar face in the crowd. My best friend is waving a hand excitedly from the corner of the bar closest to the restroom, urging me to join her. I'll be sure to thank her for her impeccable timing when I get over there.

"If you'll excuse me." I push back my chair and stand, but a hand ensnares my wrist before I'm able to exit without further explanation.

"Lex, wait!" Kade looks to me and then to Riley. "Apologize to her, now!"

I can't imagine how frightening Kade must have been on the football field, encased in an exoskeleton of foam rubber and molded plastic. He must have appeared more like a beast than a man with spiked cleats, a polycarbonate helmet, and game-day adrenaline flooding his veins. Even now, in his upscale street clothes, he looks like a warrior eager for battle.

"It's fine." I place my free hand atop Kade's and implore him to choose peace. "I don't need a half-ass apology from someone who doesn't mean it."

I shouldn't word it that way if I hope to return to the table, but I'm so tired of guys from the internet treating me like some loser who isn't meeting their high standards for adulting. Riley isn't the first guy to have opinions about my choice of work, and I doubt he'll be the last. Maybe I should stay, be more transparent, and run through the numbers, but I don't owe anyone an explanation. Undoubtedly, Riley would be shocked to find out I'm doing quite well for myself. This week, I filled and shipped a rush order that covered every one of my monthly bills, and then some. One person bought a dozen custom slasher romance novels plus artwork and spent over twenty-five hundred dollars.

Sure, that doesn't happen every day, but I make a steady income designing special editions for monthly book boxes and pad my savings with the cash I take in from my online store. Not to toot my own horn, but people know who I am and my work is highly sought after. I have a waiting list of authors begging for a spot closer to the top, but I take each job in turn and keep my pricing fair.

To hell with anyone who refuses to see the value in a passion-driven life.

"We're enjoying your company, Lex, and we'd like you to stay." The *we* Kade's referring to is himself and the ladies at the table. There's a chance even their husbands enjoy having me around. But I get the distinct impression Riley is no longer included. Kade releases my wrist slowly, leaving me free to go. "Plus, we still owe them a story."

I nod my head in acknowledgment before moving to step away, and when I glance at the television, I'm pleased to find our team leading by twelve points going into the half. It's loud in the restaurant, so I can't be certain, but as I pass beside the edge of the table, I swear I overhear Kade saying, "If she leaves, I'm telling Nero to bite your dick off when we get home."

I'm not sure who Nero is, but the sentiment is clear. If I walk out the front door without saying goodbye, my date is in for a rough end to the evening.

CHAPTER 8
ALEXIS

"I thought you were going out with the light-haired guy from the pictures. Did I get that wrong?" Skyler lifts onto her toes to sneak another peek at the table. "They're both cute, but the big guy with the dark hair is more your style, and he's still looking at you. In fact, you might want to take a pregnancy test because he was eye fucking you the entire time you were sitting next to him. Is that, like, what's his name's bodyguard or something?"

"No. Oh my god, shut up." I don't need to turn around to know that Kade is looking. I could feel his eyes on me as I crossed the bar. "That's Riley's roommate."

"Ohhhh-kay, threesome, I see you." She looks over my shoulder again and smiles wickedly. "Please, tell me you're going home with them tonight."

"How can I? This is the weirdest date I've ever been on. The guy who asked me out was cute and engaging, and I was so excited to meet him. I told you that. When we first got here, Riley seemed genuinely interested, and I swear he was flirting. But now he's distracted. Or unimpressed. Who knows?"

"Babe, guys who look that good are stupid when it comes to dating. He doesn't have to try very hard to get pussy, and it's made him complacent. But you're smart. And you're smokin' hot. And you deserve a guy who's willing to make an effort. If he can't see what's right in front of him because there's a basketball game on television, that's a *him* problem, not a *you* problem. All the more reason to make him regret it by hooking up with his roommate."

"Yeah, well, that's easier said than done. Kade's too perfect. He's obviously here as some sort of Fred Jones trap. Tall and thick and handsome and covered in tattoos. The guy is a walking wet dream. As if that's not enough, he reads books and shows a genuine interest in what I say." I sigh as reality tightens uncomfortably around my heart.

"He's too good to be true. No one that good-looking is into the shit I'm into. He's a frickin' unicorn."

"Then sit on his horn!" Skyler barks enthusiastically.

"There's no way. You don't get it. This feels like a no-win situation, and I'm trying not to look like a total asshole."

"What are you talking about? That over there is a win-win situation. The game ends in an hour, and you'll have Riley's undivided attention. Or you can select the equally impressive prize behind door number two and let Kade split you in half with the giant minotaur cock he's most likely got in his pants. It doesn't matter which one you choose because either way, you're getting your internal organs rearranged until sunrise. I guarantee both of those guys fuck like it's their job. And if you play your cards right, you'll end up like the best kind of Oreo cookie…"

I roll my eyes and shake my head, trying to look annoyed. Maybe I should boil it down to sex, like my friend is suggesting, and stop stressing over the multitude of hypotheticals.

"Double stuffed!" Skyler states the obvious in case I'm too distracted to follow along.

"I know what you meant." My failed attempt at anger breaks the dam, and my laughter gushes out, tightening the muscles in my stomach until they cramp on the left side. "But it's not going to happen. I don't think Riley's interested, and I can't very well abandon my date to run off and hook up with his roommate."

"Of course you can! Riley's a stranger, not your boyfriend. You're meeting them both for the first time tonight, and if one is showing more interest than the other, I say he's fair game." Skyler leans to her right and brushes my hair over my shoulder. "That being said, I wouldn't count the other one out. The blond guy, the one you think doesn't notice you, he's looking over here, and it's not giving me disinterested, casual glance vibes." She grips my shoulders and squeals excitedly, "You are so getting DPed."

"Who said I would even want that?" I challenge myself to play it off, but I can feel my ears burning and my cheeks giving me away. The downside of having a fair complexion is that I turn candy apple red when embarrassed. I can only pray the layer of green-tinted lotion and color-correcting makeup is doing its job.

"You do remember we lived together at one point, right? And I've seen the search history on your computer. So, let's cut the act because I'm well aware of the kinky shit you're into. Stop pretending like you aren't going to sleep with at least one of them tonight. Please. You don't have to do that with me. I'm here for it. I'm cheering you on like a best friend should, and I fully support your choices. But which one? That's the real question."

As much as I love my best friend, I think her insights are being clouded by horniness and beer goggles. She sounds like she needs to get laid worse than I do.

Skyler reaches for Nick, pulling him into our circle. "Hey hun, do me a favor and give our girl a nice big, *super friendly* hug, and make it a good one. I wanna test a theory."

"Bring it in, Alexis." Nick places a hand on my shoulder before pulling me tight against his chest. He's thinner than the guys I date, but the warmth of his embrace is not entirely unwelcome. He's a good guy. My friend is lucky to have him.

"You know what she's like when she gets a theory about something." We both laugh as he continues to hold me.

"Okay, now kiss her," Skyler prompts.

All I can do is shake my head and erupt into anxious laughter. I'm ninety-nine-point-nine percent certain Nick would never kiss me, even with his fiancée's permission, but when he leans in with puckered lips, I begin to question my certainty. I push my hands into his chest and angle my body away dramatically.

"Don't you dare!" I shout slightly louder than intended, causing the people around us to take notice of the situation.

"Oh shit! Let her go. Let her go. Let her go. Nick let go. You're about to die."

There's no time to process the words or react to Skyler's plea. One second, I'm wiggling and fighting for the safety of my lips, and the next, I'm encased in a prison of heated flesh and solid muscle as thick forearms cross my chest and stomach. The rhythmic rise and fall of his breaths, quickened by the excitement, tickle the top of my head as they rustle my hair. Against the back of my skull, I register the hammering of his racing heart and bring my hands to rest upon his wrists.

"Are you alright?" Kade's strength is not lost on anyone, and his presence feels like an executioner's axe.

My head falls to one side, propped against the bulge of his swollen bicep, leaving the sensitive skin of my neck exposed. This not-so-subtle position is meant as an invitation. A request for his kiss. A desperate appeal for a taste, a touch, a trace of the things he's been hinting at all night. He sets my body ablaze with the slightest contact, and I refuse to believe his flirtation is unintentional, especially now, with his cock pressed against me.

"I will not fail to protect you for a second time." The deep richness of his tone is even sexier when his words are meant only for me, and the sentiment is sweeter than Valentine's Day chocolates.

"I must have missed the first time because you've yet to fail me. Or is that part of our backstory I haven't heard yet?" Somehow, I'm as invested as the others, wanting to know the hidden truth, even though it was my jest that prompted the lie. "I appreciate you coming to my rescue, but I'm fine. My friends were only joking around."

"Well then, I apologize for misreading the situation. I'll go back to the table and leave you to it." The absence of his embrace is painful as his arms fall away, and he turns his back to me.

Wait! Don't leave me.

That's what I want to say, but it feels like too much, too soon, and we both know there's no path forward beyond tonight. You can't go on a date with a guy, hook up with his roommate, and think everyone will be fine with it in the morning. Life doesn't work that way.

I reach out, allowing my fingers to graze down his forearm before grasping his hand. "Please."

Kade turns, and again, his voice rings inside my head. *Mine.* The word is clear, as though it's being spoken in my ear, but my name is the only sound that passes his lips. "Lex."

"Please, stay. I want to introduce you to my friends." I smile and pull him toward me. "Have a beer with us. I'm buying."

"Good luck with that," Skyler scoffs. "It's impossible to get a drink in this place. We've been trying for the last twenty minutes."

Kade repositions himself off-center behind me and holds my waist with his hand. Again, I feel his cock pressed into me. It's situated atop my left hip instead of the small of my back, but its presence is unmistakable. How easy it would be to run my fingers up his thigh along the inseam of his jeans and find the treasure at the end of the rainbow. He raises his free hand and signals to the bartender, who acknowledges him with a smile.

She walks over, beer in hand, ignoring the crowd around us.

"Impossible. Unless you're *you*, apparently." Skyler is not easily impressed, but she smiles at me as though Kade is a pleasant surprise.

Admittedly, I have terrible taste when it comes to men. Too often, I've allowed people to benefit from my doubt. I tend to justify the rain while I'm busy dreaming of flowers, refusing to focus on the negative when there's so much happiness to be found in the simplicity of small acts. But painful disappointment usually outweighs any momentary pleasure.

"Thanks." Kade motions to the rest of us before accepting his drink from the smiling bartender, as though every woman working here knows him personally. "Whatever they want, you can add it to my tab."

Skyler and Nick quickly take full advantage, placing their order, but I turn away from the bar. I need to drive home at some point and prefer to do it with a clear head.

"You don't have to do that," I say, slipping the drink from Kade's hand and taking a sip. I hate the taste of beer, but I place a kiss on the lip of the glass, hoping it will linger there long enough for him to feel it.

"How else am I going to impress you?"

I shake my head slightly and smile. If Kade intended to impress me, that was accomplished long before now. But why would he want to? Why make a point to meet me first? Why flirt with me at all? Why chase after me?

I run through the list of obvious questions and jump to inescapable conclusions.

Because it's a setup. Or a game. A trap. Or a bet. It isn't real.

I hand back Kade's beer and take a large step toward my friends, moving away from him. It isn't long before the bartender returns with their drinks, and before she can walk away, I remove a folded hundred-dollar bill from my pocket. I hand her my winnings from the first quarter, partially clearing my debt. "Could you please apply this to his tab if it's not too much trouble?"

"Sweetie, you don't have to do that. My brother's good for it." She smiles at me for a long moment, giving me ample opportunity to rescind my offer. When I remain steadfast, she accepts the money with a nod and shouts past me. "Don't mess this up, dickhead. I like her."

I wonder how many sisters he has working here tonight. It makes sense that he was able to secure me a parking spot. I'll need to watch what I say with so many family members hidden in the crowd. I only hope our waitress isn't one of them.

"I like her too," he says. Twisting my hair around his hand, Kade guides the angle of my head and kisses my neck. The sensation warms my skin like the sincere caress of the summer sun. "I like her a whole hell of a lot, and I'm hoping she feels the same."

With my heart pounding in my chest, I look at Kade with eyes that beg for his kiss. I know better than to *like* him, but my emotions are conspiring against me, and I can't deny that I do feel something. Everything. More than I ever thought possible. I swear, his presence is altering my brain chemistry. The man has been tugging on my strings since he stepped into the building, and I handed them over like a complete idiot.

"I don't know what you want from me."

CHAPTER 9
KADE

I want you to look at me when you smile, Lex.

I want you to talk to me about your life.

And tell me about your day.

I want you to beg for me.

I want to be *your* Jax.

I want to hear you whispering that cute little nickname while I tease your pussy.

I want your eyes watering while you choke on my cock.

I want to taste you.

Tease you.

Fuck you until you cum more times than you ever thought possible.

I want to fill you with my fingers and stretch you with my cock.

I want to pour every last drop of myself inside you until my balls are wrung dry.

I want you to fall asleep in my bed tonight and wake up next to me in the morning.

I want you to stay.

I want you to stop playing games.

I want you to forget you came here for him.

And I want you to leave with me.

Goddamnit!

I want you to fucking choose me.

CHAPTER 10

ALEXIS

"I want everyone to have a good time and get home safely at the end of the night."

Seriously? I was hoping he'd say something along the lines of *a blowjob in the parking lot.*

I mean, that's fair. I also want everyone to have fun and get home safely, but that answer is the sort that goes without saying. I was looking for something slightly more selfish. I hadn't expected Kade to sound like the type of person who writes Christmas letters to Santa, asking for world peace.

Another item on the list that makes him more than I deserve. Why couldn't he be the slightest bit greedy? Then, I wouldn't have to feel so guilty for wanting him.

He fits into my friend group as naturally as I fit into his, and the conversation volleys around the small circle. Each time he releases an uninhibited, barking laugh that rings out clearly over the noisy crowd, Skyler catches my attention with a smile. *He's amazing,* she mouths as Nick recounts one of his favorite stories, and Kade listens with curious fascination.

"So, you cut cards to see who would be her date for the concert? That's a ballsy move. Not sure I could leave a decision like that to chance." Kade's grip tightens momentarily as though he's unwilling to entertain the thought of letting me go.

"Oh, trust me, I was sweatin' it, and I had every intention of chasing after her if I'd lost. But fate brought us into each other's lives that day, and we've been together ever since." Nick and Skyler exchange a knowing glance and a quick kiss.

It could be the heightened pleasure in the air or a consequence of reading one too many happily ever afters, but the evidence of true love is closing in on me. Examples keep popping up everywhere I look, sharply highlighting my single status. According to Skyler, I could take my pick. But she was referring to sex, not love.

Maybe, at some point, sex was all I wanted, when tonight was a concept, and my date's name was Riley Sinclair. I'm pretty sure that sounds right, but I can't remember. A one-night stand might have been a good time when there was no reason to hope for more. Maybe it still could be if I stopped thinking this was something it isn't. But I can hardly think at all.

Once Kade stepped into the picture, blocking all others from view, the idea of one night no longer felt like enough.

As halftime ends and the game resumes, Skyler and Nick pull me in for a hug, dragging Kade along with me. "The four of us should meet for lunch this weekend," Skyler requests.

"Yeah, Alexis could use a plus one," Nick tacks on.

"Hey! I enjoy food and good company. Anytime I'm invited, I'll be there." Kade conveys his interest but doesn't outright accept, as though the invitation he requires needs to be delivered by someone else. I can only assume that someone is me.

"You should come. But only if you want to. We meet every other Saturday at Valentine's. It's the best food around and close to where I live. I can text you the address." My pulse quickens at the thought of seeing him again, but I do my best to remain calm. Sounding too eager is a surefire way to scare him off.

"I know where it is. My buddies are obsessed with that place. One of them is married to the owner's daughter. Or maybe they both are. I'm not sure how it works. Anyways, I'd love to be your plus one if you'll have me."

"I'd like that." I would be willing to walk across broken glass and hot coals if it meant seeing him again, but if the real Kade is anything like the man I've met tonight, he'd never allow me to hurt.

"It's a date."

It's possible his words have killed me because my life begins flashing before my eyes. All the times leading up to now, when I felt alone and scared, I find him standing next to me, and somehow every-thing is better.

"And on that note, we should get going. Nick told his friends we'd swing by to watch the end of the game. Text me later. Or in the morning. I want to know you got home okay." Skyler reaches out to touch my arm, making sure she has my attention before leaning forward to press her cheek to mine. "Wherever he goes, go with him. I have a good feeling about this one."

"Yeah, I will." I smile as I choke back the flood of feelings welling inside me. This night is nothing like I expected, and the uncertainty is overwhelming. Is this a no-win or a win-win? I can't tell the difference from where I'm standing. It all feels like too much and not enough.

"You two get home safely." Kade slips a business card from his wallet and hands it to Nick. "My number is on there in case you run into trouble or need your car towed home after an evening of drinking. It's an option people rarely consider, but it's better than a DUI or a night in the hospital."

At first glance, I thought Kade was the type to rush into battle with guns blazing, or rather, axes swinging. He seemed well-equipped for combat, and I found his intimidating stature oddly comforting. Every woman wants to feel protected, and I'm no exception. But as tough as he might be, he's also kind and thoughtful. I hadn't imagined him that way when I was fingering myself in the car, but I'll need to amend my fantasy for future use.

"Are you coming back to the table or leaving with your friends?" Kade glances toward the door, his eyes landing on Skyler and Nick as they step onto the busy sidewalk and disappear.

"Looks like I'm with you."

CHAPTER 11
ALEXIS

I'm not sure what makes me part ways with Kade as we reach the table, but I retrace the path I followed when leaving, around the side where Riley is seated. The third quarter is underway, but he isn't watching the television. His eyes follow my steps until I'm beside him, wearing an expression I'm unable to read. I smile in acknowledgment.

Before I can scoot behind his chair, he pushes his seat back until it makes contact with the wall, blocking my path. If I want to get to my chair, my only option is to shimmy past his legs. It's an odd power play for a man whose attention has been mostly absent, but I'm unsurprised by his need for control.

"Am I no longer welcome to sit there?" I motion to the empty chair I'd previously occupied.

"No, you are. But I want you to sit *here* first." Riley pats his leg and grins. Whatever his intent, whether playful or malicious, I'm not sure, but it isn't worth causing a scene.

I plop down onto his legs and lift my feet from the floor, hoping the full weight of my frame is more than he expects. No matter his objective, he's toying with me. That much is clear. Perhaps this is my punishment for engaging with his friend in a way that borders on inappropriate.

A public shaming for a select audience.

Or perhaps it's something else entirely.

"I owe you an apology, Alexis. It wasn't my place to comment on your personal finances, and I'm sorry if what I said struck a nerve. Sometimes I get on my soapbox about shit and forget that no one asked for my opinion. I never intended to hurt your feelings, and I am sorry I upset you." Riley's expression of regret unlocks something in me, and I call down my guard, relaxing into his embrace. "Your passion and talent are eclipsed only by your beauty."

What a line, if ever I've heard one. Bullshit, of course, but it does make me smile. The sentiment tugs at my heartstrings, not because it conveys his genuine impression of me, but because he most likely spent the entire fifteen-minute halftime break coming up with it.

"I'll admit, I can be a bit over-sensitive when it comes to my work, but I didn't leave the table because you hurt my feelings. My friends were at the bar, and I wanted to say *hello*. I'm sorry. I should've said that before walking away." Instead of simply accepting his apology, I deflect and offer my own in return. Typical.

"If I had it to do all over again, I would've cooked dinner for the two of us, and we could've watched the game at home. I would've been greedy and kept you all to myself. Is it too late to get our date back on track?" Riley's asking for a second chance, but I'm not entirely sure I truly gave him a first one.

If Kade weren't here serving as a delicious distraction, nothing my date said or did thus far would've been a deal breaker. I would've met Riley at the door with a nervous smile and a friendly hug. I would have been a total flirt, finding not-so-subtle ways to touch him as much as possible as we watched the game together and shouted our support from the cheap seats. Despite what my best friend said to the contrary, I can't help but feel like I've been unfair. I keep trying to justify my actions by silently noting Riley's distraction, but I've been equally absent from our agreed-upon date.

"It's not even nine o'clock, so I'd say there's still plenty of time." I place my feet on the floor and attempt to stand, hoping to slip into my chair with grace, but Riley holds me in place on his lap.

"I'm glad to hear it. Maybe now, you could clear something up for me." Riley raises his voice as he turns to face Kade. "I showed you photos of her. And she saw you in my profile. Yet, neither of you mentioned that you knew each other. Care to explain?"

This is the perfect time to own the lie and tell the truth. The answer is so simple. It's right there on the tip of my tongue. *I don't know him. We've never met before. It was meant to be a joke.* But to say those words is to admit that Jaxson Kade is a stranger, and right now, that feels inconceivable.

"I didn't think she'd remember me."

Riley's embrace falls slack, leaving me to slip into my seat. A damask rose, flush with embarrassment, keenly positioned between two razor-sharp thorns. If I end this night plucked free of petals, I have no one to blame but myself.

"Right, because there are so many six-foot-seven, tattooed…"

Kade cuts him off. "Lex and I were sixteen and only met once at a party. We're talking about a night that happened almost twenty years ago. So yeah, I thought there was a pretty good chance she might not remember me."

His resolute claim has me questioning my memories.

"Well, come on then, out with it. We're all invested at this point. Tell us the story." Riley presses his hands into the table and leans forward as I freeze into a solid block of ice.

"A buddy of mine from a neighboring school invited me out. So, besides him, there was nobody at the party I recognized. I didn't even know the girl whose house we were at, and I think I met her for about five seconds. Her name was Sarah, something or other. She went to a private school. Short, skinny, blonde-haired girl. Her parents had money." Kade's expression is smug. "You would've liked her."

"Woodrich," I chime in tentatively as the weight of Kade's hand finds a home on my thigh, and my body thaws beneath his touch. It feels like he's inviting me to play along for the sake of us both. "Sarah Woodrich."

"Oh my god, you're right. That's it. Sarah Woodrich." He squeezes slightly, signaling his approval. "I love that you remember her name because I was about to make myself nuts trying to come up with it."

"Yeah." I huff out a shy laugh. "I didn't know her either, but every time I see her last name on a bottle of wine, I think about that night."

"It's the same for me, only not with wine. There was a movie playing in the living room at one point. Do you remember?" I nod my head, and he contin- ues. "Night of the Living Dead. The original, not the remake. Every Halloween, I watch that movie, and part of me feels like I'm back in that house, wishing life would grant me a do-over."

"You guys are giving me chills. Look!" Elise

stretches her arm across the table, brandishing an impressive display of goosebumps. "Keep going."

"I went out that night with my cousin. She ditched me when we got there to make out with some boy. And I didn't know anyone else. I'd love to say I talked up a storm and made fast friends, but I'm pretty sure I was invisible." Sixteen-year-old me was a bit of a wallflower, letting my art stand out so I wouldn't have to. If I had been at a party, it's likely I would've hidden in the corner or walked around cleaning up trash until it was time to leave.

"You'll never go unnoticed so long as I'm around. I saw you back then as clearly as I see you now. Lex, you've never been invisible. I just didn't know how to find you." Kade's eyebrows pull together as though he's questioning how I could think so little of myself. It's a look I've seen before on the faces of my friends when I'm being self-deprecating. He allows his statement to linger in the space between us, trapped in the duration of a pause, long enough for his meaning to sink in. And then he's back, addressing the others, resuming the story where it left off. "Sarah's parents were out of town on a two-week cruise, island hopping in the tropics, so no one was worried about getting caught. Most people were drinking and acting older than they were. I couldn't blame them for wanting to have fun, but my dad had been killed six months earlier by a drunk driver, so I made myself a rum and coke, minus the rum, and pretended to be a normal teenager."

My heart sinks, knowing that while the rest of our combined fiction is a fabrication, *this* detail is true. "I'm so sorry, Jax. I had no idea."

"It's fine. We can talk about it later." He squeezes my leg again, only this time, I wrap myself around his arm and rest my head against his shoulder, wanting to absorb every ounce of lingering pain left over from the past. "Right now, they want to hear about us."

I straighten in my chair, remembering the story we're painting is a tale of youthful romance. The only tragedy, perhaps one of missed opportunity. "After a while, the people who hadn't coupled up were getting bored, and the girls suggested we play a game. They passed around a bottle of wine, taking long swigs until eventually it was empty, and the boys cleared the coffee table. Then, they called everyone to sit in a circle. I had overheard a few girls talking in the kitchen, and they seemed to have their sights set on one boy in particular. They were all hoping to kiss the mysterious newcomer. The raven-haired hottie who stood out in the crowd. Unfortunately, for all of us, he refused to participate, and the girls were left to drown their rejection in the affection of lesser boys."

Kade laughs, ready to rejoin the story. "Yeah, well, I wasn't exactly known for my self-control back then. It's a wonder I lasted as long as I did, sitting off to the side, pretending to watch the movie flickering over your shoulder. Every time the bottle whirled around and slowed to a stop, I could feel my insides twist. When my buddy landed on the girl next to you, I'd had more than I could handle. I went outside, hoping the fresh air might cool my temper, but it only made things worse."

"Hold up. I don't understand. I thought you had a thing for Alexis. Are you saying it was the girl your buddy ended up kissing? That's who you were interested in? She's the reason why you didn't want to play?" Hailey peppers Kade with questions, temporarily halting his narration.

"No, that's not what I'm saying. I can't even picture that girl's face, and had she not been seated where she was, I wouldn't have even mentioned her. It wasn't the girl my friend kissed that had me running. It was the thought of what I would've done had the bottle stopped half an inch further to the right." He takes my hand. And for the fourth time tonight, Kade presses his lips to my skin, allowing his kiss to absorb into my bones. "I couldn't force myself to watch someone else kiss you."

I huff out a strangled breath as shallow tears begin to pool behind my bottom lashes. "Well, the gods were on your side because no one ever landed on me. When it was my turn to spin, I quit playing and went outside."

"Why?" Elise and Hailey nearly shout in harmony.

"Because the only guy I wanted to kiss never joined the game."

Hailey and Elise dissolve into a chorus of giddy shrieks, catching the attention of the tables around ours.

"Okay, so then what?" Riley leans in further. "You walked outside and found Kade standing under the moonlight like a werewolf, and he bent you over the hood of some random person's car."

"What? Where did that come from?" Riley's abrupt detour into shifter porn has me momentarily laughing until I picture Kade morphing into his wolf form so he can knot me in the grass between two pickup trucks. I bite my lip, damn near drooling when Kade cuts in to finish the story.

"If that had been the case, Lex wouldn't be on a date with you right now."

"Hey, at least you're finally willing to acknowledge that she's on a date with me."

"Riley, shut up! We didn't spend half the night hounding them for this story for you to chime in and screw up the ending. Quit acting like all of a sudden you give a shit!"

"Well, for the record, Hailey, I do give a shit!" Riley's heated tone softens as he regains his composure and reaches an arm across the back of my chair. "But by all means, Alexis, I didn't mean to interrupt. Please tell us the ending."

"There isn't much to tell. When I walked out the front door, I saw the flashing lights. One of the neighbors must have called the cops, complaining about the noise, because the party got shut down. Those of us who hadn't been drinking were allowed to drive home, and everyone else had to call their parents. The night ended, and we never saw each other again."

"Oh my god, you two are killing me right now. It can't end like that. You have to kiss. Riley, look away for a minute." Elise waves her hand wildly, motioning for him to turn his head.

"It's fine," I say with a counterfeit smile, wishing that were true. "I suppose it wasn't meant to be."

Kade releases my hand and pulls away, deepening the fissures that threaten to leave me shattered. His withdrawal is a stark reminder of his absence up until this point.

Doesn't he know I needed him back then, when we were teenagers and I was being bullied relentlessly in the hallways of my school? Doesn't he realize I could have used his strength when I was in my twenties, and men frequently found ways to push for more than I wanted to give? All these years later, I smile and flirt and act like everything's coming up roses, but if I'm being honest, I'm lonely. I crave the warmth of a lover's touch and the security of their embrace, but what I'm looking for, I'm not going to find in a one-night stand. I want mutual respect and partnership. I want inside jokes and telepathic conversations. I want take-out food and movie nights. I want brunch and book shopping. I want my soulmate to be my best friend, and I want the life we build to last forever. Why doesn't Kade see that when he looks into my soul? I needed him back then, but now, I want him more than ever.

Retrieving the buzzing phone from his pocket, Kade acknowledges the screen with a worried expression. "I disagree," he remarks as he exits the conversation, disappearing into the glow.

CHAPTER 12
ALEXIS

Like most women, I find it vexing when men make a point of having the last word, especially when they conclude a conversation in dispute before hopping onto their phone to attend to more *important* matters. It's a situation I've encountered countless times with a fair number of undeserving opponents.

But in this specific instance, with this particular man, I appreciate the disagreement.

The high I'd been riding all night dipped when I allowed myself to dive into the nonfictional parts of my past, thinking about what was instead of what could've been. But with two words left echoing in my head, Kade placed me right back onto my pedestal.

It's dangerous, this path we're on, but it's also exciting.

There's no need to wake up with regrets, and this can easily be a top-ten night if I don't get attached. That's a lesson I've had to learn the hard way. Emotions should be kept at a distance. It's unhealthy to live in the real world. As much as I might want it, and as much as they might pretend, the people out here aren't like the characters in my books. So, if engaging my heart in matters is required, I'd much rather fall in love with the chiseled perfection of fictional men who rarely disappoint me.

I turn my head toward Kade, hoping to catch his eye, but he's still too distracted by his phone to notice. A perfect example of why it's better to aim for sex and nothing more. I watch as he reads through a series of messages, reaching the bottom only to scroll back to the top and begin reading again. By the third pass, I decide to give him space.

I readjust my position and glance at the nearest television, only to find that our team has lost its twelve-point lead and is currently down by four.

"What the hell happened?" The question springs from my lips as though the words have taken on a life of their own. "We were winning by double digits, and now we're behind?"

"Yes, sweetie," Riley coos, leaning over to bump his shoulder into mine. "That's what happens in these high-stakes games. The players give it everything they've got, and the score changes as the night progresses. But I'm confident the *better* team will pull through in the end." He tops it off with an adorable, well-placed wink, and I'm certain the last line holds a deeper meaning.

Again, I glance to my left, but Kade is still knee-deep in the middle of something, hammering lines of text into his phone. Hopefully, it's nothing serious. From my chair, I'm able to see both of his sisters. All is quiet at the hostess stand, and the crowd near the bar has settled. Whatever he's dealing with doesn't appear to be a family matter.

Not wanting to be a bother or feel like a looky-loo, I turn my attention back to the television and distract myself with the action playing out on screen.

Time seems to quicken and slow to a stop as I watch with fevered interest. Our team scores two unanswered baskets in a row before getting fouled on their third attempt. Collectively, the entire restaurant looks on with held breath as the first shot is taken from the free-throw line.

Riley and I high-five in celebration as both shots find their way to the hoop, and two points are added to the scoreboard. The energy in the building is electric as the tally increases in our favor, and Riley pulls me against his chest for a hug.

"I told you, it's never too late to turn things around."

He moves his chair closer to mine and wraps an arm around my waist, pulling me flush with his chest. Kneading his fingers into my sweater, his touch makes my body tingle as his lips brush against my ear. "You're coming to the house after this, right?"

"Am I?" I ask instead of answer. "I didn't know I was invited."

Riley mentioned the hot tub and a bottle of wine with my name on it, but that was earlier in the evening. A lot's happened since then, and I'm not stupid enough to assume an invitation like that would still stand after I spent the majority of my time talking to someone else.

"Of course, you're invited. I was hoping you'd spend the night."

I've been slightly annoyed by Riley's lack of notice all evening, but now that his focus is trained on me, I'm not sure I could've handled a one-on-one date and hours of undivided attention. The way his suggestive tone makes my core vibrate, I doubt I would've lasted long enough for the food to arrive.

"But we both know you have options, and I'm not the only one hoping to extend the evening into morning." At Riley's words, my gaze shifts left.

The phone in Kade's hand no longer holds capture over his attention, leaving him free to find me. Unfortunately, he escaped in time to catch me reclining in the arms of another man's embrace. My heart sinks as I straighten in my chair.

There was a time, prior to three seconds ago, when I would've considered myself a person of unquestionable loyalty despite my internal struggle and inability to make a definitive choice between the men on either side of me. Now, as I balance between them, I find myself sitting in the category of selfish, disloyal, horny asshole who's easily distracted by pretty boys and shiny objects.

Kade's hand slips onto my leg as he leans forward in his chair.

My heart beats like a drum, banging beneath my ribs, as the tension stretches into a deafening silence. The way I see it, I have two choices. I can either apologize profusely or excuse myself from the table and run away. Each option sounds equally inadequate, and both signal an end to the orgasm-inducing conclusion I've been dreaming of, but this is what I get for being greedy.

"Lex, I need to ask you for a gigantic favor."

CHAPTER 13
KADE

I wish we had actually met when we were teenagers. Crafting a fictional backstory felt so much like rewriting the past that it's got me in my head, reliving the pivotal moments of my adult life with her by my side. I didn't know it was possible to miss someone I'd never met, and now I know better.

Her knees press into the outside of my thigh as she turns in her chair to face me. It takes a considerable amount of willpower not to kiss her. Watching her lips as they part ever so slightly. I want to knot my fingers into the length of her hair and lay claim to her body.

Being greeted with the sweet smell of her pussy has left me hungry for a taste, and after hours of playful teasing, I'm famished to the point of starvation. I want to swipe the table clean of its contents and lay her out like a buffet so I can savor every inch of her.

I want to drink dry every last drop.

This desire within me is not a temporary want. Nor is it spurred on by competitive arousal. I already knew I wanted her before showing up tonight. It was no accident that Riley was left behind with the driver, and I was the first through the door.

If he wants to make this into a competition, so be it, but we'll not be flipping a coin at the end of the night to determine whose bed she ends up in. Chance will not govern my fate. Not this time. I'll put in the work, fight for her attention, and leave the outcome in her beautifully capable hands.

"I need a ride to work, and you're the only one here with a car. Would you be willing to take me?" As soon as the request leaves my mouth, I regret the impersonal arrangement of my words.

"Oh. Yeah. I mean, of course. That's not what I consider a gigantic favor." Her smile falters as she stumbles through her response. It's as though she's disappointed. Like she'd gotten her hopes up, expecting me to ask for something else, only to be let down. "Do you need to leave right away?"

"Ideally, but you're allowed to say no." I start to feel guilty for even asking.

"I wouldn't do that. I'm not the type of person to leave someone stranded. If you need a ride, I'm happy to take you." Her sincere kindness nearly melts me.

"You know I wouldn't ask if it weren't important." She doesn't know that about me, not yet, but I want her to trust me.

"You don't have to convince me, Jax. I already said yes."

CHAPTER 14

ALEXIS

I hate when people are mad at me, but what's worse is when they're disappointed. I knew Kade's announcement to the group would go over like a lead balloon, but I wasn't expecting *everyone* to feel so strongly about our departure. The ladies and their husbands made every effort to convince us to stay. They offered alternatives and suggested we wait until after the final buzzer, but Kade insisted that leaving now was the only option.

Saying our final goodbyes, Riley stands beside me.

"Couldn't he borrow your car and meet us at the house afterward? I don't understand why you both have to leave." He tucks his fingers into the cuff of my sweater and gently tugs at the fabric. "I promise I'll do better."

"I've only had two drinks, so it's safer if I drive." I know he wants me to stay, but Riley can't argue with facts. "I'll most likely have to drive him home when he's finished with whatever he's doing. If you want, I can come in and hang out."

"You already know that's what I want." For a split second, I think Riley might kiss me, but then the moment passes.

"Okay. Well, in that case, I'll see you soon." There's a good chance this is goodbye, but neither of us says it.

Riley is attractive and successful, with plenty to offer the right girl. He isn't going to lose sleep over someone like me. To him, I'm a potential notch in the bedpost. A means to an end. An easy lay to tide him over before he's on to better things.

If he'd been interested in more than that, he would've noticed me beside him at some point in the evening prior to now.

I grab my jacket and wave farewell before following Kade through the restaurant, past the coolers, and out the back door. He seems to go wherever he chooses, and I wonder if anyone's ever dared to bar his access.

Could they deny him if they tried?

I never stopped to consider whether or not I should be scared. I'm leaving the protection of the herd, and Kade could very well be a wolf in sheep's clothing. I doubt the three other men in the group could fight him off, even if they worked together, so my odds of survival, alone, should his intentions be sinister, are virtually nil.

Kade takes my hand and links our fingers, but doesn't join them at the base like a normal person would. He weaves them together near the tip, between the joints. As we walk to the car, the warmth of his touch erases my concerns and any guilt I feel about leaving.

He pulls my keys from his pocket, unlocks the door, and opens the driver's side. "I appreciate you doing this for me, Lex. I promise I'll make it up to you."

"You don't owe me anything, but…" I toss my jacket into the back, slip into my seat, and pull on the seatbelt. "You do realize you stuck your friends with the bar tab."

Kade laughs and closes the door.

I watch through the windshield as he circles around to the passenger side, pulls open the door, and squeezes himself into the seat beside me. When he closes the door, we're alone.

Absent is the crowd that came for the game and the chaotic chatter they brought with them. Missing are the friends we shared drinks with along the way. Lost is the date I left the house for. Only Kade and I remain.

"Speaking of bar tabs, were you out here drinking in my car?" I lift the pint glass from the cup holder and raise it into the air between us. With the overhead lights on, my eyes catch on something thick and white pooled in the indent of the glasses' bottom, and realization strikes like a lightning bolt. "Did you jerk off in my car?"

He grabs the glass from my hand and attempts to explain, but I'm laughing so hard I've gone deaf. I collapse in on myself as my stomach muscles tighten and a cramp stitches into my side. I cough and wheeze, trying desperately to catch my breath, but my amusement refuses to subside.

I picture him.

Oversized.

Crammed into the tiny seat.

Dick in hand.

Rocking the small car as he works himself over.

Saying my name as he sprays his release into the bottom of a glass.

Wishing it was me.

My breaths are heavy as arousal replaces my merriment. When Kade took my keys and didn't return, I left the restaurant, trying to find him, but Riley followed me outside, insisting I wasn't safe on my own. I hadn't intended to remain alone, but I couldn't tell him that. So, I returned an urgent phone call that could've waited until tomorrow and allowed him to stand guard. After what felt like forever, Riley and I went back inside.

"Even though you're not mad, I'm going to apologize," Kade insists, slipping the glass from my view and tucking it behind the seat.

"Please don't. I don't want you to be sorry." I reach across the center console and touch his arm. "I'd rather imagine you so turned on sitting next to me at the table that the smell of me lingering in my car made you feral."

Kade takes my hand and moves it to his leg. "Would you like to feel what you've been doing to me?"

I nod, but he holds my hand firmly in place at his mid-thigh.

"I need to hear you say it."

If he wants me to beg, I will. "Kade, please. I want to…"

"No, Lex." His hand presses into mine. "Try again."

"Jaxson, please." His name comes out breathy and pleading. "I'm begging you."

"You're so close, baby. Just give me what I need."

"Jax." The single syllable hangs on a whisper. "I need to know that you were thinking about me while you were in here. Otherwise, I'm going to be jealous."

He slides my hand up his leg with a growl until I make contact with his engorged cock. "You're all I've been thinking about."

I can tell from a single touch he's thicker than any of the guys I've been with in the past, and the thought of taking him has me panting. I wish I owned an SUV. I'm not sure it would even be possible to have sex here in the parking lot. Not in my economy car.

I stroke the length of his cock through his jeans, wishing he'd allow me better access. I need to see what I'm agreeing to, and convince myself it's all for me.

"And what about you?" Kade reaches into my lap and wedges his hand between my thighs. "Who were you thinking about while you played with this sweet little pussy?"

My back arches as he rubs circles over the inseam of my jeans. "You, Jax. I was thinking about you."

He quickly pushes my legs apart and uses an open hand to pat my swollen lips. "You don't have to lie to me, Lex. It's okay if you were thinking about him. I don't care about before, so long as I'm the one you cum for now."

There are two things that get my juices flowing and have the potential to plunge me over the edge. Oral stimulation. And audio. Even if Kade stopped touching me, he could probably get me off, so long as he kept talking. But if he truly wanted to drive me wild, he'd shove his dick down my throat.

"I was imagining you. In the back seat. With your hand around my throat. You were stroking yourself and saying how pretty I'd look, swallowing your cock. And Riley was there. In the passenger seat. Telling me I'd be taking you both before the night's end." I reach down between the seat and the door, finding the lever to recline.

"Such a greedy girl." Kade unbuttons my pants and slowly eases the zipper down. He slips his hand beneath my panties and slides two fingers between my lips. "And so wet."

"Look how turned on you are." He strokes over my clit as he removes his hand from my pants and sucks his fingers clean. "You really want it, don't you? You want Riley and I to take turns fucking you until you're all used up?"

"Yes," I admit, without a second of hesitation.

CHAPTER 15

ALEXIS

Had I been thinking clearly, I might have revised my answer, but my brain stopped functioning soon after we got into the car, and I lost all sense of logic.

"Shit." Kade looks at his phone and squares his shoulders. "We've gotta go."

I've seen plenty of guys turn on a dime, but I've never had one leave me so abruptly as I'm teetering on the edge of an orgasm. It's cruel and painful. Whatever the female equivalent of blue balls is, I'm feeling it. Unfortunately, the throbbing in my clit is nothing compared to the stab of his rejection.

I'm half tempted to leave, forsake my keys, evacuate my car, and return to the restaurant. But heading back to the table with my tail between my legs would only bring further embarrassment, and I doubt I could field the group's questions with any level of tact or grace. I couldn't be honest about what happened and wouldn't want to lie.

I button my pants and tug on the zipper before inclining my seat and starting the car. "You'll need to tell me where to go."

Kade gives a series of verbal commands and accompanying hand gestures as I navigate the city's one-way streets. Any hint of flirtation is gone. There's no playful sweetness left in his voice. No relaxed confidence in his demeanor. The man I felt comfortable leaving the bar with seems to have stayed behind with his friends, and now I'm here with someone I'm not sure I can trust.

"After this light, you'll turn right at the sign. Do you see it?" He points to an illuminated, green sign fifty yards ahead. The logo is a beetle of some kind.

As I get closer, the image appears clearer, and I'm able to make out the name of the business. Cicada Towing. Available 24/7 (including Christmas).

"Not a beetle," I say as I pass through the yellow warning light.

"What?" Kade reaches over and places a hand on my leg. The weight of his touch spreads through the fibers of my muscles like glue, binding me back together.

"Nothing. I was talking to myself."

I signal for the right-hand turn, even though we're the only car on the road, and pull into the driveway at the base of the sign. It opens into a parking lot with a dimly lit building to the right and a solid metal gate straight ahead. Parked along the fence is an expensive-looking black sports car. The headlights flash as we approach.

"Any chance this place has a bathroom I could use?" My panties are soaked, and I'm uncomfortable. I'd sooner throw them away and risk chafing rather than be forced to sit and stew in the reminder of his dismissal.

"Yeah. I'll take you inside. Pull up there next to the door." He points to a spot marked as reserved.

I imagine the sign pertains to office hours and nights when the city is less distracted. I wonder if they've ever towed someone from the single reserved parking spot in the lot and forced them to pay the impound fee. In movies, tow truck drivers always seem sketchy, but they're rarely the killer.

A few years back, I hit a patch of black ice while driving 25 mph on a country road. It was the middle of the night, and there was no way I was getting out of the ditch on my own. I called for a tow, but the roads were bad, and the drivers were busy, so I had no choice but to wait. I didn't have enough gas to keep the car running and wasn't sure how long it would take for someone to find me. Thankfully, I kept a blanket on the backseat for such an occasion. The temperature continued to drop, and the minutes became excruciating. So, when I saw the headlights approaching in my rearview mirror, I thought I was saved. Unfortunately, that wasn't the case.

"I want you to stay inside while I take care of this. Do you understand?" Kade's serious tone indicates this is no time for jokes, so I remain silent and nod my head, still caught somewhere between the trauma of the past and my growing unease about the current situation I find myself in.

"I need to hear you say it."

From the corner of my eye, I catch a glimpse of the solid mass exiting the luxury vehicle to my left. He's not as big as Kade, but his body language speaks volumes. He approaches with a dark confidence that opens a pit in my stomach.

I've put myself in some stupid positions, but this might very well be the worst.

The man reaches for the driver's side handle, and I know better than to fight what's coming. I unlock the door and accept his hand when offered, exiting to stand beside him.

"I'm sorry if he's late." I lead with an apology like I often do. Only this time, it isn't *my* safety I'm concerned with. "I went the wrong way and got turned around. It's entirely my fault. Stupid one-way streets. I swear, this city's gonna be the death of me."

"Not if I have any say in the matter." The deep gravel of his voice buries me to the knees, and I'm unable to move.

Kade walks around the rear of the car and presses himself firmly against my back, wrapping his arms around my waist. "The keys are in the office. I'm gonna take her inside, and then I'll be out to open the gate." He speaks over my head to the man in front of me. Yet again, I find myself in the middle.

"No detours, you two. I want to get this done while it's quiet." The man places a hand on my shoulder, and Kade pulls me closer. "But I do like the girl-friend. She's tough."

"I'm not," I respond before Kade has a chance to open his mouth. "A little self-sacrificing, but that's about it."

The man repositions his hand so he's cupping the side of my neck and runs his thumb along my jawline. "Well, there's nothing tougher than that, now, is there? My wife would take a bullet for me. Not that I would ever let her."

If it weren't for Kade holding me upright, I'd be in jeopardy of melting beneath this stranger's touch.

CHAPTER 16
ALEXIS

The door closes behind Kade, and I hear the lock engage, leaving me securely inside. Alone. The overhead lights remain off, and an antique lamp casts the room in a hazy, yellow glow. A stack of books sits on a table in the corner next to a couch with well-worn cushions. It's not dirty or uninviting. The dated setup simply lacks the impersonal aesthetic you'd expect to see in an office.

One entire wall is lined with metal filing cabinets, each labeled with a series of numbers. I run my fingers over the back of a wooden chair, wondering how many people have sat here while being fired. In the center of the desk is a plaque that reads OWNER, so I'm careful not to touch anything else.

The last thing I need is for Kade to lose his job because I accidentally moved his boss's coffee mug.

I step across the room, hoping to find the bathroom, but on my first attempt, I locate a closet. It's mostly hooded sweatshirts and extra pairs of shoes, but there's also a small black box set high on a shelf.

"That's definitely a gun," I say aloud and shut the door, careful not to disturb anything.

The second and final door, not counting the one Kade and I came through, hides exactly the room I've been looking for. I reach inside and run my hand along the wall until I locate the switch for the light. The bathroom is bigger and a whole lot cleaner than I expected. It appears to have been remodeled within the last year, and no expense was spared.

If the couch and the lamp were a glimpse into the past, the bathroom doorway is a wormhole to the future.

The sliding glass shower doors are spotless and nearly invisible. It takes everything in me not to reach out and touch them. Oh, what I wouldn't give for a quick rinse and a massaging showerhead. It wouldn't take much to relieve the ache. Less than a minute, most likely, if I did it myself.

Maybe that's what I should do. Sprawl out on the bathroom floor like some horny teenager masturbating behind the only locked door allowed in the house. I'm turned on enough to do it, and the floor looks impressively clean, but I'm not a teenager. I'm a grown-ass woman who came out tonight looking to be expertly fucked by a whole-ass man.

I slip out of my shoes and unfasten my pants, allowing the material to drop around my ankles. Kicking the pile to the side, I consider my next move. A shower might be wildly inappropriate, but stealing a few flushable wipes from the package on the back of the toilet couldn't possibly get anyone into trouble.

While freshening up, my mind travels along a series of unrelated paths, stopping and diverting course before reaching the end of any single one-lane road.

I've been a twisted jumble of emotions all evening.

Had I stuck with the plan, I'd be watching the game with Riley and the other couples at the restaurant. He'd have his arm around the back of my chair, and every time our team regained the lead, he'd pull me close. We'd share a kiss at the sound of the final buzzer. He'd take me home. We'd have sex. And he'd promise to call me tomorrow.

Tonight could have been simple. I knew what I was getting with the light-haired, green-eyed, six-foot-two financial consultant. I've been on plenty of dates with guys exactly like him, and they always end the same.

Instead, I'm here. Hanging out in the bathroom of some random downtown towing company. Trying to talk myself out of orgasming on the pristine tile floor. Pretending I know nothing while two highly attractive and potentially dangerous men do something that's undoubtedly illegal, less than sixty feet away.

"I swear, officer. I only went with him because I thought he wanted to have sex in a parking lot somewhere. I didn't know there would be two of them." The woman in the mirror laughs at the unbelievability of my confession. So, I drop the register of my voice and try the story from a different angle. "When we found the body, she wasn't wearing any panties."

I look down at the floor where my underwear lay discarded and grimace at the thought of damp fabric touching my skin. I simply cannot do it. I consider throwing them in the trash, but the can is empty and lacks a lid. It would be too obvious. Instead, I slip back into my jeans, retrieve my shoes, and stuff the stretch lace cheeky briefs into my front pocket.

At the doorway, I pause before turning off the light and take one last look in the mirror. "You're a tough girl who goes toe to toe with killers, Bella. Quit acting scared."

The bathroom door opens, and the crisp white light cuts out, returning me to the lamp light glow.

"I'd never let anything bad happen to you, and I'd never knowingly put you in harm's way." Kade sits casually on the edge of the desk, appearing out of nowhere like an apparition.

His unexpected presence makes my heart leap, and I nearly hurl my shoes at him in self-defense. Thankfully, I recognize the voice, and my would-be weapons fall to the floor with a thud.

"That's good to hear." I take a tentative step

forward. And then another. "Does that mean we're friends again, or are you still mad at me?"

Kade pushes forward, meeting me in the middle. Seeming even bigger now that I'm barefoot. His massive hands find a home above my hips as he gently squeezes my waist. "I never intended for us to be friends."

"Oh." I mean, sure, I suppose deep down somewhere, I already knew that, but it hurts to hear him say it.

"Is that what you came here for, a cup of tea and a friendly conversation?"

My exhaled breath bounces off his broad chest.

"Well, no. Obviously not. We both know why I'm here." My clit is throbbing and my ego is bruised, but if I'm being honest, I'm more irritated than angry. "But I'm still mad at you. You can't leave a girl hanging like that. It's mean."

He spins me around and backs me into the edge of the desk. "I only stopped because I needed enough room to move, and the front seat of your car wasn't ideal for what I wanted to do to you."

Kade holds me in place while stepping around the corner of the desk, using his free arm to swipe the surface free of its contents. The unexpected crash startles me, and I turn to watch as trays of invoices and office supplies hurl toward the filing cabinets and scatter across the tile floor. A coffee mug shatters into pieces, and the nameplate is nowhere to be found. My hand comes over my mouth as I look on in disbelief.

"Now, where were we?" Kade lifts me by my ass and sets me on the desk, pushing my knees apart. Leaving me no room to question his intentions.

My breath catches, and I swallow hard, too shocked to respond.

"Tell me you still want this." Desire burns in his eyes as he slips his warm hands under the bottom hem of my sweater. "You know I need to hear you say it."

"At a minimum, you're getting fired from your job. If not arrested. You know that, right?" I press my open hand to his chest, above his racing heart. I've been horny plenty of times, but never to the point of vandalism. "What were you thinking? You can't just…"

"Oh my god, Lex, will you stop? I'm never going to get you off if you're worrying about my employment status the entire time I'm eating your pussy." He removes my sweater slowly, leaving me plenty of time to protest, and folds it into a pillow. "I promise you, we're fine. The owner isn't going to be mad."

I shake my head, troubled by his lack of concern but impressed by his boldness. I suppose, at this point, what's done is done. If we're getting arrested, we might as well make the most of it. I allow my hand to drop, grazing the front of his chest and down his stomach, stopping when I get to the bulge swelling beneath his jeans.

"You're right. I didn't come here to sip tea and start a silent book club. I don't want to be your friend. I want this, Jax. I've wanted it since I first saw you."

CHAPTER 17
KADE

I never meant we couldn't be friends.

We could be.

We are.

I should have said I never intended for us to *only* be friends.

But I didn't.

And now my vague definition of our would-be relationship title has run through that mousetrap of a mind and brought her to the conclusion that I want nothing more than sex.

I need to stop talking about it and show her. Prove to her with my actions what my words fail to convey.

When she leaves here, there needs to be no room left for doubt.

I take my time, teasing her nipples before reaching around to unclasp her lace bra. I'm going to enjoy pleasing her. The way her body responds to my touch tells me she wants this as much as I do.

Lex pulls at the opening of my jeans until the button gives way. Her touch is frantic, as though every second without my cock robs her of life. She pushes the outermost layer down my thighs and pauses to bite her bottom lip.

A small whimper escapes her chest.

Goddamn, I want her.

"I promise I'll give it to you." I move her hands and ease her onto her back, carefully supporting her head and neck with the folded sweater. "But first, I want to eat."

I've been dreaming of this moment, and after hours of waiting, I'm famished. As much as I want her to suck and fuck, she's going to have to be patient.

Lex looks gorgeous, laid out in front of me with her breasts exposed and her eyes pleading for more. I kick off my jeans and lean over her, gripping the edge of the desk for support. I want to test her boundaries, explore her body, memorize her curves, and uncover her kinks.

She hinted at something while we were flirting in the restaurant. Lex said hand tattoos made pretty necklaces. And in the car, she said she'd imagined me in the back seat with my hand around her throat. I'm dying to give her the necklace of her dreams. One she'll never want to remove.

With my thumb and four fingers, I apply increasing pressure to the sides of her neck, careful not to press my hand into the front of her throat.

Her back arches as her eyes close, and she moans beneath me.

Turns out she was right. Seeing her this way, she looks so good. My cock is practically vibrating.

"So pretty," I croon. "You're the most beautiful woman I've ever seen."

Her eyes open as she shifts beneath me. "If you're going to lie, do it by promising to make me orgasm more times than I can count. Otherwise, shut up and start licking." Her playful grin morphs into something wicked with my hand still wrapped around her throat.

For a split second, I forget to hold back. I forget we're only playing a game. I forget this is our first time together. And my grip tightens. "I'm going to lick your clit until you beg me to stop. Because I want to. Not because you told me to. I'm going to turn that pussy into a feast. And then, I'm going to fuck you."

Her fingers encircle my wrist, but she makes no effort to pull me away. This is her means of warning me that a boundary is nearby, but I haven't crossed the line. Not yet.

I receive her message loud and clear and allow my clasped hand to loosen. When I attempt to pull back, she holds me in place.

"Jax, please. Don't leave me again."

When Lex and I were in the car, parked beside the restaurant, I was so focused on the restrictions of the space and my annoyance with Darc that I completely missed the obvious. I hadn't pulled away because of her confession, but she must have taken it that way. It didn't bother me that she thought of

Riley before we met. Of course, she had. After all, it was their date I was crashing.

In the parking lot, my phone kept buzzing in my pocket, and I knew there wasn't enough time to take care of her the way I wanted to. I was horny and pissed off because I wanted to do all the things I had imagined while jerking off into that stupid glass I was dumb enough to leave sitting in the cup holder.

I wasn't thinking clearly. I was so confident she knew how badly I wanted her. It hadn't dawned on me that my abrupt stop could read as a form of rejection.

I planted a seed of doubt and nurtured it with my silence.

CHAPTER 18
ALEXIS

Great! The last thing I want is to come across as needy, and here I am, half-naked, with his hand around my neck, begging him not to leave me. I feel like I used to be better at this. Casual sex and meaningless one-night stands should never involve anything deeper than surface-level excitement. I know that. I practically wrote and illustrated the book on being emotionally detached.

"I'm not going anywhere, Lex. I just need my hands."

Dear lord, I'm an idiot. What the hell is wrong with me? This man is making me question everything I know, and not in some manipulative attempt to gaslight my reality. He's not like that. Not like them. He's different. The complete opposite of every guy I've been with in the past. Kade's not real. He's a fantasy. A combination of all the books I've read and fictional characters I've fallen in love with. He's too perfect, and I'm finding out I have no idea how to safely navigate through calm waters. I view human males through a lens that's been carefully crafted over time, refusing to ever be blindsided again. And here I am, completely thrown off my axis.

This is only for tonight. I remind myself. *And you're blowing it. Channel your inner main character energy and have fun while you can. This guy is once in a lifetime.*

I roll onto my side, tapping the edge of the desk in line with my face. With my head and neck in this position, I'll pay dearly for my choices in the morning, but for now, there's nothing I wouldn't give to get things back on track. "Could you do me one teeny, tiny, little favor and stand right here for a moment?"

Kade is eager to grant my request, possibly as eager as I am to get the ball rolling down the hill. He removes his shirt as he steps around the back of the desk, knocking into the boss's chair and causing it to travel several inches. Kade is solid and covered in tattoos. He's a bull, set loose in a china shop, unconcerned with the damage.

His swollen cock strains deliciously behind the colorful fabric of his boxer briefs, pleading to be set free. I run my fingers over his length, yet again noting his thickness and mentally preparing myself for what's to come.

"Take these off," I request as I slip my hand beneath the waistband to grip his cock. "I want you to choke me one more time, but not with your hands."

He groans in delight, and again, he complies without hesitation. Pulling his cock free. It stands, arrow straight, and I feel almost honored to be its intended target.

I encircle the girth with my hand and lap at the tip with my tongue. His precum is sweet, and his swollen flesh tastes clean, as though his skin has been recently washed. I'm guessing he had the same idea I did and made a pit stop in the employee restroom before joining me in the office. It wouldn't have bothered me had he been slightly sweaty, but I appreciate the thoughtful attention to detail and reward him for the effort.

I stroke and kiss and lick the head of his cock, testing for sensitivities and gauging his reactions. I'll need to relax and practically unhinge my jaw like a snake if I hope to please him, but I'm determined. Blowjobs are my specialty. It's a well-crafted skill I've honed over time, and it's yet to fail me.

"Goddamn, baby. How are you so good at this?" Kade cups the back of my head and shoves in deeper. As he bottoms out, I gag, and the walls of my pharynx collapse around him. He takes this as a sign of a job well done and begins fucking my mouth with long, slow strokes. "I'm going to marry you."

His perfectly timed proposal makes me laugh, and a guttural groan escapes the back of his throat.

"Oh fuck, do it again. That felt so good." Kade's request makes my throat vibrate as I laugh a second time.

I draw back far enough to catch my breath, intending to continue, but he pulls away. The second he withdraws, I miss the feeling of him inside me.

I reach for Kade, wanting to pick up where we left off, but he steps around the corner of the desk, dragging the office chair along with him. Rolling onto my back, I prop myself up on my elbows, needing to gaze upon the beneficiary of my desire.

"I wasn't finished," I whine.

I need more. More than a forbidden attraction. More than a flirtatious touch. More than half a blowjob and a kiss that never quite reaches my mouth. I need more than tonight, despite all the ways I warn myself against it.

"Too bad." Kade leans forward and kisses my hip. "Our relationship isn't one-sided. And if I had let you keep going, I'd be the one who was finished. Now, lie your head back and behave."

A part of me wants to question what he means by *our relationship*, but I know better than to open my mouth. If I keep talking, he'll keep responding, and we'll never get to the good part.

I shift my head from side to side, testing the pillow-like softness of the folded sweater by making myself comfortable. If Kade wants a compliant, *good girl* who lounges quietly on her back waiting to be pleased, who am I to argue?

Despite my arousal, Kade's got his work cut out for him if my orgasm is the trophy he seeks.

Let the games begin.

CHAPTER 19

ALEXIS

If I were the type to judge a book by its cover, at 6:01 this evening, I would have been intimidated and thoroughly overwhelmed. Kade's massive size, solid demeanor, and devil-may-care grin would have terrified me enough to send me running.

I suppose, for a moment, I considered it, but my need to flee was spurred on by embarrassment, not fear.

I learned a long time ago that people are more than the first impression they make. You have to crack the book and be willing to invest your time if you want to discover the stuff worth knowing, and Kade is a fantastic case in point. I assumed he would be guarded. A tough nut to crack. But when I met the group and took my seat beside him, everything I needed to know was laid on the table before me.

Being there with him, elbow to elbow, wasn't intimidating. It was calming. Kade made every effort to address my needs and ensure my comfort, even though I never promised anything in return. He seemed to derive pleasure from the simple act of caring, and it was hard to remember who I was originally scheduled to meet.

Riley was equally easy to read. He could well afford to spoil a girl and made sure to lead with that foot forward in every conversation heading into the night, but tossed me head-first into a tricky financial situation at the first available opportunity.

It felt like a test.

Was I supposed to bat my eyelashes, tease his cock beneath the table, and beg Daddy for a dollar? I'm sure he would have loved that.

Or was he expecting me to make a scene by shouting about how much time I'd spend on my hair and makeup, arguing that men should offer to pay when they invite a woman on a date?

That's not really my style, as I'm prone to suffering in silence. So, if an argument was his goal, I'm happy to disappoint.

Maybe he assumed I had the money on me, or I would simply walk to the ATM.

Or perhaps he thought I would opt out altogether and sit quietly as the others played. It's possible he wanted me to stay on the sidelines, dutifully cheering on the home team, but forgot the team he played for consisted of men besides himself.

Riley is attracted to the act of acquisition. He's interested so long as there's something worthwhile to be gained. Something to take. Something worth winning. Drinks in exchange for flattery. Dinner in exchange for my undivided attention. The pleasure of his company in exchange for my consent.

Dating has become increasingly transactional, or perhaps it's always been that way.

While my actual date didn't hesitate to nudge me in the direction of a pitfall, his roommate handed me three hundred dollars like it was a lucky penny he'd picked up from the grocery store parking lot. Kade saved me as if it were the easiest thing in the world. He didn't make a scene. He didn't hesitate. He didn't negotiate the terms and come to a suitable agreement. He simply added me to his total and made me an equal partner, and then he walked away.

When Kade left the table, he took my serenity with him. The peace I'd found with my arm pressed against his vanished with a smile. And I know it was stupid to mourn the loss. After all, he wasn't my date, and he had my keys, so I was confident he intended to return. But I panicked.

Thirty-four years without him in my life was already too much to bear. I couldn't handle one more second.

And this is why guys can't get me off.

The living embodiment of my every fantasy is kissing down my stomach and removing my pants after promising to devour me, soul and all by way of my clit, and I'm lying here sorting through the details of events that happened in a restaurant on the other side of the city. What's wrong with me?

"Hmmm… Now, I could've sworn the girl I was fingering in the car was wearing underwear." Kade eyes me suspiciously as he stands and makes a show of searching for my lost panties until he locates them in my right front pocket.

He draws them to his nose and inhales deeply.

"I'm keeping these," he states, pulling open the nearest desk drawer and dropping my panties inside.

My initial go-to emotional response is to be mortified, but with his eyes so full of hunger, I find myself aroused.

"Yeah. Well, I'm not going to name names, but…" I pause to bite my bottom lip, attempting to ratchet up the sex appeal beyond the breathiness of my voice. "*Somebody* got me soaking wet, and I came in here feeling like a little… dirty… sticky… mess. I thought about taking a shower, but I was afraid the boss would come in and catch me soaped and naked. And then what choice would I have but to beg for forgiveness and graciously accept my punishment?"

He slides the desk drawer closed and begins lightly brushing his hands over the top of my thighs. "If I'd known you had a power dynamic kink, I would've walked in and handed you a stack of papers. After all, if I'm here working late, it's only right that my secretary be here with me."

"Personal assistant," I correct.

"Yes, of course. How could I forget? You earned that promotion fair and square after sucking me off in the coat closet during the company Christmas party." Kade continues to fall deeper into character. "But we really should discuss your title. There's a position in the company you'd be perfect for, and the benefits package is top tier."

My lips tingle with the memory of having him in my mouth, and I want to please him again. "Would this new position require us to spend more time together?"

His pleasure is my pleasure. And I want his world to be my world.

"It's a lifetime contract, but I'm thinking of having it extended." Kade takes hold of my hips and pulls me to the edge of the desk.

I'm too far from the floor for my feet to touch, so I bend my knees and pull my legs up on either side of him, hugging him below the ribs with my ankles. In this position, I'm open and exposed. Wet and ready.

He begins tracing the line of my lips with the head of his swollen cock, making sure to pay special attention near the top. Each time Kade brushes over my clit, the air escapes my lungs in a moan.

"Are you ready for your interview?" He taps the head of his cock against my clit before slipping further down. "I need to make sure you can handle the increased workload."

"I assure you, sir. I'm more than willing to handle anything you can dish out and eager to demonstrate my capabilities." Prior to tonight, office kink wasn't on my bingo card, but it is now.

"Hmmm." The sound rumbles from the back of his throat and fills the space. "Since you're being such a good girl, I'm going to take my time and ease you into it. But make no mistake, I am fully prepared to stretch you to your limits."

"I'm ready, sir. Allow me to prove I'm a good fit for the company." I reach down and grip his cock. "Jax, please. I want this."

CHAPTER 20

KADE

So much for best-laid plans. Being greedy isn't generally in my wheelhouse, but every time she says my name, I'm prepared to betray my morals and forget my manners. "I'm going to lick and suck and savor you until the sun comes up, but right now, I need to be inside you."

"I like the sound of that," Lex says. And I'm certain she needs this as much as I do.

My cock is throbbing and dripping with precum, and I nearly explode the second I push into her. It's only the head of my cock, inside her, and it's already the best I've felt in my life. I'm almost afraid to move for fear of embarrassing myself.

"Oh, Jax." Her legs wrap around my waist, and the movement pulls me in another inch. It's exquisite. And it's torture.

She's absolutely soaked from having my cock in her mouth, which is a level of heaven all on its own.

"Jax, please. I want more." She whines and rolls her hips.

I try to force my mind onto other things. Anything to distract from the knot in my stomach, the tightness in my nuts, and the horrifying reality that I'm not going to be able to hold back.

"If you get me pregnant, you're gonna have to marry me."

And with that, I'm undone.

"Deal," is all I'm able to say before I push in deeper and begin wildly spraying every last available swimmer into the one woman I would unquestionably make my wife.

CHAPTER 21

ALEXIS

Oh my god!

I shouldn't have said that, but… Holy shit! I thought mentioning pregnancy would partially kill the mood and prolong his drive time. I hadn't considered a possible breeding fetish.

That was the quickest and hottest sex I've ever engaged in, and we barely moved.

I'm not surprised or disappointed. I'd executed a stellar blowjob, expecting him to cum in my mouth, and when he didn't, I knew sex would finish him off. But I had assumed he'd pull out.

With his cock twitching inside me, Kade pushes in

further. He isn't as engorged as he was a moment ago, but he still fills and stretches me.

"It's your turn, babygirl." His fingers find my clit as he begins rocking his hips.

I would have thought a guy our age would be one-and-done, but Kade is determined to please me. His cock swells with renewed life, but it's his fingers that tug at me like puppet strings.

"You were so wet from sucking my cock. You liked that, didn't you? Having your mouth used."

My moan affirms a resounding yes.

"I could feel how much you enjoyed showing off your skills. Maybe I should call my friend in from outside. Let him take a turn with that perfect mouth while I fill your tight pussy with more of my cum."

"Oh my god. Yes, please." Whether Kade's offer is meant as a fantasy or he truly aims to call is irrelevant. The image is already taking hold in my mind as the man from the parking lot takes shape in front of me.

"You want him, don't you? I can feel you clenching down on me."

This isn't a trick or a trap. This is his way of giving me what I need without having to share.

I drop my head to the side and imagine the other man, cock standing at attention, ready to be serviced.

"That's right. Just like that. I want you to take care of him like you did me. Be a good girl, and take his cock nice and deep. Show me how much you like it, baby. Take his big cock down your throat. I want to watch you choke on him while I'm inside you."

Kade's fingers continue to stimulate my clit as he thrusts into me.

Both men pound into me like I'm their little whore. Filling my holes. Fucking me. Using me.

A stream of Kade's cum from our previous round streams from my overfull pussy and runs over my puckered ass. This sensation is the final straw. I break apart like a firecracker as blinding orbs of white light explode behind my eyelids. My body convulses violently as I lose all understanding of my limbs and bones and blood.

It takes me a moment to get my bearings, and when

Kade pulls out, I realize it's only the two of us in the office.

"Did you cum?" The words slide past my teeth, and my tongue slips out to follow, wetting my dry, used lips.

"No. I didn't have anything left. You took it all the first time."

"I'm sorry." I open my eyes to find Kade steadying himself with the desk as he reaches for the missing chair.

"Don't ever be sorry for that." He abandons his attempt to sit and leans over me.

In the background, not too far in the distance, we hear cannon fire booming. It sounds like an all-out war.

"I've never made a woman finish so hard that the city celebrated in my honor, but I'll take it."

I laugh, even though the muscles required for the action are spent.

"I think we won." The game must have finished at the same time we did.

"I agree."

It's cute the way he does that. Kade says things that could mean more than what they are on the surface, like the truth lies further than words can travel. He's been doing it all night, and as a romantic, I appreciate the sentiment. In fact, I'm a complete sucker for it.

"Can I be honest with you?"

"Of course." Kade leans close enough to kiss my collarbone. "That's all I've ever wanted from anyone."

"I feel like a pile of mashed potatoes."

Kade laughs and collapses into me. He's exhausted. Even with the top half of his body crushed against mine, I'm not sure how he's maintained the ability to stand. My knees would unquestionably buckle if I even thought about setting foot on the floor.

"You know, your stomach thinks all potatoes are mashed."

I'd laugh, but there isn't enough oxygen in my lungs. After all, half a giant is quite a bit of weight to have crushing down on your chest. I tap Kade's shoulder, needing him to find the strength to support his own weight, and he does me one better.

He jumps to his feet and scoops me up into his arms. I'm already in the air before I realize what's happening.

"Let's clean up so we can get home."

All of a sudden, Kade sounds keen to leave, and I'm reminded that a certain roommate is waiting for us to return. This means the shower and car ride will be the last moments we share. I have no intention of going into the house, regardless of Riley's request. How can I? Not after what just happened. Even if I could go another round, I don't want it to be with him. Not anymore.

I'm ruined for all other men, and I'm about to say goodbye to the man who spoiled me.

CHAPTER 22
KADE

Holding Lex in my arms is my new favorite pastime. It feels natural, as effortless as breathing. The length of her naked body pressed against mine as the steam from the hot water floods the space around us fills me with the urge to kiss her. She regained her ability to stand a full five minutes ago, but I refuse to let her go.

That's going to be the hard part.

Letting go is going to require a great deal of effort, and I'm not sure I have the strength.

I'm so tired of being strong.

"Come on, let me wash your back." Her soaped

hands slip along my wet skin, and I'm not sure how I'll ever be able to shower without her.

I'm completely obsessed.

Unfortunately, I'm not entirely confident in my ability to tell her that without scaring her away. It's too much too soon, and she'll assume I'm love-bombing her with bullshit lies like every narcissistic asshole on the internet. And then there's this mess with my roommate to consider. I'll need to sort it out at some point, but first I need to speak with her and figure out what's what.

As much as I want her to be mine, I won't deny her other options or take away her choice by pounding my chest and sharing the details of what we did. I won't kiss and tell, even though I want them all to know. Not that Riley would care. He'd screw her just to prove he could.

The horror stories I've heard from my sisters and the shit I've seen firsthand from my roommate, it's no wonder so many women choose to stay single. It's not worth it anymore. The hope of finding happiness is easily outweighed by a history of pain caused at the hands of those who claimed to love them.

Lex has undoubtedly fielded her fair share of discomfort. Heartbreak that I could have protected her from had I only found her sooner. Her last relationship ended eight months ago, and she's been single ever since. This incredible woman. This stunningly beautiful, intelligent, and immensely talented woman. A woman any man should be proud to have by his side has been alone.

There's got to be a reason.

"Okay, now you do mine." The sweetness in her voice has me spinning on my heels.

Calling me back to her.

I want to drop to my knees and worship at her feet.

I'm so fucked.

If I never see her again, or worse, she winds up dating my roommate, I'm done for. I'll have to move to another country, abandoning the life I've built here. I'll never be able to handle the idea of them together. Seeing her with anyone who isn't me would be torture.

Her back is right there, turned to me, waiting patiently to be cleansed of our mutual sin, and I want to give her what she's asked for. It's such a simple request. But I also want to give her more. Everything. Always.

"Hey, it's okay. You don't have to if you don't want to." She turns off the water and faces me with a strained smile. "We should get going. The heat's making me lightheaded, and I have to be able to drive."

I reach past her and turn the water back on, setting the temperature significantly cooler, and dispense a glop of liquid soap into my hand.

"I'm okay to drive." I realize this is the first thing I've said aloud since carrying her into the bathroom. Everything else has been relayed through touch.

My massive hand covers a third of her back, making quick work of her request. Even with my languished strokes, the shared moment is brief. I try to soak in the sensation. Store the memory deep inside. But it's over before I realize, and again, the water disappears.

There's only one towel hanging on the rack, and she hands it to me as though I'd ever take it from her. As though I'd leave her to stand naked and uncomfortable while prioritizing myself.

"Come on, it's your towel." She's finally riddled it out.

I accept the offering, but only to wrap it around her and watch as she dries herself from shoulder to ankle. When she drops to pat the water droplets from the tops of her feet, my cock twitches. Seeing her there, nearly on her knees, is giving me ideas. Flooding me with memories. Reminding me of how good her mouth felt.

She must sense it because she looks up with doe eyes before stealing a glance at my swelling cock.

Lex doesn't say anything. She doesn't have to.

She drops to her knees and hands me the oversized white cotton towel. It's damp and warm and smells like her bathed in my scent. I fist it tightly in my grip as she takes me into her mouth.

The expert way she pleases me, as though it's her chosen profession, makes my muscles tighten.

"You're too good at this," I say.

Far too good for me to share.

I want to ruin her. And I want to be greedy. So, I

drop the towel and fist my hands into her hair. Thrusting into her mouth.

"Oh my god."

The soft moans combined with slurps and gags make me feral. I push in deeper and feel the back of her throat tighten around the head of my cock even as she allows me access. When she pulls back for a breath, her hands take over, unwilling to leave me unattended.

This blowjob matters to her.

It's important.

She cares about the quality of her work, and I feel her commitment in every stroke.

A few minutes in, I nearly stop her, concerned for her well-being and fearing I have nothing left to give, but then I feel it. That all too familiar tension at the base of my spine. It swells and constricts until my nuts tighten. It's as though a hidden reserve was tucked away in my tail.

I reclaim my grip on her head and pump into her mouth wildly. Violently. Desperately needing to give her the prize she deserves.

And when it's over, she looks up at me, slowly swiping across her bottom lip with the back of her hand, then reversing to make a second pass with her thumb. Her jaw must be on fire, but she shows no sign of discomfort. Merely beams with pride and a satisfied smile until I'm lifting her by the arms.

"Tell me I get to keep you." I pull her tightly into my embrace, needing this more than the release.

"Does that mean I've gotten the promotion, sir?" She says with a small laugh, still committed to the role.

And for the first time in my life, I hate sex and foreplay and orgasms. I hate how we could say anything right now without meaning it. I hate that she'll question my sincerity and brush aside my honesty. But she asked the question, and now I have no choice but to tell her.

"You're the only one I'd ever consider."

CHAPTER 23
ALEXIS

There's still the occasional firework seen lighting the night sky as we exit the building, and a gunshot pops too close for comfort.

"Why idiots shoot stray bullets into the air is beyond me." His voice makes my heart leap.

I'd forgotten he was there, or assumed he'd already left. Although now that I see him, I'm not sure how I missed the car and the shadow that seems to reflect his darkness.

"We're headed out." Kade's tone is matter-of-fact and to the point.

"Yeah, well, it certainly took ya long enough.

Thought I was gonna have to come in and hurry things along."

I swallow hard at the idea and find myself rewarded with a jolt of pain. My throat is sore, having taken quite the beating. I can't even imagine what this man could have done to me. The punishment he would've inflicted, simply for my presence.

The air escapes my lungs all at once, and Kade tightens his grip on my hand.

The headlights of the black luxury vehicle illuminate, making my heart jump for a second time.

I've been struggling to properly work out the state of their relationship, and I never stopped to ask. I thought Kade said they were friends, but now I'm not sure. With so much uncertainty sewn into the edges, I can't be sure of anything.

There's so much tension between the two of them that it seems to charge the air. Or maybe it's me. Maybe I'm the reason for the static. I shouldn't be here. Shouldn't be a witness to whatever dealings they see fit to conduct in the dark of night.

And it's cold, as though the temperature has

dropped since our arrival, and hell is officially frozen over.

A shiver runs up my spine as a second man, identical to the first, steps through an opening in the gate. He pulls the metal door shut and locks it before tossing Kade the keys.

I squeak and duck out of the way, but Kade catches the keys easily, barely needing to lift his arm.

"Jumpy little thing. Thought you said she was tough?" The man from the gate joins his carbon copy.

"She is," Kade and the other man respond in unison."

"Okay, well, it was lovely to meet you both, but *we* should be going." I find my voice and hope I haven't overstepped as I raise my hand in a small wave of farewell. "Jax is hungry and said something about *eating until the sun comes up*. So, I should get him home before he dies of starvation."

Kade laughs as we walk forward, and the two men mirror the movement, repositioning the teams on common ground in the middle.

"And what about you? Not feeling hungry."

My breath hitches, giving way to renewed nervousness.

"I've already eaten, thank you."

"In that case," the man says with a grin, "put her in my car. And do it quickly."

I recognize the command in his voice for what it is, and my heart drops. The man isn't asking Kade politely to do him a favor. He's giving him an order. There will be no terms to negotiate. No arguments heard. The choice is to comply or die.

Without a word, Kade takes hold of me with both hands, gripping tighter than he has all evening.

"That's not necessary," I say, pushing at his hands.

"You're mistaken if you think I'm letting go of you." Had Kade said that to me inside the office, it would've made me smile, but the words take on a different meaning out here.

I walk to the passenger side of the black Lamborghini and suck in a sharp breath as the door opens.

This is it.

This is how I die.

The door closes and locks, and I wonder if this is anything like a normal person's car. Couldn't I simply unlock it from the inside and run away? Or have his serial killer friends had it modified? No point in even testing. I'm not much of a runner, and the three men standing in a huddle in front of the car look like they would enjoy the chase and take pleasure in hunting me. Perhaps that's part of the game, and they want me to run.

Didn't this thought cross my mind as we were leaving the restaurant? And now, here I sit with my prophecy come true. I gave Kade the benefit of my doubt and swept my prediction aside as though it were nonsense spurred on from reading one too many dark romance novels.

I watch incredulously as the men exchange handshakes and slaps to the shoulder. I swear the world is one big members-only club, and ladies need not apply.

Does it matter?

Do I even care?

My life feels so meaningless. It always has. I knew something was missing. Something important. For a long time, I thought it was love that I needed, so I went searching. I looked under every stone I could turn, but all I ever found were soul-sucking leeches.

I should've been afraid of Kade when I met him, and I wasn't. Instead, I felt comfortable. I felt whole.

"You deserve this," I say, dropping my eyes to where I'm mindlessly flicking at the seam of my pants. "You deserve everything that's coming to you because you acted with your heart instead of thinking things through."

The door unlocks, and a massive figure fills the space beside me. I want to block it out, but I can't. I hear the seat adjust to the will of the driver, and I close my eyes. I want to go back in time. It doesn't matter which one is in the driver's seat. I doubt I'd be able to tell them apart.

I refuse to look up.

I don't want to see Kade standing out there when he should be beside me. If I have to shut my eyes tight and never open them again, so be it. I'll live in the memories of us together. I'll lock myself in the office and be his willing assistant, fulfilling my indefinite contract.

The engine roars to life, pulling me into the present, and I want to claw my way back to him. Scratch this stranger's eyes out if I have to.

How dare he come out of nowhere and ruin the best night of my entire life! Why am I sitting here like a well-behaved child when I should be fighting? Fighting to get back to…

Kade.

I'm sitting here, keeping my head down and my hands to myself because of Kade. He brought me here. Handed me over without a word. Gave me away like I meant nothing. And still, all I want to do is protect him. I'll play the part of the obedient hostage and die without a single word of protest so long as he's safe.

"Babe, look at me." A giant hand slips into my lap, taking my empty hand into his, and I open my eyes. We're pulling onto the street when I glance out the side window, past the glowing sign with the jade cicada. "I'm sorry they scared you."

The voice is familiar, but doesn't seem real. Maybe I'm in shock, or this is a coping mechanism brought on by intense stress. My mind's attempt at self-preservation.

"I don't value my life enough to be scared." Sadly, this is true.

"We're gonna need to work on that." Kade shifts his gaze toward me as we stop at a red light.

"I wasn't scared, but I am confused." Nothing about this night makes sense.

"Darc wanted us to take his car because we're leaving the city, and instead of asking us like a normal person, they decided to pull that shit."

"So, they were what? Testing your loyalty. Seeing if you would give me up to save your own ass. Is that even a question? We barely know each other."

Kade pulls his hand away and turns his pointed attention back to the road ahead, taking a deep breath before he speaks.

"You can't be serious!" The deep breath doesn't seem to help. "You honestly think I'd give you up because they snapped their fingers and told me to?

You think I'd be so careless! No, worse than that. Compliant!"

The light turns green, and Kade takes off like a shot, flying past the line of parked cars.

I thought it would be busier now that the game is over, but the side streets are still relatively quiet, with no signs of life. I imagine it's absolute chaos around the stadium. But here on the outskirts, we're alone.

"They weren't testing me." His voice calms as he eases off the gas pedal. "They were testing you."

"Well, I'm sorry I failed to impress." My voice comes out hoarse, and I'm not sure if it's my bruised throat causing the change or the tears I'm struggling to choke back.

Kade lets out a ragged breath and shoots up the on-ramp headed east. "Everyone's impressed by you, Lex. How could they not be?"

I don't know how to respond, so I stay quiet. In the face of danger, I should've been scared or hurt or mad, but I wasn't. I shut down those emotions as they attempted to breach the surface, stuffing them back into their boxes. And now all I feel is disappointment.

As stupid as it sounds, I wanted to prove to Kade that I was a worthy endeavor. I thought I could show him that I'm not the kind of girl who goes out with one guy and leaves with another because regardless of how you spin in, that shit makes me look horrible. And how did I attempt to prove my loyalty? By abandoning the guy I arrived with so I could leave with another.

Bloody hell, I'm an idiot.

"Do you remember what I told you in the office?" Kade slips his hand back onto my thigh and gives it a squeeze. "I said I'd never let anything bad happen to you, and I'd never knowingly put you in harm's way. I made you a promise, and I meant every word of it. So, if you think for one second that I would've let them touch you, you're wrong. Now, I'm not gonna lie and act like it would've been easy. Those two aren't afraid to get bloody. But it sure as shit would've been a fight."

"You think they could beat you?" The guys in the parking lot were in good shape, but their size was comparable to Riley's, and I remember thinking he wouldn't stand a snowball's chance in hell. Even with Jakob and Chuckie by his side, I still would've bet on Kade to emerge victorious.

"Maybe. Probably. They pretty much live for that shit. And they cheat."

"Then, what's the point?" Guys keep offering to defend my honor in fights they don't think they'll win. As if dying and leaving me vulnerable on my own is some romantic act of heroism.

"I'm not sure what you're asking?"

I rearrange my thoughts and try again. "What's the point of fighting if you don't think you'll win? I mean, I know they didn't want to hurt me, but…"

Now that the danger has passed, I'm fairly confident my well-being was never in jeopardy. I was, however, less certain in the moment.

"Let's say, hypothetically, their intentions had been less than friendly. What would be the point of getting hurt or worse if it wouldn't assure my safety? Wouldn't they step over your body and kill me anyhow?"

"No. They wouldn't have the chance."

"But in this scenario, you're dead and I become the helpless victim."

"You still don't get it, do you?"

"I guess not." I shake my head and sink into the seat, realizing Kade and I are no longer on the same page.

"Lex, if I had to die to keep you safe, so be it. But rest assured, I would've dragged that twin demon to hell with me."

CHAPTER 24
ALEXIS

The mood in the car lightens once I drop the topic of Kade getting killed and me being raped and murdered by his friends. We take turns asking each other random questions, and as we pull off the freeway, my cheeks hurt from smiling.

"…Okay, but what shade of blue is your favorite? There are tons to choose from. You can't just say blue and leave it at that." I ask as though his answer to *what's your favorite color* holds all the secrets of the universe.

"I don't know. I can't put a name to it. Not dark or light. Blue like clear ocean water. The kind where you can see your death coming from forty meters away." He describes it in a way that shuttles me into a fully immersive vision.

"The blue of a serene death. I like it. It's peaceful and quiet. Unmuddied by the inevitable plumes of red."

"Exactly. I knew you'd be able to see it." Kade laughs and moves on without elaborating further. "I have a two-part question. What's your favorite kind of romance, and why do you love it so much?"

"Oh my god. Seriously?" The light in my mind goes out, and I'm momentarily plunged into the pitch-black nothingness that signals a full shutdown.

At least he didn't ask me to choose a favorite book. It's such a panic-inducing ordeal to be asked to narrow the selection to one, like asking a mother to admit which child she favors. Sure, not an impossible task, but the answer changes depending on my mood, the time of day, and the current season.

"Like a favorite romance trope. Something you're drawn to. Or happy when you stumble across it accidentally." He narrows the scope of his question to make it simpler, and slowly the answer comes into view.

"Well, I suppose my favorite has always been soul-mate connections. Not insta-love, per se, but insta-certainty. Like, they meet, and they know beyond a shadow of a doubt. It feels like electricity and tunnel vision and timelessness. It's like finding your way home and feeling comfortable for the first time since you can't remember when, and it all comes flooding back. Memories from lifetimes long past. But it's more than just knowing. My favorite is when they find each other, feel all that in their souls, and then life keeps them apart. They're forced to love one another from a distance, convinced their feelings are one-sided. It's cruel and painful, and most of the time, I cry like a baby, but that's what I love about it. Their pain becomes my pain, and when one of them finally drums up the courage to make a grand declaration, their happiness becomes my happiness. I'm obsessed with the feeling of falling in love, and I'm a total sucker for starry-eyed sentiment. So, I read romance. Because men in real life are disappointing. They never say the right thing when it matters. And they sure as shit don't come with a guaranteed Happily Ever After."

Kade finds my hand and pulls it towards him, placing a kiss on yet another part of my body that isn't my lips. It's intoxicating and mildly frustrating.

"You deserve a man who says all the right things because he means it."

The car begins to slow, and I want so badly for him to pull over to the curb so he can kiss me with the unabashed passion I know he's capable of. Bruise my lips to match my throat. Then pull back just enough to tell me how much he needs me.

"I know this most likely goes without saying, but you have to keep quiet about the last hour or so. This group of friends wouldn't understand..."

"I get it!" I snap, cutting him off. "There's no need to explain."

If there's one thing I understand better than anything, it's the terms and conditions of being a secret. What happened between Kade and me didn't happen. Nothing happened. It's as though we've never met. In fact, we haven't. We don't even know each other.

He pulls into the driveway and turns to look at me. "Lex, I didn't mean..."

"It's fine. I know the drill." I make a show of silently locking my lips and placing the invisible key into his hand.

He nods, his lips turned down in the corners, and tucks the key into his front pocket.

This is the moment I've been dreading. The time in the night when I have to say goodbye. Only, I can't. I can't say anything because my lips are sealed, and I can't leave because I don't have my car. My heart drops further as I realize, for the first time, that my wallet and cell phone are in my jacket, which is in my vehicle, currently parked in a tow-away zone.

But hey, I got the best sex of my life, and our team won the game. Wasn't that all I'd wanted coming into the evening?

A figure jogs over from the front steps.

I didn't notice him sitting there when we pulled in, but the movement captured my attention.

He's in shorts and a t-shirt, and I wonder how long he's been waiting. Riley catches me through the windshield and splits off for the passenger side. When he tries the handle, the door doesn't open.

"I meant to ask before we got here." Kade sounds defeated as Riley knocks on the glass. "I want to know what your plan is. If you still intend to go out with him."

Inside, I'm screaming. I'm throwing punches wildly and pounding on his chest. He still doesn't get it after everything I said. I wasn't talking about book tropes and morally grey, fictional men.

Riley knocks again. "Everyone's waiting."

Kade pauses momentarily to glance between me and Riley, as though he's resigning himself to some truth I never agreed to.

"I'm sorry I put you in this position."

Kade's as bad as I am, apologizing for every minor infraction, and I hadn't realized how annoying personal accountability could be until now.

"Come on, we're celebrating!" Riley says through the glass. He reaches for the handle but doesn't pull until he hears the locks disengage.

I swallow my guilt and fix my face with a smile as the door swings open, fully aware of the part I'm expected to play until I can find a way home. I'm a bad person. I know that. I'm nothing if not self-aware.

I wanted to have sex with Kade, and I'm not sorry I did it. But let's be brutally honest. By bailing on Riley and hooking up with his roommate in some dark downtown office, I painted a pretty unflattering picture of myself. I look like a cheating whore. And sure, it takes two to tango, but Kade wasn't out with someone else. And we all know guys are never held to the same standard when it comes to meaningless one-night stands. If the group finds out what happened. If Riley finds out. It'll be a fight, for sure.

I'll be walking home in the middle of the night with no jacket, no money, and no GPS to tell me where I'm at.

"Goddamn." Riley steps into the opening and squats to eye level. "Had I known you were pulling in this kind of money as an artist, I would've kept my mouth shut at dinner. Way to put a guy in his place, Alexis. Nicely done."

If only I'd known sooner. All I needed to impress Riley was a borrowed sports car from a well-dressed criminal.

I silently laugh to myself.

"Where've you been? What happened? Why aren't you saying anything?" Riley looks from me to his roommate. "What did you do to her?"

Kade pulls something from his pocket, lifts my hand at the wrist, and sets the invisible key gently in my palm. I use it to unlock my lips as he exits and slams the door behind him.

"What was that about?" Riley's eyes follow Kade as he stomps off toward the garage.

"It's nothing. A stupid joke. Guess he didn't think it was funny."

"Yeah, well, Kade's weird. Forget him." Riley says it like it's the easiest thing in the world.

Forget him.

As if such a thing would be possible.

But that's exactly what's expected of me because I don't know Jackson Kade. I barely met him. And I've certainly never kissed him.

CHAPTER 25
ALEXIS

"You weren't kidding. That's literally a bottle of wine with my name on it." I set the chilled bottle on the counter next to a stack of twenty-dollar bills, a black two-piece bikini, and a pair of empty wine glasses.

"I told you, Alexis, I had our second date all lined up and ready to go."

Something about that hurts and soothes all at the same time. I didn't give Riley enough credit. I was quick to write him off based on a series of educated guesses, assuming our night together would be a one-off. I hadn't planned for a second date because I didn't want to get my hopes up, but it turns out he did. Riley had faith in our connection, and now I feel even more guilt-ridden.

"I'm sorry I left the restaurant." It feels good to say it, even though that's only the tip of the iceberg.

I'm sorry I walked out on our date so that I could have sex with your roommate. I hope you guys don't hate each other because of what I did.

That part, I keep to myself.

"There's no need to apologize. Kade's intimidating. It's nearly impossible to say no to someone three times your size. If anything, I should be apologizing to you. The situation had to of been awkward for you, and I should've been more insistent that he piss off and find another ride."

"It was fine." I don't know what else I'm allowed to say. Probably nothing. And thankfully, I don't have to lie.

The other couples round the corner, loudly spilling into the kitchen. The girls scream when they see me, literally scream, as they run over to where I'm standing at the counter.

"You're here! Oh my god! You're finally back! Tell us what happened! Was it hot? Did you guys make out? Riley, go away so she can tell us everything!" They shove him out of the way and encircle me, attempting to create a cone of silence.

"I swear. There was no kissing." I raise my hands as if to prove they're still clean.

Just then, Kade walks through a side door, and for the briefest of moments, the kitchen is plunged into complete silence.

"After all that, you didn't even kiss her? Jesus Christ, bro. I figured that was the whole reason you left." Riley throws a playful jab that lands with a thud against Kade's chest.

In my mind, I see it happening. Kade grabs Riley by the throat and beats him to death while we all look on in horror. Somehow, it feels like the logical response. Even blissed out on rage and covered in blood, he doesn't scare me. He could walk over and kiss me right now, and I would wrap my arms around his neck to pull him closer. I would sit in the front row every day at his trial and send him love letters in prison. I would wait thirty years, or the rest of our lives, and if he never got out, I would find him in the next life and try to do it better.

"Why would I? She isn't on a date with me." Kade steps back to lean against the counter, glancing at the girls on either side of me and the guys over my shoulder. Looking past me like I'm not even there.

I know why he's playing off the *nothing* that happened between us as meaningless, but it still hurts. Even though I'm far from innocent, I hate that we're here.

"I guess I'll get changed so we can go in the hot tub." I turn to retrieve the black bikini from the counter, wanting to be anywhere else. "Is there a bathroom I can use?"

"Upstairs on the…" The two men speak in unison. One finishes the sentence with 'right,' and the other says 'left,' but I don't look back to register which is which.

I hurry toward the stairs, eager to make my escape. On the heels of my retreat, I hear the conversation in the kitchen resume, but I'm up the stairs and well beyond earshot before anything important is said.

The second floor is a hallway, lit by a decorative nightlight plugged into an outlet, with a single closed door on either side. The door to the right is closest to the top of the stairs, so I duck inside to change. There's a flat-screen television mounted on the wall. It's powered on, but nothing is playing. Merely the dim glow of a scrolling home screen, as though the owner of the bedroom left in a hurry. Or maybe it was left on intentionally, as a light source to fend off the darkness. I suppose when you can afford to live in a house this size, paying the electric bill isn't a concern.

I pull off my sweater and drop it on the bed.

The bikini is the kind that ties together and fits nearly everyone. I wonder if it belongs to one of the ladies downstairs, or if Riley picked it out with me in mind. It's cute. Sexy. Easy to remove in the heat of the moment.

Without a hint of stiffness, I doubt it's been washed. As I remove my bra and tie on the top, my fingers rub the soft fabric. It feels new, like the tags were removed as I walked in the front door. If I had a mind to look, I bet I could find them sitting at the top in the kitchen trash.

I move quicker when it comes time to take off my jeans and secure the tie-on bottom in place. At any minute, someone could walk through the door, and I'm not sure who that person might be. I'm not even sure who I'd want to find me here.

Well, that's not true. I have a good idea. There's only one person I'd go all in on.

Now that my eyes have fully adjusted to the lighting and I have unrestricted access to my vision, I turn to take in my surroundings.

There's a floor-to-ceiling bookcase that spans the length of one entire wall. Its shelves are stuffed with an impressive collection of books and a mask that makes me yip. I move towards it, wanting a better look and not believing what I see, when a low growl comes from the corner of the room. I stop abruptly in my tracks, too afraid to move or look or breathe.

"You must be Niro," I say with a shaky voice.

The black figure rises, walking on four legs. Moving slowly. Intentionally. Stalking me down like prey.

I step backward toward the bed, never taking my eyes off him. Watching his muscles tighten as he readies his attack, I try to remain calm.

"Niro. I swear, I'm friends with your dad. He's downstairs in the kitchen. Probably getting you a treat for being such a good boy. Please don't kill me."

He moves so quickly, I don't stand a chance. Niro lunges, and I scream as the pair of us crash onto the bed.

CHAPTER 26

KADE

"Like I said, winner takes all." Riley thrusts his hand into mine, setting the terms in stone.

One minute, we're finalizing plans to go our separate ways, and the next, I'm using every available muscle group to hurl my body up the stairs.

When I heard her scream, I knew what had happened. Yet again, I'd been careless with her life, not seeing the danger in deadly things because their harm never saw fit to threaten me.

I hesitate, a fraction of a second, with my hand on the knob to the bedroom, adequately ill-prepared to accept the damage I've inadvertently inflicted. The door flings open, and I catch sight of Lex. Her arms are pulled tightly across her face as her legs kick wildly.

"Place!" The command should elicit an immediate response, but the beast holds still, unwilling to sacrifice his target.

"Place!" I shout again as I step forward, and this time, Nero pauses, takes one final lick, and retreats to his bed in the corner of the room.

Lex is silent and unmoving, frozen by shock.

I plant my knee on the bed beside her and prop myself up with one arm. I'm too late to protect her, I know that, and she'll never forgive me. Not after this.

"I'm here. I'm sorry. Please. You need to show me your face." I wrap my free hand around her delicate forearm and wait. "Where did he bite you?"

Nero is a working dog who has been programmed to kill on command. He could easily remove flesh from bone if he thought my security was questioned. I take him to the office with me because he keeps me company and keeps me safe in a city that has enough violent crime to warrant several layers of protection. Nero was a present from Darc, and until tonight, he's never failed me.

Lex sucks in a breath, and I watch as her lungs expand. It's a good sign and a pleasant sight, considering she's half naked and lying beneath me on my bed, but it does little to quell my panic.

"I don't know who's scarier, you or the hellhound. I swear, if you ever yell at me like that…" She laughs playfully as if trying to lighten the mood. "Fucking hell, Kade. I nearly peed my pants."

"Monroe, please." I take hold of both arms with one hand and reposition them over her head, still needing to see her face.

"Oh, it's Monroe now, is it? I see what you did there." She smiles, and it nearly breaks me. "Alright, fine. You've made your point."

The sight of her unmangled face causes my spike of adrenaline to plunge as my forehead drops to her chest.

"Oh my god!" The alarm rings in her throat. "Jax, are you okay?" She strokes the back of my head as I hold myself up enough to keep from completely crushing her.

As my heart rate slows, my hold on reality tightens.

Lex is wearing a small tie-on bikini that I could easily remove with my teeth. Her soft skin smells like a combination of us, and her touch aims to comfort.

"Jax, look at me."

I lift my head as she settles her hand against my cheek.

"Babe, you scared the shit out of me. I heard you scream and…"

"I'm okay. I promise. It was an accident. I didn't mean to yell. It slipped out when your dog knocked me onto the bed. I wasn't trying to scare anyone." She lifts her face to brush her nose against mine. "I'm not hurt, I swear. He didn't bite me."

She holds me in place, and her eyes soften almost painfully. "You don't have to worry about me or feel bad about anything that's happened. We can stick with the plan, and no one needs to know. It's probably for the best. We're not friends, we don't know each other, and nothing happened."

I pull back, slightly enraged by her suggestion. "That's not what I want. I never said that. In the car, you didn't let me finish." I straddle her legs and lean in close. I'm a breath away from kissing her. It would be so easy. "I don't care if you tell them about us. I want them to know. You just can't mention the other one. They're a bit– dodgy."

"Yeah. That's putting it mildly." She laughs, and when her eyes refocus on mine, I feel the pull between us. "It's funny how you talk about them like they're a singular person in two bodies."

"Because they are." The guys are interchangeable because they've made themselves that way. A deal with one is a deal with both. The same can be said for trouble. "They're the human equivalent of a pair of pants."

She laughs again, erasing the last remaining whisper of my previous concern.

"Lex, I want you to enjoy your time here, and if that means finishing your date, I understand." With her pinned beneath me, she feels fragile. "But there's something I have to tell you."

"You keep acting like I care about this stupid date, but I'm only going downstairs because I made a deal with Riley so I could leave with you. And maybe it's dumb that I'm trying to keep things friendly, but I assure you it's not for my benefit. I know you're tough and can take care of yourself. Trust me, your strength is not lost on me. But I don't want what we did to be the reason your life gets turned upside down."

"So, what do you want me to do? Sit back and watch. Say nothing. Keep my hands to myself and let you end up with him. How friendly are you planning to be?" The thought of them together opens a pit in my stomach, like a black hole threatening to suck me inside out.

"No. What? I'm not saying that. It's just..."

"Just what, Lex? What do you want from this?"

"Nothing. I don't know. I'm trying not to get attached, and..." She closes her eyes and pulls an arm over her face. "You keep making me want more."

"Okay, well. You're not the only one who feels that way." I should be greedy and keep her to myself, but I don't want to snuff out her flame by smothering it.

"I'm not?"

"Will you stop? I haven't exactly been subtle."

"I suppose that's true, but maybe I need to hear you say it."

I swallow the words on the tip of my tongue, even though she's asking me to share them. It's still too much and far too soon, and I don't want to lose her.

"I like that you get along with my friends, and I want you to have fun." I dip my head lower to kiss her breasts. "But these are mine."

Her breath hitches as her body reacts to my touch. "Okay, I can agree to that, but you're gonna get us caught. We should shut the door."

I snort at the thought of getting caught because that's the least of my worries. Riley and the others couldn't be further from my mind if I stuffed them into a box and mailed them to Japan. They feel like they exist in another life. The people downstairs are a distant memory. All I need is her.

"Guard." I give the command, sending Nero to his post at the top of the stairs.

"Trust me, no one's coming up here. And since you're in such a giving mood." I kick back so I'm standing and pull her to the edge of the bed. My fingers brush along the inside of her thigh and over the smooth bikini. "This is mine."

Lex is free to make her own choice. She can have as much fun as she wants. If she chooses to make out with everyone in the hot tub, so be it. But I want her in my bed and in my arms when it comes time to shut her eyes.

She bites her bottom lip and lets out a nearly silent moan. "Okay."

I drop to my knees and bury my face between her thighs, kissing the layer of fabric that's keeping me from her clit. "Use your words."

I want more. I have to have her. The taste of her arousal is essential to my continued existence. More vital than oxygen.

"If you want it, it's yours." Lex rakes her fingers through my hair.

"*If* I want it? No, baby, there is no *if*." I hook the bottoms with my thumb and pull them to the side, exposing her lips. With my other hand, I slip two fingers inside enough to hit the ridges that make her eyes roll back into her head, and with each slow circle, her body trembles. "This pussy belongs to me, and I say when and who you cum for."

"You're not playing fair, Jax. You know I'll agree to anything while you're doing that."

"In that case." I slip my fingers out of her and continue lower, painting a trail to the one place I've yet to explore. "I want this as well."

She looks momentarily horrified. "Are you crazy? Your dick's never getting in there."

I push the tip of my finger inside and smile as her body practically folds in two. "It doesn't have to be my dick. I'm not that mean."

I resigned myself to the fact that anal was out of the question a *long* time ago when an overconfident ex-girlfriend was feeling frisky and ended up blacking out from the pain.

"Alright, fine. Promise not to hurt me, and you can add it to your list."

"That's fair."

She reaches for me as I pull back and fix her bikini. "What are you doing?"

"I need to take the hellhound for a quick walk, and then I'll join you in the hot tub."

Lex stares daggers at me but smiles. "I don't care what you say. You're so mean. I don't even know why I like you. I should get myself off and make you watch."

It's tempting to take her up on the offer, but I grab her wrists and press them into the bed at her sides.

"Is she alive, or do we need the shovels?" Riley calls from the bottom of the stairs. He must assume I would have yelled for help if it were serious.

"She's coming!" I shout, and Lex bites her bottom lip.

"No, she isn't actually, but she's about to." Her playful quip makes me grin.

So fucking tempting.

I should lock the door and please her the way I promised to. Until the sun comes up and death do us part. But she gave her word to my friends, which means something to her.

I push myself up using the edge of the bed and find my footing before offering her my hand. This hug needs to linger in my absence, so I make it a good one, attempting to convey with my touch all the things I fail to say. I only wish I were as equally undressed as she is.

"Heartless and mean." She wraps her arms around my waist and tucks her face into my chest. "I'll see you downstairs then. You promise?"

I could promise her the world and find a way to deliver. Diamond rings. Sports cars. All-inclusive vacations to the best places on earth. I have connections and resources that far exceed anything this group of friends is aware of. But that's not what Lex wants from me.

"I give you my word." I release the bonds of our embrace and watch as she steps out the door.

"Hey, Lex," I call after her. "Can you do me a favor?"

Her head appears in the doorway. "You leave a girl hanging and then ask for a favor. Seriously? You're lucky I'm so nice."

"I feel lucky."

"Well, come on then, what is it?" She smiles

wickedly as if every thought is filled with sexual favors.

"Don't kiss him before I get there."

CHAPTER 27

ALEXIS

Nero wags his tail as I approach and allows me to pat his head as I pass. "I don't know what your dad's so worried about. You're as scary as he is."

"A pair of sheep in wolves' clothing," I say as I descend the stairs.

Kade and his dog look like main event prize fighters. Dangerous, even deadly, should they care to be. But beneath the intimidating outer layer, they're total sweethearts. Loyal to a fault, should they choose to be.

"It's nice to see you still in one piece," Riley calls over from the couch. His shirt is gone, and when he stands, I get an eye full of the body he's been keeping under wraps. "I knew that suit would look amazing on you."

He isn't covered in tattoos like Kade is. Riley's hands and throat are free from any hint of color. Even his forearms are bare. But he's been hiding things from me, impressive things that accentuate the muscular curve of his form. And while I'm not typically a fan of six-pack abs, the definition in his body pleases my eyes in a way that's making certain parts of me tingle.

Or maybe it's because a certain someone upstairs dropped my mind in the gutter and left me there to rot. Again.

I hadn't thought about grabbing a towel from Kade's bathroom, but now that I'm on full display in front of a guy who deserves to grace the cover of a fitness magazine, I'm feeling self-conscious. Working from home, I don't necessarily eat foods that one might consider a meal, and I haven't been to the gym in weeks. Even when I work out, it's mostly strength training and the occasional self-defense class.

It was my choice to go with Kade's scary friends, even though I didn't want to leave. I was willing to play along in order to protect him, and who knows, it's entirely possible I would've fought back at some point. Though it's hard to say, in hindsight, considering it was only a test. With the twins, I didn't feel like a victim. But that's not to say I've never felt that way.

"Would you like to lead the way?" The thought of hiding my flaws beneath the surface of the water gets more appealing with every step Riley takes in my direction.

"I didn't get a chance to properly thank you for coming out with me tonight." Riley cups the side of my face and tips my chin upwards. His lips brush past mine and linger within reach. "I appreciate you giving me a second chance."

"Of course." I'm so hungry for a kiss that I have half a mind to take it. There's joyful chatter spilling in from the kitchen, heavy footfalls on the stairs, and warm, inviting breath that smells of mint as it passes over my lips.

"Two minutes, Monroe." The deep baritone of his voice brings me up short. "I leave you alone for two minutes, and you're already getting into trouble."

"You told me to have fun." I shoot back with a smirk as Kade drops the leash, and Nero runs over to wedge himself between me and where Riley once stood.

"Kade, get your dog away from me!" Riley's panic is evident. He's unnerved at the sight of Nero unrestrained, so I reach down and retrieve the end of the leash, hoping to calm the tense situation. "And since when does Alexis need your permission?"

"It was a joke, dude. You should try to relax." Kade gets bigger the closer he gets.

I shake my head and make my exit, hoping to redirect their attention. "Come on, buddy. Let's go outside."

When I step toward the kitchen, heading for the patio door that I assume leads to the backyard, Nero moves with me, practically attached to my hip. The conversation rotating around the ladies and husbands falls silent as we pass. Riley doesn't move, but Kade follows closely behind.

I leave the sliding door open, and as it closes behind us, he says, "I asked you for one thing."

I turn around, feeling mildly frustrated, as though everyone is screwing with me. "Was it my tits, my pussy, or my ass? Which one thing are you referring to? You're gonna need to remind me." I know it isn't any of those. Kade asked me not to kiss Riley, and then I ran off to do exactly that.

"You know what? Forget it. Do whatever you want." Kade reaches for my hand, but I pull away.

"You're being stupid." I raise my voice and solidify my tone.

"I'm being stupid?"

I square my shoulders and jut out my chin. "Yeah, Jax. You're being incredibly stupid."

I hear the door open behind him and see the others pass in shadow.

"Would you care to explain why you're pissed at me?" He reaches again, and I pull away as Nero begins to growl. "And how you've managed to turn my dog against me?"

"I haven't," I say, handing him the loop of the leash. "And I'm not. But I hate it when you do that."

"Do what, exactly?" Kade steps forward, closing the distance between us.

I drop my voice to a whisper. "I hate it when you get me worked up and don't finish me off."

"Will you two kiss already?" One of the ladies shouts as the husbands pull the cover back from the hot tub.

I don't know what he's waiting for, and I lack the courage to ask. Kade's been flirting with me all night. He let me suck his dick, we had sex without a condom, he came in me, we took a shower together, and a moment ago, he had a finger in my ass, but apparently, kissing me is a bridge too far. Too intimate. I keep waiting for his girlfriend to walk through the door, or a recent ex he's hesitant to get over.

"Spend the night with me." Kade pulls me against him, so not even a sliver of light exists between us. "Tell me you'll stay with me."

"You know you're being super obvious, right?"

I'd say I don't understand Kade, but that doesn't seem right. I feel like I know him. Like I've always known him. Most of the time, I think we're implying the same thing without actually saying it, but I'm not confident enough to truly believe that could be the case.

"Kiss! Kiss! Kiss! Kiss!" The group begins to chant.

"Or don't." Riley's voice comes from around Kade's back as the pressure of my non-decision collapses in on me.

I want to be here, but I hate that everyone's looking at me. I want to leave, but I have no means to make it happen. I don't have my keys, so even if I could make it home, I wouldn't be able to get inside. I need to get my car, keys, phone, and wallet, but that requires a goodbye I'm not ready to make. And who knows if Kade would take me, or if my car would even be there?

I've made a mess of things, and I'm not sure what to do. How do I untangle this web without being devoured by spiders?

Riley and Kade are coming at me from both sides, in full view of one another, as though it's a scheduled expedition and I'm nothing more than the unsuspecting prey.

I'd like to think I'd know if I were being played for a fool, but my track record reflects otherwise.

After tonight, I'm done with online dating. Even the casual hookups are far more stressful than they ought to be. All I wanted was to get out of the house, watch the game, get laid, and go home. Instead, I'm being toyed with while onlookers cheer from the cheap seats.

Kade is fiddling with my heart, and Riley is getting off on watching me squirm.

This is not the threesome I envisioned.

CHAPTER 28

ALEXIS

Kade kissed the top of my head before walking away. The ultimate manipulation, if ever there was one. He's an absolute pro. If I didn't know any better, I'd think this night was something it wasn't. I'd get caught up in the romance of it all and assume our meeting was fate. Or worse. True love.

If I didn't have a wealth of experience dealing with liars, I might've convinced myself we were soulmates. But, of course, that's ridiculous. And thankfully, I know better. Sure, I make new mistakes every day, but that doesn't mean I haven't learned from the old ones.

The hot tub is large enough for couples to pair off and spread out, leaving me in Riley's crosshairs.

"It's an impressive house, but don't you think it's overkill for two single guys?" I attempt to steer the conversation onto a topic that'll get him to stop staring at my lips.

"You're right. The house could use a woman's touch and a couple of kids running around. I never thought that future was in the cards for me. Until tonight."

And there it is. That's exactly what I needed to hear to confirm my suspicions. He's messing with me for the sport. Riley barely gave me the time of day during the game, and now he's casually suggesting that matrimony and reproducing are still on the table. He can't seriously think I'm that stupid.

The number of times I've had guys propose marriage after a week has been a lot. When Kade alluded to it earlier, I chalked it up to sex talk. We're all guilty of saying things in the heat of the moment, and promises of forever are a good way to send a girl over the edge. I can appreciate that.

But this, what Riley's doing, is something different. He's baiting a hook and setting a trap right in front of me, thinking I'll be too blinded by his charm to notice.

"Oh?" I raise an eyebrow. "Did you meet someone at the restaurant after I left?"

He barks out a laugh and pulls me onto his lap. "You're adorable."

"I'm not." I reach for the edge, but my hands are wet, and I can't get a grip. "That's the drinks talking."

"You're a tricky one. I can't quite figure you out." He allows me to settle on the seat beside him, but keeps my legs draped over his. "When you agreed to come out with me, I thought you were somewhat interested, but now I'm not sure. If you don't find me attractive, Alexis, you can tell me. I promise I won't get mad."

"Okay. I'll say it, but remember, you promised not to get upset. If you want to know the truth, I'll tell you. I'm willing to be brutally honest, even though it might get me into trouble." When I look up, the other couples are gawking. "If you would've told me the six of you were a group of swingers, and you were inviting me back to the house for an orgy, I would've gotten here faster."

"Come again?" Riley stammers.

"Exactly. We're talking multiple orgasms. I mean, look at all of you. It's not hot tub steam clouding our vision. It's a smoke show. I'd make out with any one of you."

Riley attempts to pull me closer, but Hailey gets to me first. Her lips press into mine, and I forget what we were discussing. I've needed this kiss. I've wanted it so badly. But I hadn't imagined the kiss I craved coming from a married woman. Our lips part, and our tongues exchange pleasantries as she moans softly.

"You're just in time for the show." The water level rises, and the atmosphere around me shifts.

"I'm next." Elise taps in, and I have enough time to open my eyes and see Kade smirking before the next girl braids her fingers into the back of my hair. Her lips are soft, but her kiss is hungry, and when she brushes her free hand up my leg, I gasp.

It would be easy to cross the line, but I had friends like this growing up. Girls who like to play around when they're drinking typically regret anything past second base come sunrise.

"Rock, paper, scissors for next?" One of the husbands says, putting an end to my playtime.

Kade might enjoy watching me kiss other women, but it'll be over a pile of dead bodies that he'll sit back and let another man do it. He might not want that part of me, but it's clear he doesn't want anyone else to have it, either. Before Elise can plant her final pucker, I'm hooked around the waist and dragged in the direction of the newcomer.

"You should let her decide for herself. As you can see, we were all having fun before you got here." Riley looks as annoyed as he sounds.

As I settle into place, my head spins. I thought being pulled in two directions was a lot, but now I've gone and added to it.

Shame on me for suggesting an orgy.

CHAPTER 29
ALEXIS

There appears to be a conversation taking place beneath the surface of my understanding. The tension builds as I move off Kade's lap and position myself between the two men. But it isn't only Riley and Kade who appear to be in on the joke. The glares and giggles from the other side of the hot tub remind me I'm the odd man out.

I lean towards Kade, and he seizes the opportunity to wrap me in his arms, making our conversation seem more intimate than I originally intended.

"I think I might have been better off getting abducted by the scary pair." I keep my voice low.

Kade tucks a strand of hair behind my ear and leans in closer. His lips brush against my skin as he makes his bold claim. "I can fuck you as well as they can. But if you don't believe me, I can give 'em a call and ask 'em to stop by."

I try to limit my reaction, but fail miserably. I don't need a mirror to know the smile on my face is positively wicked. It isn't that I want to have sex with the twins, although I'd have to be an idiot to turn it down. I live for the idea of being shared. In my twenties, I had a handful of threesomes that live rent-free in the back of my mind. And while I yearn for the concept of forever, and I'm not one to shy away from commitment, I have questioned the notion of monogamy and the implied benefits of polyamory.

"I don't think their wife would appreciate that."

"She can come too, since you're into that sort of thing. I'm sure between the four of us, we could get you off." He holds me tightly as I attempt to smack his arm.

"It's not like you aren't capable of doing it on your own. You're just mean."

Kade drops a hand under the water, but I break free before he can slip beneath my bathing suit. In my haste, I practically dive into Riley's lap. I reach for my glass of wine, attempting to play it off, but he catches my wrist.

"It's gonna cost you." Riley licks his bottom lip, drawing my eye to the movement.

"Well, put it on my tab, and I'll swing by an ATM in the morning." I know it isn't money he's after, but I can't help throwing the not-so-playful jab. I'm still pissed about the bullshit he pulled at the restaurant. "Hey, come to think of it, who won the final score?"

Kade and I were otherwise engaged during the fourth quarter. Based on the fireworks display, we assumed our team came out victorious in the end, but neither of us checked to confirm the outcome.

Riley hands me the wine glass, but doesn't answer my question. "So, you're planning to spend the night?"

"I don't know. I guess I..." I stammer, looking for the words, but they evaporate into the air.

Now is a good time to drink.

The glass of wine empties in three gulps, which is not nearly enough time for me to come up with a suitable response. I reach over Riley's shoulder, trading my glass for his, and repeat the process.

"I take it you aren't planning on spending the night with me?"

Stealing Kade's phone and calling the twins for an emergency evacuation is looking better and better by the second.

"Since we're drinking, I thought it might be okay." My voice cuts out, and my confidence is carried away in a cloud of hot tub steam.

"Lex is staying with me." Kade's voice comes from over my shoulder. "She's made her choice."

"Sounds to me like you're the one making the decisions for her, and I'm wondering where you get the nerve."

The onlooking crowd reaches for me, taking hold of my arms and shoulders. Without looking, it's impossible to tell who's who. They pull me into the safe zone as Riley gets to his feet and prepares to strike.

Kade sits there, unimpressed by the show.

"I'm so sick of tripping over your shoes and dealing with that goddamn dog. The list of shit I hate about you grows by the day. There's constantly a sprinkle of protein powder left on the counter after you leave for work. And hair in the sink when you shave."

"It's my bathroom. Why are you in there?"

"I'm not. I don't go into your room. But you leave your door open, and women assume I have a teenage son living with me. I have to waste time explaining that all the childish shit in the house belongs to my loser roommate. And at this point, I'm not sure which is worse."

"You're what? Mad that I play video games on Sunday morning."

"I'm mad that you drive a fucking tow truck and are still riding my coattails. I'm mad that women compare us as if you could even see my level from where you're at. And I'm pissed that you came out tonight, acting like you're something you're not, and stole my fucking date."

"Lex was never yours!"

I want to dwell on those words and their meaning, but I never get the chance.

CHAPTER 30
KADE

The muscle in his chest tightens, telegraphing the swing, and I'm able to block it with my arm.

Since freshman year in college, Riley's been fixated on the idea of fighting me. He brings it up every time he's drunk but never pulls the trigger. Maybe because I'm the biggest guy in every room, it threatens his position at the top, but that's his hang-up, not mine.

I never cared about being named the captain, and never understood why girls compared us. Riley and I couldn't be more different than one another, and we weren't exactly fishing for pussy out of the same ponds. If his exes were secretly interested in what I was keeping in my pants, I was none the wiser, and even if I had been, I wasn't interested.

Blonde teenagers with daddy issues aren't my type.

"Stop! Okay. I'm leaving." Lex wedges herself into the middle of the fight with absolutely zero regard for her safety.

Why am I not surprised?

"Alexis, move. Why are you protecting him? Aren't you the one who said Kade would kill me in a fight?"

"When was this?" I chime in, letting my curiosity get the better of me. I like that she was talking about me, but even more so, I love hearing that she bet on me.

"At the restaurant, before we sat down." Lex presses her back against me as I wrap a protective arm across her chest.

"Shut up, and let's settle this once and for all." Riley's always been a sore loser. That part of his personality goes hand in hand with his arrogance. He thinks he's better than the rest of us. Thinks he can take whatever he wants and assumes we'll hand it over without a fight.

The other guys might have been willing to play along, but I'm not.

"Oh, that better of been directed at me." The matter of Lex and I ending up together was settled the moment I took her hand, but if Riley refuses to acknowledge the obvious, I'm happy to kick the shit out of him, per his request.

"Riley, please don't do this. I'm sorry, okay?" Lex flattens her hand against the front of my thigh, holding me in place behind her as she begs him to stop. "You have every right to be mad at me. I deserve that. But please, don't mess up your face and destroy your friendship over some stupid girl you were never interested in."

"Respectfully, I disagree." He raises his hands in surrender. "But since you asked politely, I'll stop and we'll play a game instead."

I wish I could kiss her and end his reign of terror, but the rules are clear. Whatever Riley chooses to even the playing field or stack the odds in his favor, I don't care. Let him keep the house if he wants it so badly. Had he let things play out, it would've been his.

"What sort of game?" Lex has to be the one to decide, and she's the only one who doesn't realize what's at stake.

"Oh, I think one round of spin the bottle would do the trick."

CHAPTER 31
ALEXIS

They're in love with each other. That's the only logical explanation. The sexual tension I've been picking up on has nothing to do with me. I'm not the rose between two thorns. I'm merely the annoying aphid singularly focused on sucking the sap from their tender stalks. I keep putting myself between them, but what Riley wants is for me to get out of the way.

I've read a handful of books like this. Two tough-guy alpha males with a girl sandwiched between them. Afraid to admit what they're genuinely after.

You go into it thinking, *damn, what I wouldn't give to be in her shoes*, only for things to take a turn. One minute, she's the center of attention. The next, she's an unnecessary addition. The girl excuses herself to the kitchen for a glass of water while the guys finish each other off in the bedroom.

Is this my life?

Is this the story I've walked into?

I was certain Riley had hooked up with Hailey when he and Jakob exchanged a look across the table, but it's entirely possible I misread the signs.

"Alright, Alexis. Are you ready to put us out of our misery?" Riley leans forward with his hands pressed into the edge of the table.

I understand the mechanics of spin the bottle, even though I've never played, but I don't understand how this helps to settle things.

"So, whoever it points to, I have to kiss. But what if it lands on me? Do I kiss my hand? Then, it's someone else's turn?" I know the answers, but I'm too afraid to start the game, so I'm stalling for time.

Kade and Riley are equal distance from me, but the table is divided into three parts by a series of imaginary lines.

"If the bottle lands on you, you have to choose between them." Elise reiterates the stipulation added at Kade's behest.

"Why don't you guys kiss each other and leave me out of it?"

Kade laughs, and Riley rolls his eyes.

"No offense to anyone who's into that, but there's a reason *you're* the one spinning."

Now, I'm more confused than ever.

"Come on." Hailey urges.

"Pretend you're sixteen, and you're back in Sarah's living room while her parents are out of town. It's your turn to spin, and the guy you hoped would play finally took a seat at the table." Elise paints the picture of a memory I didn't know I had. "Finish the game, Alexis, before the cops show up."

My hand is shaking when I reach for the wine bottle marked with my name.

Thirty-four years old, and I'm playing a children's game with a group of strangers from the internet, for reasons I'm not quite clear on.

"Lex, look at me," Kade says my name like it belongs to him.

I flick my wrist and send the bottle whirling.

"No matter what happens, it's you and me." He motions back and forth between us. "I'll not allow a day to come when I have to love you in secret from a distance."

I waited my entire life for this moment, for it to all turn to shit.

CHAPTER 32
ALEXIS

All at once, the pieces fall into place.

Kade steps around the edge of the table as the spinning bottle slows. He cups my cheek, I close my eyes, and for a split second, I'm the awkward sixteen-year-old girl who's about the kiss the most sought-after boy at the party.

"Damn, Kade, that's low. Telling a woman you're in love with her just to win a bet." Riley continues to talk, but I'm no longer listening. After all, what is there left to say?

Normally, I value honesty, as brutal as it can be, but this truth feels like a bomb going off in my chest.

All evening, I've been trying to read the situation like a book when I should have been watching it like a movie.

Kade pulls me to his chest, wanting to compound the lies and no longer finding an audience. "Babe, please let me explain."

My body goes rigid beneath his touch as the factory settings for self-preservation take effect, and a prerecorded message plays over the speaker. "It's fine. You don't have to explain. Everything makes more sense now. I would say I had a nice time, but that would make us both liars."

"Please, stop." He's got some nerve, sounding heartbroken when I'm the one who's shattered.

I take a step back, adding physical detachment to my emotional absence. Might as well toss another log on the fire if I have to stand here and watch my future burn. "I don't care that you had sex with me in order to win a bet. I wanted you to do it. But you didn't have to lie to make it happen, and you really should've pulled out."

The ladies gasp, and Riley unleashes a series of curse words and a flurry of insults, but they're little more than noise. Nothing that's said matters anymore.

"Let's go upstairs and talk." Kade wraps his fingers around my wrist with a weak grip. I could easily pull free if I wanted to, but I allow the last of our connection to linger and fade slowly.

"There's nothing to talk about, Kade. I don't even know you." I slip my hand through his enclosed fingers and turn to walk away.

"Maybe not, Lex, but my heart would recognize you anywhere. In any form." Kade steps in front of me, cutting off the path to my retreat. "I'm sorry it took me so long to find you. I promise next time, I'll do it better."

I want to push past and tell him to piss off. I want to kick him in the shin or knee him in the balls. I want to jab the base of my palm into his nose and drive bits of bone into his brain until he's twitching on the floor like a fucking cabbage being eaten by a worm.

But worse than all of that, I still want to kiss him.

I glance over my shoulder at the table and the bottle and the people looking on as though they're waiting for something to happen. As fate would have it, the choice is mine to make. But why are they still making observations and hypothesizing the results, as if the outcome wasn't clear within the first thirty seconds?

Standing in the restaurant, in front of god and everyone, with my hand in his and my secrets laid bare, I knew I belonged to Kade. Why I bothered with the song and dance and multiple rounds of charades, hoping to spare Riley's feelings, I'll never understand. I should've ended the date before it started. I should've given Kade my number, walked out of the restaurant, and left the outcome of my future securely in his hands.

But I didn't, and now I'm here, and if I had to do it all again, I would.

I would do it again. And again. And again. And I wouldn't change a goddamn thing because the time I spent with Kade was effortless, even though everything else was chaos.

Even if our connection wasn't real, my heart didn't know the difference.

"Will you tell me if it was worth it? Having to hook up with some average-looking nerdy girl from the internet. Did you get something good out of it?" Now that the anger has worked its way out of my system, I'm back to being self-deprecating. One-night stands were never meant to be this complicated.

"That depends on whether or not you forgive me." Kade is still trying to say the right things for reasons I'm unsure of.

"I don't understand why that has anything to do with it." The emotions of a pawn are irrelevant to the game of chess.

"Riley bet the house, but all I ever wanted was you."

I hear it before he says it. I feel the words growing inside me. Twisting around my bones. Taking root in my heart and feeding my soul. They lock me in place, unable to dodge or duck or weave as his declaration hits me head-on.

"Lex, I love you."

CHAPTER 33

KADE

"I hate you for making me believe that." A single tear streaks her face, and I'm gutted.

My eyes trail Lex to the stairs, and I feel our shared disappointment with every step that takes her from me. I desperately want to be the man she deserves, but everything good inside of me dies the moment she rounds the corner.

"You stupid mother fucker." I'm at the table with my hand around Riley's throat in seconds. I could kill him, but that would be too easy.

I slam him hard against the wall as our friends fail to pull me back. Wanting to inflict pain. Needing to see him suffer. I want to make him bleed.

"She's no one. Just some random girl." He manages to get out, prompting me to slam my fist into his stomach. He'd double over if I didn't have him locked in place. Instead, he sucks in a sharp breath. "You've known her for five hours."

"I've been looking for her my entire life!" The force of my confession makes my chest heave. "You wouldn't understand because you've never cared about anyone besides yourself."

I throw him to the side and kick his feet out from under him, not thinking about the sofa table we use as a minibar. Riley crashes into the bottles, sending shards of glass and wasted booze spilling out in all directions.

With broken glass littering the floor, nobody moves.

"All this for a girl who doesn't even like you." Riley tips his head from side to side and presses a hand against his ribs, surveying the damage.

"Oh my god, will you shut up? It's your fault for making that stupid bet. We've been telling you all night they like each other." Hailey triple-checks the floor beneath her feet before tentatively stepping toward the kitchen.

"If she likes him so much, why didn't she kiss him?" It's clear Riley has a death wish and wants to go out with a bang.

Elise picks up the fight, as Hailey slips away. "Because you've both been acting possessive as fuck since Alexis walked in the house, and she could tell something was off. The woman's not an idiot."

"The girl rolled up in a Lamborghini. You think she's gonna slum it past tonight with a guy who drives a tow truck?"

I check the floor around my feet and turn toward the stairs. If walking on broken glass would prove my devotion, I'd smash every bottle in the house. I'd stand on hot coals and a handful of Legos if it meant she'd forgive me.

"In case you failed to notice, dickhead, she didn't kiss you either."

CHAPTER 34
ALEXIS

I drop to my hands and knees in the dimly lit room and lift the corner of the comforter, peering under the edge of the bed as far as I can see. Nero seizes his opportunity, walks over with his tail wagging, and licks the side of my face.

"Come on. I thought we were friends. Help me out. I promise I'll play with you. Just tell me where your dad hid my clothes." My begging falls on deaf ears as Nero returns to the comfort of his bed, unwilling to betray his favorite human.

I'm beginning to understand why Fred, Daphne, and Velma kept a box of Scooby snacks at the ready.

I can't fault Nero for being loyal. Even though I'm unhappy with Kade's lies of omission, I wouldn't gamble against him or his ability to come out on top. I might not fully understand what happened this evening, but I know he's so much more than his friends give him credit for.

The sound of raised voices and shattered glass coming from downstairs reminds me of the time my ex threw a beer bottle at my head and broke the kitchen window instead. Somehow, I was to blame. I can't remember what the fight was about or what I had cooking on the stove, but his accusation remains.

You're worthless. No one will ever love you.

A low growl sounds from the dark corner of the room, and I hear footsteps coming up the stairs.

"Shit." I hop to my feet and scurry into the bathroom, shutting the door behind me. I engage the lock on the handle and steady myself against the sink.

I should've used the time I had to locate a set of car keys instead of worrying about my sweater and jeans.

"Can you please let me in?" Kade's voice is low but clear.

"Just a minute." I grab the bathrobe from a hook on the back of the door and pull it on like an oversized coat, hoping to preserve a shred of dignity.

"I need to know you're okay."

"I'm fine," I lie. "I couldn't find my clothes. Do you know where they are?"

I hear him opening the drawers of his dresser before returning to knock gently on the door. "Lex, please. I'm asking you nicely to unlock the door."

"Well, where was all this nice guy shit earlier while you were ruining me for all other men?" When I'm nervous, I default to humor.

A distinct sound signals what's to come, but I'm powerless to stop it. Metal rubs against metal as the lock disengages and the handle turns slowly. A half-naked Kade enters the space, making the decent-sized bathroom feel cramped. "If that's the case, I'll need to amend my apology."

I hold the thick robe firmly in place and step toward the wall. It's stupid to think it'll happen now, but I want him to finish the game. Feeling his lips against mine would add value to our experience. Then, maybe I wouldn't have to feel so cheap.

Unfortunately, Kade doesn't kiss me. Why would he? I gave up the milk, the cow, the whole goddamn farm, for free, and now I have nothing left to barter. I'm surprised they haven't kicked me out of the house for all the trouble I've caused.

"I heard something break. It wasn't Riley's face, was it?"

"His face is fine." Kade sets the small stack of clothing on the counter and looks me over.

"Oh, thank goodness." I over-exaggerate my relief, although I am genuinely happy to hear that no one's hurt.

"There was never a bet to see who could sleep with you. There was no bet. Not until we got to the house. And even then, it was never about sex. I wouldn't do that. I'm not that type of guy." But even now, he looks starved, like he did in the office. As though having me is the only thing that will feed the craving and silence the hunger.

It's hard to see him like this and not give in, especially when he's shirtless. I know I'm meant to be mad, confused, and disappointed, and a part of me still is, but I also want him to touch me. There will be plenty of time to sort through my feelings later, when I'm crying at home over how much I miss him. For now, I want to feel significant. I want the fantasy. But I also want the truth.

Needing to feel like I'm the one calling the shots, I shrug off the bathrobe and allow it to fall around my feet. "So, everything that happened prior to us getting here…"

"…was because we both wanted it." Kade licks his bottom lip and hones in on the ties holding my bikini in place.

"So, then, what? What happened after we got here? What changed? I thought we were good, and then we weren't. I was a secret, and then I wasn't. Riley didn't give a shit, and then he saw your buddy's Lambo and was suddenly all about it. I feel like I took crazy pills, and now I'm trippin' my balls off."

Kade laughs and steps forward, slipping his hands around my waist. "You're adorable."

"I'm serious. Be honest with me. Then, I can decide if I should be upset with you or not." Even though he's seen me naked, I feel exposed. There's more I want to say, but I'm worried about what the words might do.

"I like you," he says, removing my top and dropping it into the sink.

"You like me? Funny, that's not the way you described your feelings downstairs." It's easy to be playful when we're on the same team.

"Yeah, well, when I said it downstairs, you yelled at me." He pulls the loose ends of the bikini ties, rendering my bottoms useless.

There were so many things I wanted to share with the man who brought me here, but I can't move forward leading with my emotions until I know the truth, for better or worse. If there are red flags, I want to see them. I want to fully understand what he's capable of before I adjust my blinders. No matter what, I'm still here, but in what capacity, I'm unsure.

"I promise I won't get upset, and we can have sex again if you want to, but I need you to give me a few more details. Otherwise, I won't be able to stop thinking about it, and I'll never get off." I tack on the last part, knowing that's important to him.

Instead of touching me, Kade hands me a folded t-shirt and a pair of black sweatpants from the top of the pile. "Whichever one of us you kissed got to keep the house. There were some rules. We couldn't kiss you first, and someone else had to be there to confirm it happened. But that's the gist of it."

I shake my head in disbelief and set the clothes down beside me.

"A kiss from a girl you both met tonight determined who owns this house? This giant mansion. Are you both out of your minds? What were you thinking?" My hands wave wildly in the air and I'm so caught up in my rant that I nearly miss the flash of Kade's cock as he removes his shorts and pulls on a pair of grey sweats. I stammer and regroup. "If that's the case, Hailey won the bet when we kissed in the hot tub."

I grab the pants from the counter first, wanting to cover my sexy bits in order of importance. Kade watches as I struggle to pull the string tight enough to hold the pants in place while I reach for the shirt.

Well, it might have been a shirt at one point, but it could hardly be described that way now. He's removed the sleeves and half of the sides. It's cut in a way that the strip down my chest struggles to cover both of my nipples at the same time. "You've got to be kidding me?"

I would exchange it for his shirt, but he didn't bother selecting one for himself.

"Damn, you look good in my clothes. I don't even remember what you were yelling at me about."

"Yes, you do." I playfully smack his arm, inviting him to grab me by the hips and set me on the counter.

"The wives didn't win because, technically, they kissed you, and they were never in the running." He pushes my knees apart and wedges himself between my legs.

"So, if I kissed you right now?" I wet my lips and smile.

"I would die a very happy man."

"Because of the house?"

"No!" Kade cups my face in one hand and runs his thumb across my cheek. "Go downstairs and kiss Riley in front of everyone. Give him the house. Let him have it. I don't care. If that's what it takes for you to forgive me, then do it. I don't want the house."

"Then why agree to the bet?"

"Because I knew you and I were gonna be together, and I was going to make you my wife the first chance I got. Had Riley left well enough alone, the house would've been his. But he's so damn arrogant. And that arrogance made him careless. He saw what was happening, heard what everyone was saying, and thought he could take you from me. And sure, it was stupid on my part to agree. Had I known it would lead to this, I would've.left things the way they were. But..." Kade runs a hand through his hair. "I wanted to stick it to him and prove, once and for all, that he isn't better than me."

"That part, I understand." Being confident is one thing, but Riley takes it too far. "Even the bet makes sense, in a weird way, but there's one thing I can't figure out."

Kade leans in with clear eyes and a raised brow as though this moment determines all others that follow. "Whatever it is, babe, I'll make it make sense."

"If the rules weren't in place until we got here, and they're all but irrelevant now…" I tip my head back and focus on his lips. "Why won't you kiss me?"

I know it's pathetic. I'm practically begging. If I'm not careful, I'm going to end up guilting him into kissing me, which is not my intention. But if there's something holding him back. Someone else his heart belongs to. I need to know. I'd rather he tears off the band-aid now while I'm semi-recovering but still slightly wounded. That way, I can walk away and find the will to never look back.

Oh, who am I kidding?

It catches me by surprise when his lips meet mine, and the world around us disappears.

If his kiss is guilt-ridden or half-hearted, Kade doesn't let on. He takes his time, savoring the press of my tongue against his as though indulging in dessert for dinner.

"I should've done this at the restaurant," he says, pulling back.

"Then, why didn't you?" My arms cross the back of his neck and ease him forward, still needing more.

"Because I didn't want our first kiss to taste like beer-soaked garlic."

The confession makes me giggle.

Imagine being so flawless that your biggest worry is the lingering scent of barley and herbs on your breath.

Kade lifts me with ease and carries me to the bed, navigating the transition seamlessly. In his arms, I'm as light as a feather, and when we settle on the bed, I find he's stiff as a board. Feeling him hard against me is as impressive as it is flattering. My exes were usually good for a single round of affection once a week, and in some cases, once a month. It feels good to be wanted. Kade conveys his desire in every stolen glance, each secretive touch, and every sincere promise.

Now, I can add his kiss to the growing list of things I can't live without.

We make out like a pair of high school kids hopped up on teenage hormones and freedom from responsibility. Oh, what I wouldn't give to stumble back in time so I might find him sooner.

If heaven is a moment we live in for eternity, let tonight be mine. I promise I'll be a good person. I'll pay my bills the day they appear in my email, I'll meet deadlines well before they're due, I'll brush my teeth twice a day and floss religiously, and rescue stranded earthworms from the concrete.

Whatever it takes to get the deal done, and regardless of whom I need to make it with, I'm willing to sign my name on the line for the chance to see him again.

Only, god and the devil aren't here right now, and neither of them is interested in my soul.

I reach into the front of Kade's grey sweats and brush the back of my hand against his cock, causing him to grown.

"You're insatiable. You know that, don't you?"

I smile and lean in for a kiss. "We don't have to do anything. And for the record, I am plenty satiated. You're the one who got hard."

"Which is entirely your fault." Kade gets up from the bed and adjusts his pants, but fails to hide anything. "Quit being so goddamn sexy and I'll stop getting hard every time you touch me."

"Why would I agree to that? That sounds terrible." We both laugh.

He pulls a black hoodie from his dresser and yanks it on, denying me the visual pleasure of his bare chest and tattoos. "Is there anything you're into that I should know about?"

"You mean, besides personal assistant kink and hand tattoos?" I say jokingly.

"And threesomes," Kade adds. If he's trying to have a conversation and get my mind off sex, he's going about it the wrong way.

I point to the shelf over his shoulder. "That mask is kinda doing something for me."

"Yeah. Well, I'm not *him*, if that's what you're wondering." Kade removes the lifeless Goblin King head from the bookshelf and holds it in one hand.

I sit in the middle of the bed and cross my legs underneath me. "I know you're not him, but…"

He fastens the mask over his face and pats the side of his leg. "Nero, heel!"

The sight of them side by side, stalking toward me, makes my heart flutter, but it's the hellhound who's the first to strike, springing forward and landing on the bed in front of me. He rams his head into the center of my chest, knocking me onto my back.

I laugh uncontrollably as he attacks my face with puppy kisses.

"So much for being sexy." The mattress indents beside me, alerting me to Kade's presence, and before long, Nero has settled.

I open my eyes expecting to see the face of a Goblin King, but am pleasantly surprised to find the monster turned back into a man. I stroke his cheek and stare into his eyes like some love-drunk goober. "Out of all the faces I've ever seen, I like this one the most."

"Oh yeah? You think I'm better looking than Riley?"

"Mmhmm." I hum in affirmation.

"And the twins?"

"Okay, let's not get crazy." If I were a cartoon, my lips would curl into a grinch-like grin. "Technically, I never uttered the words better-looking. You added that. I merely said it was my favorite."

"Oh, you brat." Kade hooks an arm between my legs and pulls me toward him, eliminating what little space existed between us.

I squeal and twist as he begins tickling the exposed skin above my hip. As I work to unscrew myself from his grasp, the front panel of my borrowed shirt slips to one side, leaving my breast exposed. He clamps his lips to the sensitive skin before tonguing the fleshy bundle of nerves as though it were a secondary clit.

"Okay. I take it back." I struggle to secure purchase as Kade's body drops lower. "You're better looking than the twins and all your other friends combined."

"I don't know. Jarreth might have me beat. He looks better in the mask than I do." Kade slips a hand past the waistband of my oversized sweatpants.

"Now I know you're messing with me."

With gentle pressure, he brushes over the lips of my pussy. "I'm playing with you, but I'm not lying."

I should give in to his touch and stop talking, but I enjoy hearing him speak. I find myself gathering details about his life like a squirrel collecting nuts during the mild autumn months. I need enough to hold me over, and no tidbit is too small when looking down the barrel at an endless winter.

"Are you part of a local hot guy secret society?"

In a way, it makes sense, but at the same time, it doesn't. They're all around the same age and on the same level of attractiveness, making them cohorts but also making them competition. I can't help but wonder how many times they've swapped dates or shared partners.

"It's more like an underground fight club."

I place my hand over his and pause the movement.

"Well, whatever it is, my money's on you."

CHAPTER 35
ALEXIS

I'm filled with a desire to make the most of the time we have left, but I'm physically exhausted and mentally drained, and I know Kade won't stop until I'm a boneless glob of goo. Could I have sex? Sure. Do I want to? Kind of, but not really. Is it lame that I would rather cuddle and talk? Definitely.

Long story short, I could go either way, so I'll leave it for Kade to decide. "Not to be weird, but do you think you could get off again?"

As a woman, I have an endless supply of orgasms, each one progressively more difficult to obtain, but not impossible. I can't speak on the issue with any certainty, but I don't think it's the same for men.

"I could have sex with you, and it would feel amazing, but I'm not confident I have any swimmers left, and I'm worried you'll take it personally." Kade wraps his arms around me in a bear hug and rolls onto his back, taking me along for the ride.

"You say that like I'm trying to get knocked up." I tuck my knees in on either side of him and sit up. Careful not to break his dick, I straddle his waist slightly higher than normal, feeling his hard cock as it rubs against my ass. "Which I assure you, I am not."

"I'm fine with it either way." Taking hold of my hips, he guides my movements. "I like seeing you like this, but we don't have to do anything if you don't want to. I'm good just being with you."

"Me too." I lie forward and rest against his chest, tucking my face into the nook between his shoulder and neck. I could close my eyes and drift off to sleep as easily as I could wiggle out of my pants and ride his thick cock until we're too worn out to continue.

I don't want to have regrets, one way or the other, but Kade isn't helping to steer my choices. We're both towing the center line, keeping it cute, and focusing on the needs of the other. It's an adorably respectful stalemate that's ultimately getting us nowhere.

I'm seconds away from suggesting we watch porn, have sex, and fall asleep, when Kade offers an alternative. His plan runs in the same vein but lands on the opposite end of the spectrum. "Should we put on a movie and snuggle under the blanket?"

I love that he uses the word snuggle.

"There's a good chance you'll lose me halfway through."

I'm torn between wanting to stay awake as long as possible and needing to know what it feels like to fall asleep in his arms. Typically, I'm a night owl. It's not unusual for me to crawl into bed after sunrise and sleep until lunchtime. I get my best work done when it's quiet and the world around me is dark.

"That's the main thing I'm trying to avoid." He brushes his hands over my exposed skin, and my arms prickle with goosebumps.

"I didn't mean it that way." I'm so accustomed to

guys half listening that I'm not used to choosing my words carefully.

"Let's call it a night and save the movie for another time." The mood in the room drops out from underneath us, and Kade and I are both caught in the fallout.

"Yeah, that's probably for the best." I sit back and slip to the side before climbing off the bed completely. "I need to get up early so I can figure out how I'm getting home."

"You can take the car, and the guys can pick it up from there." Kade moves to the end of the bed and sits on the edge. "I don't want you to feel like you're trapped."

"It's fine. I don't have my keys, so I wouldn't be able to get inside." This isn't meant to make him feel worse, but it lands that way all the same. I'm starting to regret my decision to pump the brakes. If we'd had sex, this awkwardness could've been avoided until tomorrow.

"Well shit, I'm an asshole." He pops up and grabs his phone from the dresser. "I was so happy you decided to spend the night. I never realized it was because I took away your ability to leave."

"Hey," I say, touching his arm. I'm unsure if this is a misunderstanding or merely reality crashing in on us, but whatever it is, I need it to stop. "I want to be here."

Kade eyes me intently, looking for any hint of hidden reservation. Perhaps he's used to people being afraid of him, tiptoeing around tense situations, and telling him what he wants to hear.

I'll admit, I'm guilty of being accommodating with men in the past. Sometimes, it's easier to give in and stay quiet in order to avoid escalating negativity. Girls are like butterflies. They learn when to close their wings and make themselves small. They're taught how to blend in with their surroundings. And they're excellent at morphing into something whose beauty is revered. But they're also delicate and easily damaged in the wrong hands.

I grip his wrist and pull him toward me, needing his arms around me. "I'd like the stay with you, if that's okay?"

I wish I could convince Kade that this is me being greedy. Wanting to be near him is an act of self-preservation, but not in the way he's used to. If I had it my way, I'd never leave. I'd avoid saying goodbye until we were old and grey and prepared to depart side by side for our next adventure.

And sure, I know that isn't going to happen. Like clockwork, the sun will rise, and my carriage will turn back into a pumpkin.

But a girl can dare to dream.

CHAPTER 36
KADE

It doesn't take long for Lex to get comfortable, tucked in beside me. With the television off, the room is dark, and the house is quiet. I focus on her breathing and the tempo of her beating heart as she draws invisible patterns with her fingertips across my bare skin.

"I want you to stay." I brush a strand of hair behind her ear, looking for an excuse to touch her.

"Yeah, I think I agreed to that when we got into bed together." Her palm flattens on my chest, and she tips her chin forward.

I claim her lips, hoping, yet again, to convey all that my words fail to say.

I want you to stay tonight.

And tomorrow.

And the day after that.

I want to make you breakfast.

And watch you work from home while you're still wearing my clothes.

I want to extend our evening indefinitely.

Because I don't want you to leave.

I'm afraid I'll never see you again.

And I can't bear the thought of losing you.

I don't want to return to the life I had before.

Not after knowing how good it could be.

I can't.

I won't.

I don't want to miss you.

I nip at her bottom lip before placing a final kiss on the end of her nose. "Goddamn, I fucking love you."

If I haven't ruined things prior to now, this has surely sealed my fate. If I'd had sex with her, I could've gotten away with saying it, but here we are.

Lex hesitates before letting out a breath. "If I say it back, can we get some sleep?"

She's willing to utter the words simply to placate me, but she won't mean it, which sucks, but it doesn't change the fact that I want to hear it. "You don't have to."

Lex flips onto her other side and pulls my arm over her like a weighted blanket. Even with her back to me, I appreciate the way our pieces fit together.

I should've kept my mouth shut and let her float off to sleep without giving us a reason to drift apart.

But what's said can't be unsaid, and I wouldn't take it back, even if I could. I'll suffer the consequences, but at least she'll know. The last time I said it, she told me she hated me. Maybe she'll say the same this time.

"Hey, Jax." Her voice is steady, and I ready myself for the blow.

"I love you, too."

CHAPTER 37
ALEXIS

I'm a big fan of reality TV dating shows. In my downtime, while nursing a creative hangover, I enjoy binge-watching episodes that claim love is blind and couples get married at first sight. If I'd met Kade on an island, would we be a perfect match, or would the temptation of others be too great? Why is it so easy to cheer for strangers seeking love in unusual circumstances, but I regard myself with criticism when put in the same position?

If true love isn't real, what are all the stories based on?

I thought finding my person would feel like butter-flies hatching in my digestive system, which is horrifying when I stop to think about it, but being with Kade is peaceful. It's calm and quiet. I feel safe from the world around me. Like, everything might be violent, but fear is unnecessary because I'll never have to face the difficult situations alone.

If I had a choice, I'd stay tucked away in my cocoon, safely wedged between him and his dog. This space they carved out for me is my new happy place.

I close my eyes and lock away each detail of the memory, desperately needing to hold on a little longer.

When I roll over, Kade is on his phone, silently watching a highlight reel from last night's game.

"What was the final score?" I inquire, for no reason other than to have something to say.

"Ninety-three to Eighty-nine."

"Three and nine. Do you remember who had that square on the board?"

"I think we did." Kade leans over to kiss me, and his breath tastes of mint.

I'm wondering when and how he was able to escape the bed without alerting me to his absence. Normally, I'm a light sleeper. Then again, wine tends to knock me out.

"Do you think I could borrow some toothpaste?" I bring a hand over my mouth, hoping to stifle any unpleasantness, but Kade encircles my wrist, gently removes the barrier, and kisses me again.

"I put a toothbrush on the bathroom counter for you. Just toss it in the drawer when you're done."

"Is it yours?" I've never borrowed a guy's toothbrush before. It sounds unhygienic but also deliciously intimate.

"Mine is in the drawer if you'd rather use that one, but I thought you'd want your own."

I blush at my inane assumption. "Yeah, that makes more sense."

My options for evacuation are climbing over the top of my massive overnight companion or disturbing a sleeping Nero. Allegedly, Kade's four-legged companion is something to be feared, though I've seen no evidence to support this claim. Regardless, I know better than to wake a sleeping dragon.

I wiggle beneath the comforter like a worm in an underground tunnel until I'm spit out onto the floor at the end of the bed.

"We would've gotten up, had you asked." Kade laughs, and Nero lifts his head to issue a judgmental stare.

"I was trying to be considerate." I pick myself up off the floor and steal the hoodie Kade left discarded at the end of the bed.

The smell of him envelopes me as the cotton fibers playfully brush against my skin. It reminds me of his fingertips and the tender caress of his palm as he massaged my back. "By the way, I'm keeping this."

I disappear into the bathroom, shutting the door behind me.

"I can take Nero for a walk and give you some privacy," Kade calls from behind the locked door. "I left a clean towel on the rack in case you want to shower."

I pop the lock on the handle and swing open the door.

Standing near his dresser in shorts and nothing else, Kade's as handsome in the morning light as he had been upon first meeting. Maybe even more so. His dark hair is playfully messy and utterly careless, which stands in contrast to the body that clearly requires effort and attention to maintain. The sight makes my heart beat faster, even as he pulls on a t-shirt.

I know the only shame I'll feel while walking out of his bedroom will be the regret of not having more time.

I wasn't originally planning to shower, but now it's all I want to do. "Hurry back, and you can join me."

Two steps are all it takes before he's filling the doorway with his arm bent, gripping the trim so he can lean into the space I once occupied alone. Trapping me inside. If he were anyone else, I'd be mentally scanning the room for weapons, running through rapid-fire escape plans, and calculating my odds of survival. But the closer Kade gets, the quieter my mind becomes, until pin-drop silence signals the press of his lips to mine.

"I'll be back before you have a chance to miss me."

I smile in response, choosing to receive his message in the spirit it's given.

Perhaps Kade doesn't realize the depths to which I've fallen. Considering the swift descent took me by surprise, I can't blame him for not understanding. Even if he could harness the speed of Hermes, my heart would use the minutes apart to torture me. Taunting me. Teasing me. Reminding me that this is merely an echo of life before our meeting and a memento of the emptiness yet to come.

I'm unrehearsed and ill-equipped, and I can't help but slip into the comfort of my impending depression.

"I already miss you, and you haven't even left yet."

CHAPTER 38
KADE

I pace the length of two boards as Nero meanders along the perimeter of the back fence. I swear he's doing it on purpose. Ninety percent of the time, he's the best dog a guy could ask for, but the other ten percent, he's pure evil, and I swear, he secretly loves to mess with me. This is my punishment for leaving him at home and going out without him. They say dogs are man's best friend, but even best friends can be vindictive little shits.

I hear the door slide open behind me, and for a split second, my heart leaps as I turn, expecting to see Lex. Unfortunately, my excitement takes a dive, leaving disappointment in its wake, and quickly, my frustration morphs into anger.

"Are we good?" Riley asks.

I know we're outside, but his continued inability to read the room is astounding.

"I haven't decided."

"That's rich, considering the circumstances." Riley takes a single step forward, then thinks better of it and falls back.

One could easily argue that I'm the asshole in the situation after actively pursuing the woman he was on a date with. But it's not as though I had a choice. Sure, I didn't have to steal her away mid-dinner conversation, but I couldn't very well leave without her. And yeah, maybe I shouldn't have introduced her to the twins or had sex with her in my office, but it was going to happen eventually. And I definitely shouldn't have leveraged my certainty to screw him out of the house, but he's the one who changed the rules and proposed the wager.

"You told her it was a bet." Despite everything I did to deserve his wrath, I can't forgive him for hurting her. Riley didn't merely cause her to distrust my intentions. He inadvertently made Lex question her value, and in my eyes, that is unforgivable.

"I was wrong for that."

"You said she was no one. Just some random girl." I take a step forward, and he flinches.

If nothing else, Riley's presence is good for one thing. Once Nero registers what's happening, he abandons his bird-watching expedition and joins me on the deck. With his attention trained on a new target, he takes his place by my side, awaits my command, and mirrors my steps as I walk toward the house.

I pause at the door, gripping the handle tightly. A conversation needs to occur if our friendship is meant to endure, but now is not the time. I'm on edge, caught between opposing versions of forever, and until the matter is settled, I don't have room in my headspace for Riley Sinclair. Plus, there's someplace I need to be.

I don't bother looking at him, which sends a message all its own, but I amend my answer to his initial question.

"You and I are only *good* because she's still here."

CHAPTER 39
ALEXIS

I'm in the final stages of my morning routine when Kade joins me in the shower. His arms wrap around me from behind as he presses himself into my back. Instinctively, my head falls to one side, and he leans down to kiss my neck. I love the way his body feels bound together with mine, like two sides of a book cover sharing a spine.

"You look unbelievably sexy with your hair tied up. You know that, don't you?"

After brushing my teeth, I found an elastic in one of the bathroom drawers and was able to pull my hair into a messy bun. Part of me considers asking him who it belongs to, and another part of me doesn't want to know. We both have a past, and body count is only an issue for people who lack the confidence and ability to get things done in the bedroom.

"I was hoping you would think so. I enjoy turning you on." I place my hands on his arm and feel the muscles tighten beneath my fingertips.

Flirting with Kade is easy. Maybe it's the heat from the shower melting us together, or perhaps it's a trick of the mind. When I twist in his arms, it's as though he's reading my thoughts. We suck in a shared breath as his lips meet mine.

My eyes are closed when the water cuts off, and I'm lifted from my feet. I laugh as I imagine my naked body slipping through his barrel grip and landing on the floor like a pile of laundry, but with all the soap rinsed clean, he's able to keep from dropping me.

Kade doesn't bother grabbing a towel or pausing at the mat. He carries me straight to the bed and plops us down in the middle.

"We're gonna get the sheets wet." It goes without saying, and clearly, he doesn't care, but I find myself pointing out the obvious. Kade makes me nervous as much as he calms me, and my anxiety doesn't know what to make of the quiet.

"Then we might as well get 'em dirty."

I shift back on my elbows until my head finds the pillow, and Kade drops between my thighs. When it comes to cunnilingus, plenty of guys promise the world, but few have the skills or a desire to deliver. Lucky for me, Kade is an exception to the rule in every exquisitely conceivable way.

He starts slowly, teasing me with well-placed kisses and confident, feather-light strokes until I'm wet with arousal and buzzing. In my mind, he's praising me for how good I taste and how pretty I'm going to look taking his cock.

With two curling fingers, he works the ridges of my g-spot while licking my clit with the flat of his tongue. He's almost too good. Too perfectly in tune with my body and willing to see to my needs. Add to that, his voice in my head, silently muttering a series of *good girl* praises and a handful of derogatory pet names.

It feels selfish to lie here on my back, chasing my pleasure, when I've yet to touch him.

"I want to suck your cock."

The thought of having him in that way makes my mouth water, but Kade latches onto my clit in response and hums a muffled sound of disapproval against the most sensitive part of my body. The vibration makes my spine arch, and his unwillingness to stop makes my eyes roll to the back of my head.

"Jax, please. I want to make you feel good." If I have to resort to begging, so be it. Saying it aloud will only make the visuals stronger.

He can't hold out forever, and honestly, neither can I.

It's that perfect pressure that's getting to me. Making me come undone at the edges. I don't mean to say it, sincerely, I don't, but politeness left the room the second his fingers slipped inside me, and I've been losing my grip on reality ever since.

"Should I yell for Riley since you refuse to give me what I want?" I dig my fingers into his hair and pull, but he doesn't stop.

"Goddamnit, Kade! You're gonna make me cum."

Of all the verses in the English language, these are the magic words.

Kade springs to his knees and pulls his fingers free from my body. The sensation ripples along muscle fibers and nerve endings before disappearing through my fingers and toes. But there is no time or need to mourn the loss. He grips onto my hips and pushes inside. The blinding pressure is almost too much to bear, and I forget to hold back.

"I could go at any time. Just say when." Kade drives into my sturdy frame with hard strokes.

"I'm so close." In an effort to give us both a win before I'm split in two, I reach down and begin stimulating my clit.

"Fuck. I like watching you do that. Keep going, baby."

I suck in a breath and hold it. Refusing to let it out. I draw in more air, taking small sips until my lungs are filled to capacity. And I hold it. I keep the air inside until it's depleted of resources. Until it's painful. Until my vision blackens at the edges and orbs of white light pepper my sight. I hold the used air and push myself to the brink, not caring about the damage.

When the orgasm comes, my body spasms, and carbon dioxide releases from my lungs in a moan, making room for something new. Seconds later, Kade finishes inside of me, extending my pleasure until it's so ingrained with his that I'm no longer sure they can exist separately.

Kade crumbles down on top of me with his cock still twitching inside me.

"Stay with me."

I'm not sure what he means exactly. His request could be taken several ways.

Remain in this moment.

Hang out with me for the day.

Or perhaps my lack of breathing has him concerned about my ability to remain conscious.

"I want to, but I can't. I have to work, and I still need to get my car. I was hoping to get a ride with you to your office, but…" My words trail off as I read the lines of disappointment etched into his features. "I'm sorry."

Kade dips his head to kiss me as he pulls out slowly, making sure to replace one sensation with the next so that I never have to go without. His words brush against my lips. "You don't have to be sorry."

I should stay. I should definitely stay. I should put on his clothes, cuddle into his arms, and take a nap as we watch a movie. I should give him my heart. I should dig in my heels. I should tie myself to the bed and allow him to lay claim to every part of my body. I should stay. I should call this place home. I should make him so happy that he forgets about the rest of the world and never leaves my side. I should stay until he calls the cops and threatens to have me forcibly removed from the premises. I should die here and haunt this house like a poltergeist so he never feels alone.

Or, for everyone's sake, I should go.

I should stop being a needy psycho in the making, say goodbye, and find a way home.

"Do you think I could get my jeans and sweater back?"

Kade looks at me with a flash of annoyance, as though I mistakenly punched him in the face instead of asking a simple question. He practically flees the scene, retrieving his shorts from the floor on his way to the bathroom. "I don't have your clothes, Alexis. I told you I didn't take them."

The shower turns on, and I'm left contemplating my next move. If I get up too quickly, it's going to be a mess. And I can't very well throw on sweatpants and walk to the nearest gas station with cum running down my legs. I suppose I could lie here, naked and confused, wondering what the heck just happened, and pray Kade goes downstairs for breakfast.

The smell of bacon and coffee has filtered into the air, and I hear the muffled voices of the group's chatter.

"Oh shit!" I sit up, looking toward the blankets in the corner, and notice for the first time that the bedroom door is wide open. My heart beats wildly in my chest as realization strikes. I jump out of bed and hurry to the shower. "Babe, Nero's not in here."

Kade turns with a smile and reaches for my hand, guiding me into the shower. "Did you call me *babe*?"

"Yeah, sorry. It slipped out." I wrap my arm around his waist as he pulls me closer.

"Slipped out, accidentally, huh? Interesting." Kade turns the pair of us so I'm in the water and he goes without.

"How is that interesting? You've called me *babe* more than once. Anyways, that's not the point." I get flustered and regroup. "Did you hear anything past that? Nero's not in your room."

"Mhmm." His hand glides along the side of my neck and tips up my chin.

"Did you send him out to guard the stairs?" I should've thought of that before allowing my panic to get the better of me, and now that it's come to mind, I feel a bit silly.

"If I had to guess, I'd say he's in the kitchen, waiting for someone to drop food on the floor." Kade's touch soothes me more than hot water ever could.

"But I thought..." Or rather, I assumed. Incorrectly.

"He's fine. I told him to play nice." When Kade leans in for a kiss, I meet him halfway. "But I like that you're worried about him."

I smile and laugh to myself, thinking about those videos online of fearless women who adopt gigantic pit bulls from busted dogfighting rings, take them home, feed them a four-course steak dinner, give them a spa treatment and a daily facial routine, put them in a pair of onesie pajamas, give them a silk eye mask for when it's sleepy time, and call them Winston Mackrell Jefferson III. Named in loving memory of their beloved great-grandfather, who fought bravely in the war. Which war? It doesn't matter. We can assume one of the big ones where he stood proudly on the right side of History.

"Can I help you get cleaned up? Since it's technically my mess."

I've never dated anyone who was attentive. The guys in my past weren't the sort to concern themselves with the wants or needs of others. Selfishly, they took until there was nothing left, and then they moved on without so much as a glance in the rearview mirror.

I nod my head, granting Kade permission.

Last night, I wondered what it would be like if two givers found each other. Could that relationship dynamic work, with no one there to take? It's interesting how a person's past can influence their perspective. You get so used to being treated a certain way that you start to think it's normal. You convince yourself that better doesn't exist because you've yet to stumble upon it yourself.

Then, one evening when you're on a date with some random guy from the internet, you find everything you've been searching for. And while the man you've been dreaming of is sitting beside you, he isn't the one who asked you for a date.

Finding true love sounds great in theory, but perhaps it's better not to know. Because what if you don't get to keep him? What if he asks you to stay but doesn't intend for it to be forever? What if he says, *I'll call you later* and he means *I'll call you never*?

"Ow." I flinch away from his touch before thinking better of it.

Kade freezes in place. "Why didn't you tell me that I hurt you?"

"Because I didn't want you to feel bad." I guide his hand back to the soreness between my thighs. "And because I liked it."

He holds me closely in way of an apology, and we finish rinsing off in silence.

Even on my best days, I'm a voracious overthinker, scrutinizing each micro expression and seemingly insignificant gesture. Kade shuts off the water and hands me a towel before taking one for himself.

Me and then him. Permanently in that order.

He prioritizes my comfort and meets my needs before attending to his own.

"Do you want me to check Riley's room for your clothes? He could've taken 'em after you changed, thinking you'd go looking and accidentally fall asleep in his bed." Kade laughs, but barely.

"Yeah, I don't know. I guess anything's possible." I replay the timeline of events in my head, moving the players around the board like a game of Clue. Kade was the only one here, as far as I know, but if he says he didn't take them, I'm willing to believe him and drop the subject completely. "Honestly, it doesn't matter."

I hang my damp towel on the bar and steal his bathrobe from the hook on the back of the door. It's warm and comforting, like a hug I didn't know I needed. If I were staying, I'd pull a book from his shelf, crawl back into bed, and use his robe like a blanket with arm holes. If I had my choice, I'd take quiet days at home over going out every time.

I wonder if Kade knows that about me since he seems to know everything else.

I locate my borrowed hoodie and sweatpants and take a seat on the edge of the bed. "Do you mind if I wear this home?"

It feels silly to ask since I can't very well leave here naked, but I don't want to be accused of stealing. The set he gave me feels high-quality and oversized, as if it were custom-made for him. These aren't the type of sweats you buy from the local store and discard after a season once they lose their softness. They feel like a luxury purchase. Something you splurge on when you have extra money and take a moment for yourself.

"Anything that's in this room, you can take home with you," Kade says with a wink, and the implication is clear.

I only wish he wasn't joking.

Getting dressed feels like the beginning of the end, like we're in the final stretch of the fourth quarter and the clock is counting down to zero. I want to call a timeout and pause the game, but I keep waiting for the right moment, not wanting to leave with misgivings about where we stand. But leaving is a regret all its own.

"When you went downstairs to take Nero outside, what was the overall mood of the group? Is everyone mad at me? Should I tie the sheets together and go out the window?" I doubt I have the physical strength required for the climb. More than likely, I'd drop like an egg and shatter on the deck below.

"No one's mad at you."

I raise an eyebrow as if that couldn't be true.

"Well, there's still the matter of my car, and I should help put your office back together." Normally, I leave a place better than I found it, but last night, I blew through like an F5 tornado. Best-laid plans, the owner's desk, clean bedsheets, and life-long friendships, all ruined because of me.

"I can sort out the office when I'm there tomorrow. You don't need to worry." Kade opens his arms like a bear trap, and I walk straight in. "As for your car…"

"Don't tell me you had it towed. I can't afford the impound fee." I laugh against his chest as his arms clamp tightly around me.

"They dropped it off this morning. It's in the driveway. I wanted to tell you when you woke up, but I wasn't in any hurry to say goodbye." Kade says it like he's apologizing for lying, but I miss not knowing it was there.

I take a deep breath, drawing in his scent, making sure to memorize the details.

I don't let go, and neither does he.

We sway gently in the warmth of our shared embrace as something greater than the halves we came in as, and all is quiet as a heartbeat.

CHAPTER 40
KADE

We're about to walk into the hallway, hand in hand, when I spot something poking out from beneath Nero's favorite blanket. "Are you kidding me?"

I'm not surprised, and honestly, I should've thought to look there sooner. Nero is a magpie, constantly hoarding treasure in his nest. He likes to steal things from around the house when no one's looking, but he's never taken something that wasn't mine.

I pull back the blanket to find a cache of women's clothing. Lex's sweater, jeans, bra, and even the shoes she left by the front door. I'm not sure when he brought them up here or how I didn't notice, but I appreciate the sentiment. Nero wanted to make

Lex part of his world. He wanted to keep her. And it's possible he thought that she belonged to me.

"Well, I guess that solves the mystery." Lex picks up her shoes and leaves the rest. "We'll call it an even trade."

"I'll consult with my sisters on the proper method for washing all that." The last thing I want to do is shrink her sweater and ruin her bra.

"It's fine. I can take it with me, so you don't have to worry about it." Lex moves to retrieve the items, but I stop her.

"Leave it," I say, wrapping my arm around her waist. "I wanna worry about it."

I need something to prove she was real.

That she was here.

And for one night, she was mine.

There's an unspoken tension between us as we enter the hallway and descend the stairs. Maybe Lex is mad that her clothes smell like a dog, and I insisted she leave them behind. If she doesn't intend to return, she might view the evening as a net loss and our time together as a mistake.

When I hit the base of the stairs, I turn back, but Lex stops short. She drops her shoes and wraps her arms around my neck, using the final step to cut our height difference in half.

"Can I count on you to keep me safe?" she asks.

"Always." I look at her intently before leaning in for a kiss.

I realize I've screwed up. If I'd done things properly, Lex wouldn't have to overthink it. She wouldn't have to question my strength or worry about everyone being mad at her. She wouldn't have to look for excuses to leave or consider alternate exits.

Had I done it right, she'd be staying.

CHAPTER 41
ALEXIS

I'm not sure what I expected, but now that I'm here, nothing is as I imagined. Nero is sitting at the island begging for bacon, the ladies light up when I enter the room, the husbands wave hello between bites of food, and Riley nods in my direction.

"Morning, Alexis. Coffee or tea?" Riley asked, holding a mug.

"Um." I feel like I'm in an episode of the Twilight Zone. "Whichever. I'm fine with either."

"It's your choice."

"Yeah. Well, I think I've made enough choices to last me a lifetime."

He smiles and fixes two cups of coffee. "Oh, I don't know. I think there's still a decision on the table."

I look over my shoulder and see the wine bottle lying lazily where I left it.

"Come on, you two. Make a plate and pull up a seat. There's plenty of food." Hailey motions to the full continental breakfast spread covering the kitchen island.

I turn my face toward the front door, contemplating my next move, but all I see is Kade standing beside me, and with a smile, my decision is made. "Yeah, I guess I could stay for a quick bite."

There's only one available bar stool at the counter, and of course, Kade insists I take it. We each make a plate, and he stands behind me, never beyond arm's reach. When Riley sets two mugs of coffee in front of me, Kade responds with a curt "thanks."

"Alexis, if you're free later, I thought we could get dinner together." When Riley asks me out in front of everyone, I nearly choke on a bite of toast.

"She has plans tonight," Kade responds on my behalf.

While he's not wrong, I wouldn't necessarily say I have plans. I mentioned that I would be busy, so perhaps he's referring to my intention to work through the evening and into tomorrow morning.

"What about this weekend? We could meet for drinks and go from there." Riley smiles playfully, as though he's toying with me.

"She's busy." Kade lays a protective arm across my chest, or maybe it's a claim of ownership.

"Next week?"

"Until she suggests otherwise, consider her schedule booked." I understand why he doesn't want Riley to ask me out, what with the bet still unsettled, but Kade hasn't exactly made plans to see me, so I'm not sure why he's acting like I'm officially off the market.

"Interesting," Riley remarks. "And to think, you ladies said I was the one being an asshole."

"You *were* being an asshole, and here you are giving us a repeat performance and making everything awkward," Elise interjects.

"He's so controlling, Alexis is too intimidated to

speak." Riley is talking about me like I'm not sitting right in front of him. "And he assaulted me."

Kade's arm falls away, and he steps back so we're no longer touching. I feel the absence deep in my bones like ice threatening to split apart stone.

"Okay. Well, for the record, I'm not afraid to speak, and Jax isn't controlling me. So, while I appreciate the offer, I'll have to say, no thank you. I actually am quite busy. And honestly, Riley, I don't think you and I are a good match. I'm sorry about last night. I should've handled the situation differently. That's entirely on me." I get up from my seat and turn to walk away, but Kade is blocking my path of retreat.

"Alexis, wait!" I turn back in time to see Riley drop a stack of twenty-dollar bills onto the center of my breakfast plate. "Don't forget your money." He says it with disgust, like I'm a used-up hooker who over-stayed her welcome.

I've never been more embarrassed in my life, but there isn't time to fixate on the emotion when Kade is on the verge of a full-blown explosion.

"Nero." The name is a command for attention, and we all know what comes next.

"Wait. Whhh, whhhh, wait. Wait." My childhood stutter kicks in as I panic and reach for Kade's arm.

"Please don't do this," I whisper.

"Nero, let's go for a walk." I'm not sure what I'm saying, or why I think he'll listen to me, but the dog heels beside me as though my pockets are stuffed with bacon, which reminds me I owe him a treat.

I grab the six hundred dollars from my plate and the uneaten strips of bacon. "If you walk me to my car, these are for you." I wave the bacon in front of Nero's hungry eyes before stuffing the cash into the pocket of Kade's shorts. "And all of *that* is yours."

Kade's thick fingers braid into the back of my hair as his forehead presses to mine. I close my eyes and allow his words to sink into my skin. "You don't have to leave. I'm sorry I spoke for you. I shouldn't have."

"I don't care about that."

"Oh my god, kiss him," Jakob says aloud, reminding me why I'm here.

In a way, this feels like the right moment for a kiss, if my reason for being with Kade was simply to stick it to Riley. There would be no need for arguments or apologies, no space for accusations, name-calling, or phony dinner date requests. With one kiss, I could end it all and settle the terms of their wager.

I could put Riley out of his misery.

That would be the humane thing to do.

But what do I care about settling their bet? What does it have to do with me? Why should I cheapen myself further so someone else can have a win?

Then again, that *someone* is Kade, and if anyone deserves the world, it's him.

CHAPTER 42
ALEXIS

I'm pulling on my second shoe and using the front door for support when there's a knock on the other side. The perfectly timed jump-scare makes me drop Nero's treats and causes my heart to beat wildly against my ribs. The dog inhales the sliced meat from the floor and starts barking as Kade tucks me behind his back and opens the door.

I appreciate that he promised to protect me, but I'm not sure my heart can take much more.

"Thanks, have a nice rest of the day," Kade says to the anonymous visitor.

"You too." It's a man's voice I don't recognize. "I've got a spring in my step after last night's game. Did you see it?"

"I watched the highlights this morning."

"Oh man. I can't believe you missed seeing it live." The man sounds like he's walking away.

"It was a good night, to be sure."

Kade attempts to keep his back to me as he closes the door and maneuvers something outside my field of vision. He's acting strangely all of a sudden, but in a way that's playfully secretive, like a teenager withholding information about their first kiss. They don't want to tell you outright, but they're dying for you to find out what they're hiding.

"Chuckie, can you help me out for one second?" Kade calls to the man in the other room, and Chuckie appears from around the corner with Elise following closely behind.

"Take this to my room, please," Kade says. Then whispers the next part. "And don't let her see it."

I try peering around his arm, but he's boxing me out.

With his hands free, he ushers me toward the wall, laughing all the while.

As Chuckie ascends the stairs, I catch a glimpse of the mystery item and spot a familiar logo stamped on the side of the box. The curling M with the pointed tail and devil horns is the symbol for Monroe Custom Books.

It's not very often that I ship boxes that size, so it's not hard to connect Kade with the order.

"Have you been stalking me online?" I ask, pushing against his arm.

"No. I swear, I wasn't. I clicked on your site after Riley showed me your profile and saw that you had some special-edition horror books. I wanted them for my shelf, and I like supporting local businesses." Kade keeps me trapped against the wall. "I thought you were cute, so I looked at your photos. And the more I saw, the more I realized how wrong I was. Because you aren't just cute; you're absolutely stunning. And I haven't been able to stop thinking about you."

"I should be mildly creeped out, but your order made my house payment, so I'm going to let it slide. Plus, I may or may not have looked you up after seeing you in Riley's profile." I lift onto my tiptoes and drop my voice. "I really was thinking about *you* before I went into the restaurant."

I suppose fair is fair. If Kade has my car towed from his reserved parking spot and forces me to pay the impound fee to get it back, so be it. Last night was worth every penny. As for looking me up online, I can't exactly fault him for engaging in an activity I'm equally guilty of. After all, a person can't be too careful these days. You never know who's on the other side of the screen.

But in a way, I feel like I did know. Somehow, I recognized him. Riley was good-looking, but Kade intrigued me the moment I saw his face. There was a devilish look in his eyes and a playfulness to his smile that captured my attention in a way that no other has. Seeing him felt like remembering, but I couldn't piece together what was forgotten until he took my hand.

Pinned against the wall by a man who's twice my size, I can understand why someone might find Kade intimidating. If he ever yelled at me, I'd cry on the spot, and yet, I feel like he would go out of his way to show me kindness and understanding, if for no other reason than to spare my tears.

He has a considerate nature, a giving spirit, and a protective temperament.

Instinctively, I knew I could trust him. I could feel it in my gut, my head, and my heart. It was as though my entire body was being pulled in his direction.

I know what it feels like to be lured in by the false charms of a predator masquerading as a nice guy, and Kade isn't that. He's genuinely good.

Stay with me.

His earlier request plays over in my head.

If he asked me again, I would stay. I would stay for as long as he would have me.

But he doesn't ask. He doesn't say anything. He simply kisses me.

The intense press of his lips to mine and the accompanying heat of his closeness make me nearly melt into a puddle, but any strength Kade takes from me, he returns tenfold. I feel powerful in his embrace, as though the pair of us could bear the weight of the world without breaking a sweat. I strap myself to him, ratcheting my arms across his shoulders until I'm locked into place.

Somehow, I sense it's coming, and yet, the action steals my breath away. Kade takes a hold of my ass and lifts me from the ground, never pulling back from our kiss. He presses my back to the wall and leans into me as my legs wrap around his waist. It feels like an act we practiced a hundred times until the motion was ingrained into our muscle memory. We move without thinking. Without pausing to confirm that the other will be there. We know it in our hearts, and that's good enough.

"I think that should count." Elise and Chuckie descend the stairs behind us.

"Rules are rules. You know how he is." Their hushed tones are like a bucket of cold water.

"The rules are bullshit." Before they reach the final step, the mood has shifted, and my time with Kade has come to an end.

He takes me by the hand and ushers me out the front door. The morning sun is momentarily blinding as we exit our darkened sanctuary. I want to scurry back into my hole in the corner, but there is no going back. Hand in hand, we walk to the car with silence pooling where conversation once flowed freely.

"I hope you like the books." That's all I can think to say. The only safe topic. The only words that don't divulge how much I'm going to miss him.

"I already love them. They're my new prized possession."

"There's one I'm working on that belongs on your Goblin King shelf. I'll mail it to you when it's finished."

"Yeah. Let me know how much I owe you."

Normally, I live to discuss books with a fellow reader, but right now, I hate everything about this conversation. It's too impersonal. It feels like a business transaction. And I hate that this is our way of saying goodbye because it's clear we'll never see each other again.

"You don't owe me anything." What I give, I gift freely.

At the car, Kade's arms frame my body like I'm a priceless work of art.

Prior to last night, I'd never known what it felt like to be held in high regard. Sure, plenty of people praise my work, but those items are separate from me. Leaving here, I'm going to miss feeling special.

Over the years, I've struggled to figure out how to love myself, and perhaps that's why I was unable to unearth what I was searching for.

I needed Kade to find me, to quiet the voices, and to make me feel whole. He calms the chaos, and I wonder if I have the same effect on him or if the peace we share is one-sided. All I know is, he merits so much more than I can give him, but I'm happy to leave him with one last parting gift.

Kade tucks his hands into the kangaroo pouch of my hoodie as I lift to kiss him.

We both deserve to win.

The mutual thought is shared between us, but neither of us lends it our voice.

CHAPTER 43
KADE

From the front steps come the sounds of celebration. Whistles, applause, and cheers. Even Nero joins in with a round of joyful barking.

"Did you know they were there?" I turn my head to survey the onlooking crowd.

"Riley was stupid to bet against you, Jax. You're twice the man he is." She says it like I should feel better now that I have a big house to call my own.

As if she isn't ripping my soul in half by leaving.

ALEXIS

"I had a nice time with you."

When faced with the soul-crushing reality that I can't live in a fantasy forever, I lose my ability to say what's in my heart and fall back on empty phrases that dance around goodbye.

For his part, Kade looks uncomfortable. "Yeah. Me too."

"Okay, well…" There's plenty I could say, several things I should, and even more I would if given the chance, but the final buzzer has sound, and it's time to go home.

I turn and reach for the door handle, but Kade beats me to it. A true gentleman to the end.

This is stupid. I should tell him I want to stay.

"Is it alright if I call you later?" Kade's one-question survey brings me up short.

This isn't the empty goodbye I recognize from first and last dates prior, though it is similar enough. I'm sure that all said and done, these words will hold the same weight and later will never come. I could point out that we never exchanged numbers, but what's the point in making things more awkward if he has no intention to call?

The time has come to tear off the bandage, though I fear this pain will linger far beyond anything temporary.

Slipping into the driver's seat, I detach from the emotion of the moment and formulate a plan by running through my list of next logical steps.

- Buckle seat belt.
- Pull up directions.
- Stop for gas.
- Dive headfirst into my career.
- Make art my entire identity.
- Never date again.

I pause before closing the door, noting the size and position of Kade's hand. I draw in a breath, preparing to speak, but think better of opening my mouth. Instead, I release my grip on the handle and retract my arm, allowing Kade to close the door for me. Sealing me inside. It feels as though we're worlds apart, like we're on opposite sides of an airlock, and I'm about to smash the control panel with the button that opens the door.

Next to me, in the passenger seat, not remotely where I left it, my jacket is neatly folded. My phone and wallet are tucked underneath with an edge sticking out only slightly. Hidden but not. I can't help but wonder why my things were moved. What were they looking for? And who was sitting in the backseat? I doubt the twins used my car as a rideshare to make a few extra bucks after the game.

I turn on the car, expecting to see the low fuel light, and find the tank has been filled. Well, damn. Part of me was hoping I'd run out of gas on the way to the station and be forced to call for a tow. Instead, I'm indebted to a pair of guys who look like the type to stockpile favors. I only hope that when the time comes for them to collect, they bring Kade with them.

When I lower my window, his stoic demeanor cracks, and Kade looks like this small action is a welcome surprise. He smiles as though he's found hope where none existed before. Or maybe I'm projecting.

"Would you mind checking the trunk?" My vague request seems unexpected.

"Sure." He shakes his head and steps toward the back. "What am I looking for?"

"A body," I call out the window as I pop the lock on the hatch.

Kade takes a moment to indulge my flights of dark fancy before closing the trunk and walking around to the passenger side. He opens the door, and I clear off the seat so he can get in.

"You're good to go." His words make my heart drop into my stomach, and I feel sick. Looking up, they seem to have the same effect on him.

"Okay." I've been trying to leave for the last forty-five minutes, but it's like taking a morning swim across the La Brea Tar Pits.

"I hate this." I can sense that Kade is struggling to hold it together. He's being nice and keeping it cute, but barely. The dam is about to break, and I feel powerless to stop it.

"So do I." My voice shakes as I look away from his face.

"Then why are we doing it?" He tucks his hand between my legs and squeezes my thigh, pulling my full attention back to him.

"I don't know." Somehow, over the course of my overthinking, I convinced myself that leaving was in everyone's best interest, but now, I can't remember how I came to that conclusion.

"I don't want to say goodbye to you, so I keep saying nothing, which feels even worse."

"I know." I should say more to comfort him, but I'm at a loss for words.

"Lex, I want to see you again. I want to spend time with you. I want to ask you out on a real date and make plans. Hell, I want to beg you to stay. I considered getting into my truck and following you home, but I figured that was so far beyond crossing the line it actually made me a legitimate stalker." His confession makes me laugh.

"I mean, if you bring the mask, we could definitely act out a few scenes at my place." I brush my fingers up his flexed forearm. "Just sayin'."

"Is that what you want? To get fucked by a stranger who's secretly obsessed with you? Because I'm pretty sure we did that last night." He cups the side of my face, and I melt into the warmth of his touch. "If that's what you want, I need to hear you say it. I can pretend to be okay with a sex-no-strings relationship. I'll even break into your house to leave flowers on your bed if that's what you're into. But I'll be in love with you the entire time."

If it were anybody else, it'd be bullshit, but I know Kade means every word.

"I don't want to cry. I'm afraid if I do, you'll think I don't want this, and that couldn't be further from the truth." I laugh nervously as salty tears catch in the nets of my eyelashes.

"What's keeping you from staying?"

"It's not you, I swear. It's everything else. Riley's pissed at me and I feel guilty. Especially now that you've won the bet. He's probably in there, punching holes in the walls. And I really do have to work. I was hoping to get everything finished and submitted tonight so I could drive my car into a ditch tomorrow." Even with my deadpan delivery, he catches the joke that's not a joke. "I figured I'd need some way to get a hold of you. You know you don't have my number, right? Were you planning to buy out my website and send me cryptic messages in five-star reviews?"

Kade pulls a cell phone from his pocket, and a second later, mine begins to ring.

"Kold sent me a text from your phone when he noticed I wasn't in your contact list. He had a good laugh when I told him we'd only just met, but said he completely understood."

This piece of information leaves me with more questions than answers. "Why would he…how did he even…when…I just…you know what, never mind. It doesn't matter."

"You're important to me, Lex. So that means you're important to them. It's not something I can fully explain, and you'll have to be okay with that."

I don't know what doors my importance unlocks, but I have a feeling most of them lead backstage or underground. "Does this mean I get to join the fight club?"

Kade laughs, and a genuine smile lights his features, reminding me that pain is temporary. Even in sadness, a silver lining can be found.

"So long as you're on my team."

CHAPTER 45
ALEXIS

Leaving now feels different than it did a moment ago. Even as I back down the driveway and the distance between us increases, the weight of my guilt is no longer dragging me beneath the surface and drowning me in sorrow. I'm practically floating. I glance toward the house as I pull onto the street. Kade is where I left him, and Nero is at his side, where I once stood. I smile at the sight, taken by the image of a man and his dog, confident I'll see them again soon.

My phone rings and I reach for it, fully expecting it to be Kade. "I miss you."

"Yeah, I miss you too. I drove past your house, but your car wasn't there. Thought I'd check in. Did you have a good time with..." Skyler trails off, leaving the rest of her sentence to my discretion.

I laugh at myself for not checking the caller ID, then jump into the conversation, needing to share the details of my night. "Yeah, he's amazing. I just left. You know how when you have a choice, but not really, because the answer is so obvious? Last night was kinda like that, but I also kissed two girls."

"Nice. I think the last girl I kissed was you." We both laugh.

"Yeah, probably. I turn into a bit of a lip slut when I'm drinking." I put the phone on speaker and stuff it into the hood of my sweatshirt so I can use both hands to drive.

"Nothing wrong with that." Skyler pauses. "So, this amazing guy who was the obvious choice, that would be..."

It's like she doesn't want to guess for fear of guessing wrong, and I'm starting to wonder if my choice wasn't as obvious as I assumed.

"Kade. I left with Kade. The big guy with the dark hair and the tattoos. The one who almost killed Nick."

"Oh, good. I liked him."

I smile and roll my eyes. "What made you think it would be Riley?"

"Because I know you, and you have an absurd sense of loyalty. I saw it at the bar. There was a fifty-fifty chance you were going home with the light-haired guy simply because he was the one who asked you out. It was a coin flip."

"A bottle spin." I correct.

"What?" Skyler sounds confused.

"Nothing. There were no coins involved. We played spin the bottle."

"For real?"

"Yeah. But Kade and I had already had sex by that point." I fade out as I stop at the corner and look both ways before pulling out onto the main road.

"Why are you skipping over the good parts? And what happened during spin the bottle? Is that when you kissed the two girls?"

"No, that was in the hot tub. Spin the bottle was when Kade told me he loved me. Well, I guess he also kinda said it when we had sex, but you know that shit doesn't mean anything."

Skyler laughs. "Were you like, 'okay, thanks. Bye'? That's what you do whenever I say it."

"No." Now that I play it back in my head, I wish I'd responded that way. "I told him I hated him."

"Oh my god. You're the worst," Skyler chuckles, "but that's what I love about you."

"Yeah, well, I hope that's one of the things he loves about me, too. I wasn't mad at him, not really. Mostly, I was upset about the timing and the situation. Before we went to bed, he said it again, and I said it back." I bite my bottom lip to keep from grinning.

"You what?" There's a rustling on the other end of the phone, and Skyler begins shouting from some distance away, as though she dropped the phone.

"Hello?"

"Sorry. You couldn't see it, but I was kicking my feet in the air with *giddy excitement*." She says it like she's narrating stage directions, and I have no trouble visualizing her action. "You never say the L word. To anyone. You've dated guys for months and broken up without saying it. Do you think you might actually love him?"

"I don't know. Never saying it makes more sense when I stop to consider the fallout, but last night, I was feeling sappy, and I wasn't thinking clearly. It felt right, in the moment." Even now, it feels the same. "But you know me, I have the worst taste in men. He'll most likely turn out to be a serial killer or something."

"At this point, who cares? Kade strikes me as the type to prey on bad guys. And if you're happy. I'm happy. I'm sure the lake is full of bodies. Someone has to put them there. Does he have a boat?"

"I can't even let my mind go there. Is this seriously what dating looks like for women in their mid-thirties? The pool is so shallow that murder becomes acceptable." I'd laugh if this weren't my life.

"Could be worse. He could have a girlfriend or two stashed away somewhere."

"Well, on that note," I groan.

"I'm only kidding. Kade seems great. When are you seeing him again?"

"I'm not sure," I admit. "Hopefully sooner rather than later."

Talking to Skyler keeps me from overthinking, and I hope work has the same effect when I get home. I left Kade with a sense of certainty but no real plan to hang out, leaving ample space for my mind to spin.

"I'm sure he'll call. And if he doesn't, I'll leave a scathing one-star review on the towing company's website." If Kade isn't careful, he's going to find out how petty some girls can be. "Hurt my best friend, and I'll get you fired!"

"I appreciate that, but considering he had sex with me on the owner's desk and left my panties in the drawer, I don't think he's worried about losing his job."

"You guys hooked up at the towing yard?" She sounds shocked.

"In the office," I respond like it's no big deal, and these things happen every day.

"Come again."

"I did. This morning," I say, without missing a beat.

"What the hell?" Skyler laughs uncontrollably. "I need details. Nick and I stopped at the house to change our clothes, and now we're headed out the door. Do you want to join us for breakfast?"

"I can't. I've got work. But I'll call you later." If I'm not otherwise engaged.

"Sounds good. And, hey. Alexis, I like this devil-may-care version of you. It's nice to hear you excited about a guy."

"Yeah. I hope I'm not setting myself up for disappointment. I keep reminding myself that whatever happens, it doesn't erase the facts. I had an incredible time, and that kind of night doesn't come around every day." Now that the call is ending, my confidence is slipping.

"He's gonna call. But even if he doesn't, you're amazing, and I love you. If you want, maybe I can convince Nick to be in a throuple."

"For you, Alexis, anything," Nick calls from the background.

"You guys are the best. I love you, too."

"Oh my god. Kade is an angel sent down from

heaven. I can't believe you said it. I can die a happy woman."

"I'm not sure which realm he comes from, but I can confirm his dick is otherworldly."

"Babe, how do you feel about making it a foursome?"

Nick is a good sport, and I know his response without seeing it. "Whatever you want, dear."

"I'll let you two work out the details over breakfast." I shake my head and smile. "Talk to you later."

"Okay, bye," Skyler hangs up, leaving me alone with my thoughts and memories.

I'm lucky to have people in my life who care about me and a best friend who checks in to make sure I'm still alive. I'm privileged to have a roof over my head, paid for by a career that fills me with a sense of accomplishment. There are moments in my past better left forgotten, and in truth, I'm lucky to be here, but even the bad moments played a part in my story, making me who I am today. It was a stroke of good fortune that I gave dating one more chance, allowing fate an opportunity to play its hand. The night didn't turn out the way I thought it would.

Instead, it was everything it was meant to be. Sure, a part of me wishes we'd met sooner, as kids at a party playing a round of spin the bottle. But who knows what popular teenage Kade would have thought of nerdy teenage me?

Could he have fallen in love with an angsty version of me who constantly struggled to hold it together?

Or the broken dove binge drinking through her twenties?

Would he have appreciated the time I shaved my head in the university courtyard during breast cancer awareness month?

Or the years when I got sober and obsessed over working out?

Could he understand that there were times when I did what had to be done to survive?

Or would he feel the need to avenge me?

Would Kade have joined me in the mud when I was wallowing at my lowest point?

Or was I meant to go it alone?

Maybe I was destined to be this version of myself when he found me.

As much as I would've appreciated his company during the times when I wanted to give up, I take it as a sense of pride that I'm still here. I picked myself up and stood on my own two feet, knowing I would get knocked down. I found the strength to drag myself through the hard days, even if I did so while hiding in bed.

I put in the work and made every effort to learn from my mistakes. I found a community that embraced me and a sense of purpose with my work. Of all the versions of myself, I'm certain this is the best one yet.

With or without Jaxson Kade, I shine.

CHAPTER 46
ALEXIS

I'm at my desk, still responding to emails, when the text alert vibrates my phone.

I check the time on the clock and question my ability to accomplish anything meaningful with images of a naked Kade filling my headspace.

I want a meal of substance, not simply a burger and

fries, but I don't want to wait until this evening to see him.

> Text me your address and leave the back door unlocked.

I swallow hard, understanding this is what I asked for, but not the least bit mentally prepared for what's to come. I don't know what to make of these feelings and the certainty Kade brings. He feels stable, like a solid base to build on, and I wonder if the materials I bring are enough to construct a life. But I suppose that's the benefit of being on a team. For the first time, it doesn't all fall on my shoulders.

I text Kade my address, unlock the back door, and draw the curtains. The darkness is part of the ambiance, and I don't want the neighbors to worry if they accidentally catch sight of something they aren't meant to see.

I'm fairly certain I met my soulmate fifteen hours ago and fell for him soon after, which is weird on so many levels. As much as I pine and burn for the idea of forever and consider myself a hopeless romantic, the romance is typically reserved for my bookshelf, while my dating life is entirely hopeless. Or rather, it was.

Two hours from now, I'll be on an official date with Kade. He'll be here in my personal space, and I'll get the opportunity to openly adore him while simultaneously pretending to fight him off. We can be loud without worrying about the friend group overhearing. And affectionate without pissing anyone off. We can be ourselves, for better or worse, and discover if that's what the other is looking for.

In two hours, I'll be on a first date with a man I just met, and I'll be in love with him the entire time.

CHAPTER 47
KADE

I triple-check the address on the front of the house, comparing it to the one saved in my phone, before casually walking past her car. The large bushes on either side of the back door create a visual barrier between me and the neighbors, while a thicket of woods lines the back of the property. I use the green sanctuary to collect my thoughts and secure my mask.

I've seen zero signs of home security. No doorbell camera, barking dog, or locked door in sight. It's as though she's inviting trouble.

She's making it all too easy for me to get to her, as well as anyone else who might have a mind to try.

I'm going to need to scare her in order to protect her. Hurt her enough to keep her safe. I need to give her a taste of the darkness before I can guide her back to the light.

I will be her savior and her destruction.

I will be her everything.

Silently, I remove my black leather boots and place them neatly on the rug, leaving my backpack propped beside them. I plan on being here for a while, so I might as well make myself comfortable, and the items in my bag are meant for after.

The smell of medium rare steaks and garlic-smashed yellow potatoes fills the small mudroom attached to the back of the kitchen. I lock the door and bolt it shut, cursing myself for not doing more to smother the scent of our dinner. I don't want to alert her to my presence.

Not yet.

Thankfully, I can hear the water running in the shower on the other side of the wall and the sweet hum of her muffled voice as she sings. I follow the sound through the small house. A private concert meant only for me.

The bathroom where she's showering is an en suite attached to the bedroom where I'm going to make her fantasies a reality. The blackout curtains are drawn, plunging the room into an impressive level of darkness. Unsurprising, considering she gets migraines and frequently posts project updates throughout the evening and well into the morning.

My little night owl.

I half expected to find her asleep in bed.

I shut the bedroom door and engage the worthless lock. It's the sort that pops when you twist the handle, so it won't do much to keep her inside. That'll be my job. Keeping her in the room and relatively quiet until I can break her.

I will make her submit, and then I will let her worship me.

The bathroom door is slightly ajar, allowing a sliver of light to filter into the darkness. I maintain my post as I survey the room. If she leaves the light on and opens the door, my presence here will be revealed too quickly, giving her the distance and opportunity to get away.

I'm confident I could break through the hollow white door with the pathetic excuse for a lock, but if the bathroom has a window, it might leave enough time for her to escape. And I can't allow that to happen. Not when I have so many fun things in store for our evening.

As the water cuts off, I move to the other side of the room. Standing beside her desk, I'm relatively well hidden in shadow. As much as a man my size can be. When she enters the room, her back will be to my new position, and I'll have the upper hand. The element of surprise. I can overpower her, and then she'll be mine.

She continues to sing the verses I don't recognize, and I wonder if it's a song she's written in her mind. I imagine what she looks like as she dries herself with the towel. I'd give anything for a peek. A private show. A playful flash of nipple and a quick glance at that perfect ass.

She's taking her time. Teasing me. Making me wait.

The bathroom light cuts off as she steps into the bedroom, and I see her flawless figure, dressed in a tiny pair of shorts and a cropped tank top, and I know she's chosen this outfit for me. She called me here like a siren, using secret codes and hidden messages tucked into the descriptions of her various posts. She knows I've been watching her, so she gave me the key to decipher her personal invitation to come inside.

She'll say she doesn't want it. She'll beg me to stop, but that's all part of the game. I know in the end she'll see it my way. She'll see that we belong together.

I have the advantage. My eyes are attuned to the premature night, whereas hers are still adjusting.

I slam into her from behind, knocking her onto the bed. It's not hard enough to hurt her. Not yet. But the sound she makes tells me I've taken her by surprise. Before she can roll onto her side or scramble onto her knees, I cover her body with mine. Weighing her down. Pressing her securely into the mattress.

"Shhhh." I twist her damp hair around my hand and run my nose up the side of her neck. "You are so pretty when you pretend you don't want me."

"Who are you?" She tenses beneath me as my cock begins to stiffen, pressed firmly against the swell of her ass.

"I came all this way to see you. You should try being a little more appreciative." I grind my cock slowly against her. "I want that pussy nice and wet when I fuck you."

"I don't know you." Her voice cracks, as though she's fighting back tears.

"Oh, but I know you. I've been watching you for a while. I was at the restaurant last night, stroking my dick under the table while you threw your pussy at other guys." I use my grip on her hair to angle her face to the side. Not that she would recognize me. Last night, I wasn't wearing my mask. "Do you have any idea how that made me feel?"

"I'm sorry. I didn't know. Had you come over and said something, we could've…"

"Liar." I cut her off, unwilling to hear her out. "You saw me. I know you did. You saw me watching you from across the bar. You smiled while you stood out of reach in that black v-neck sweater, showing off those perfect tits. You liked hurting me. Making me jealous. Laughing while another man touched you like the little cock-tease you are."

"Please. I swear I wasn't trying to hurt anyone."

"So, this is my fault?" My head swims as her whimpered pleas send every available ounce of blood to my erection.

"No. It's my fault. I shouldn't have talked to those other guys."

"It made me so mad, watching you with them when you should've been with me." I sit back on my knees, straddling her legs. "I wanted to tuck you under the table cloth and let you suck me off while everyone was distracted by the game."

She moans in response and reaches back to press her palm into my thigh.

"You'd like that, wouldn't you? Taking my big cock down your throat in a room of two hundred people until I fed you my cum."

She wiggles beneath me, parting her thighs as I begin massaging her ass. Through her thin cotton shorts, I pull her cheeks apart and imagine her holes opening, granting me access.

"Please, stop."

It's cute the way she pretends not to want me, but her body gives her away. I rub circles over the lips of her pussy as she soaks through the fabric of her shorts.

"Keep telling me to stop." I slip my fingers between the fabric, drawing out her juices. "I like it."

"Please. You don't have to do this." She grinds herself against me as I push two fingers into her. "Stop. Please. I can't believe you're inside me."

"Oh, fuck. You feel so good." I add a third finger, knowing the thickness will hurt.

"Oh my god. Stop." She humps the mattress as I pump inside her.

"You're doing so good for me. That tight pussy is almost wet enough to take my cock."

"No. Please. I swear I won't tell anyone. You can stop, and no one needs to know you were here."

"You want me to leave?" I give her ass a hard smack and she cries out in surprise. "You want to keep hurting me? Is that what gets you off?"

"No."

"Oh, I think it is." I leave her on the bed with a false sense of control, knowing she won't risk running when she's so close to getting what she asked for.

There's a lighter on the bedside table. I noticed it when I came into the room and was surprised to see it there, knowing she's not a smoker. I was momentarily jealous, thinking it might have been left behind by a previous sexual partner. Then I saw the candle I initially mistook for a coffee cup at first glance.

Stepping around the edge of the bed, I hold her in my periphery while I strike a flame and light the wick. The flickering orange glow dances on the wall and gently kisses her skin. If she gets off on hurting me, there are a few things we can do with hot wax. If nothing else, let her get a good look at who she's saying no to, and we'll see if she still refuses me.

"Which one of these books is your favorite?" I ask, casually walking over to a display shelf that doesn't appear to be mounted to the wall.

She scrambles to her feet, sensing my target has shifted. "Wait. Oh, god, stop. Don't."

"Tell me which one is your favorite."

She tries to shield the treasured possessions with her small frame, but her attempts are laughable. Pulling a random paperback from the center, she holds it out in front of her like a crucifix fashioned from two pencils as if I'll be driven away by bullshit.

"Do you think I'm stupid?" I yank the book from her hand it throw it aside, recognizing the cover and knowing it's nothing special.

"No." A moment of annoyance flashes in her features, and I know I'm getting close. "It was a good story."

"Is that what I asked for, a book club recommendation?"

"If you know me so well, why don't you pick it out yourself?" she says under her breath, and it's clear that candlelight and bodily autonomy have filled her with a counterfeit impression of safety.

Cockiness is an interesting choice, given the circumstance.

I reach over her head to the top shelf, where the books are displayed with their spines turned in and their painted edges facing out. There is a gasp of genuine horror as she claws at my arm.

"Quit it, Kade. I can't replace that book!" She realizes what she's done, but it's too late to stop.

I grab her by the throat with one hand while holding the book out of reach with the other. "What the fuck did you just call me?"

Her eyes shift between my masked face and her beloved special edition hardcover.

I knew exactly which book was her favorite. The video of her opening the box the day it arrived in the mail will be forever burned in my mind. The giddiness in her voice and the smile on her face glowed through my phone screen like a flashbang.

"I'm sorry. Please. I'll do anything you want. I swear I'll behave. Please. Please put down the book." Her hands encircle my wrist as she offers herself in sacrifice.

"Get on your knees. And if I feel teeth, I'm ripping the cover off. Are we clear?" I lay the book across the tops of those on the middle shelf, returning it to its bedroom without tucking it neatly into bed, in case my threat requires a revisit.

"Okay." She nods in agreement, and I consider the matter a signed contract. Her precious books are safe so long as she pleases me in whatever manner I see fit.

With a shaking hand, she notches the zipper of my hoodie slowly downward, exposing my bare chest underneath. Once the two sides fully release, she returns to my shoulders and slides her hands over my skin. Her touch is like fire, branding me with her fingerprints and asserting full ownership.

I was meant to be the one claiming her, but with one touch, the tables have turned. I shrug out of my sweatshirt as she drops lower, and the sight of her on her knees before me, with her hands pressed flat into the front of my thighs, renews the stiffness in my cock.

"I'm not entirely sure I trust you." Her submission is too abrupt for my liking. "Not after you called me by another man's name."

"I'm sorry." Her fingers work to unfasten my belt.

"I wasn't thinking clearly, and I misspoke." With a tug, she unhooks the button on my jeans.

"I want you to trust me." The teasingly slow manner in which she unzips my pants is deliberate. Meant to drive me wild with desire.

"After all, you've been watching over me. Keeping me safe. And you came all this way to see me." Her voice is soft and sweet like a lullaby.

"Please let me show you how much I appreciate you." Gripping the waist of my jeans at the hip, she pulls them to my ankles, and I quickly kick them to the side.

"I know you came here to make me feel good." With a feather light touch she brushes her hand over the length of my cock currently straining to break free of my boxer briefs.

"Will you let me make you feel good?" She looks at me and licks her bottom lip before dragging it through her teeth.

"Fuck." I push my hand through her thick hair, bunching a tangle at her crown as any pretense of being in control dwindles by the second. "How badly do you want me?"

"So badly, daddy." The way she says it makes my cock twitch. "Will you take your mask off so I can see your handsome face?"

"Not yet, babygirl. If you want to see me, you have

to earn it." I'm not typically into age play, but I'm beginning to understand the appeal.

"Like this?" She leans forward and kisses my shaft. "Is this what you want?"

I groan in response, wishing I'd packed my underwear into my bag instead of wearing them. I want to feel her soft lips.

"Does this feel good?" The glint in her eyes and playful smirk tell me she knows it does. "Is this what you wanted me to do last night at the restaurant? Get on my knees under the table and please you."

"Yes." I'm not even slightly ashamed to admit it.

"If I suck your cock, will that make you feel appreciated?"

"Yes." I want to feel her tongue and the warmth of her mouth.

"And then you'll take off the mask for me?"

"If that's what you want." How could I say no when she's asking me so sweetly?

"Okay." She hooks her fingers into the waistband of my underwear and looks up at me. "Do you trust me?"

I drop my head back and groan.

"I need to hear you say it."

What have I gotten myself into? I crept into her lair, looking to brandish my sword and slay the beast, only to fall under her spell and willingly allow her to swallow me whole. I'm not much of a knight. Or a stalker.

"I trust you."

KADE

I should see it coming, but I don't. I'm too deep in the hallucination. There are plenty of signs a sober man would perceive as dead giveaways, but I take them another way. Nervous excitement over what's to come.

She yanks down my boxer briefs and springs up from the floor, taking off for the door.

I lunge toward her, but my ankles get caught in the fabric that stretches like an exercise band before landing me on the carpet. From my hands and knees, I scramble to get back in the game. Summer two-a-days and endless play calls feel like the echo of another lifetime that my body fails to forget. I might be big and guilty of falling hard, but I'll continue to get back up.

And I'll never stop chasing her.

In the living room, at the corner of the couch, I catch her around the waist and swing her up from her feet as she paws at my arm without claws.

"Let go of me!" She calls out with a hushed shout. "I'm not having sex with you. I have a boyfriend!"

The admission makes me pause, but my grip remains firm. "Liar. You haven't been in a relationship since Halloween last year. And that guy was a fucking loser."

She goes rigid in my arms as though I've struck the nerve that shuts down her motor function.

I want to stop momentarily and break character, apologize for what I said, and make sure she's okay, but if I do that, our time together will be over. Or, at the very least, altered beyond restoration. I have to continue following the plan with a mental side-note to circle back and fix things later.

With lumbering steps, I carry her to the bedroom and kick the door shut behind us, blocking her path of daylight. "Did you think I would let you go? That I would allow you to get away so easily?"

"No, but I had to try. I really do have a boyfriend. And he's definitely going to kill you when he finds out about this." She switches tactics on a dime, fully committing to each campaign. "He's scary enough on his own, but when he comes for you, he won't be alone."

"Is he alone when he *comes* for you, or does he bring friends?" I grin beneath my mask.

"Hmm. I'm not sure how to answer that." She relaxes into me. "Yes and no on both counts."

"Then he won't mind if I take a turn."

"No pussy is worth getting killed over." She stuffs her laughter into a box and remains in character, but I feel the smile and its effect on her body.

"I think you underestimate your appeal. And if your boyfriend is as terrifying as he sounds, I'm a dead man no matter what I do next." I slowly release my hold on her, leaving her standing beside the bed as I make myself comfortable. With my back supported against the headboard, I scooch toward the center and begin rubbing my cock. "So, I might as well enjoy myself."

"Take the mask off." Her eyes shift down my body as she bites her bottom lip.

I kind of thought she might like watching.

"And make it easier for your murderous boyfriend to find me? No thank you." I stifle a laugh as I begin pumping my fist.

"Take off the mask, and I'll behave." Her voice is sweet but pleading.

"It's too late for that. Plus, you've made it clear that you're not interested."

"Yes, I am." She kneels on the bed beside me and takes hold of my wrist, bringing my hand to a stop. When her eyes return to my face, the candlelight catches in her pupils and sets me ablaze. "I don't want to have sex with the Goblin King. Or Jareth Cole. I want *you*."

"And what if I'm not enough?" I know she wants things I can't provide on my own.

"Please, take it off, Jax. I'm sorry I asked you to

wear it." She strips off her tank top and slips out of her shorts, matching my nakedness.

"I'm sorry I threatened to call for Riley this morning." She straddles my waist.

"And I'm sorry I offered to go with the twins last night." She grips onto my shoulder as she eases herself down my cock.

"I don't want them." Her head drops back as she seats my full length inside her. "I only want you."

Unhooking the clasp on the back of the mask, I free it from my face and toss it to the floor, wanting to rid it from her eyesight. Then, I wipe the sweat from my brow and run a hand through my messy hair, hoping any flaws will be softened by the darkness.

"I know." I let my hands trail over her body, lingering in the places I know she likes to be touched.

If she's sore from last night and our time together this morning, she's kind enough not to let it show. Lex doesn't hold back. She rides my cock like *too much of a good thing* is a foreign concept.

With one hand, I take hold of her neck, applying steady pressure to the sides, while using my other hand to guide the movement of her hips. Of all the ways I've seen her, I think this might be my favorite. I pull her in for a kiss, needing to taste her lips.

"Goddamn, I love you." It practically comes out in a growl.

She pulls back and quirks a smile. "How much?"

"Enough that I know I never want to lose you." I lean forward and kiss her again.

"So, a tiny bit then? Just enough to keep me around."

If I could manage it, I would shuffle us around and roll Lex onto her back so I could properly rail her clear into tomorrow, but I'm stuck like a turtle on its back, and she is the radiant sun baking me into terrapin pies on the pavement.

"There's nothing tiny about me or my feelings for you." I thrust my hips upward, and she moans. "Eighteen hours or a few thousand lifetimes, it doesn't matter."

"And why's that?" Lex grinds against me in a spiral.

"Because my love for you is beyond measure." Lust might play a part in it, but that barely scratches the surface.

She falls forward with a laugh, tucking her face into my neck as she settles her head against my shoulder. "You're too damn good at that."

"At what?"

"Saying everything I want to hear. How will I ever know when you're telling the truth?"

"If it comes out of my mouth and is directed at you, it's the truth. Always. Every time. Without fail. I have no cause to lie to you, and I won't give myself a reason." I wrap my arms around her and squeeze. "It doesn't serve me to hurt you."

If Lex wants me to lie to her, I can't do it. That will be the one and only time I say no. I'm pretty open-minded and can go along with any fantasy she's willing to share, but roleplay isn't the same as deception. I could never keep the truth from her, or knowingly upset her and then lie to save my ass. The guilt would eat me alive from the inside out.

"Why don't we take a break and eat our lunch

before it gets cold?" I suggest. Emotions are running high, and maybe it's a bit too much.

"Yeah, we could do that. Or you could fuck me from behind and finish what we started." She says it like a matter of fact, leaving me no space for a retort.

Not that I have anything to say beyond, "sounds good to me."

We quickly reposition ourselves on the bed, and within seconds, Lex is fully surrendered to my control.

Surely, this is what she wanted all along.

CHAPTER 49
ALEXIS

I settle onto the couch in the hoodie and sweats I borrowed from Kade this morning. Hopefully, he realizes I have no intention of returning them, and he all but signed over ownership the second he let me wear them home.

From my seat in the living room, I can hear him in the kitchen, opening and closing cabinets and drawers, clearly looking for something he's yet to locate.

"Do you require assistance?" I call out.

"Nope. I've got it under control." He sounds confident, so I leave him to do his thing. "I'm getting the lay of the land, so to speak."

A moment later, he walks in carrying two plates of steak, potatoes, and some of the longest string beans I've ever seen. He sets one on the table and hands me the other.

"I need to grab your drinks." He's out of the room and back again before I can offer to help.

Pulling my legs up and crossing them in front of me, I use the makeshift table to set down my plate and accept a soda from Kade's hand. He jostles the other glasses a bit, and I watch with held breath as the liquid curls into waves like a miniature ocean. Caught in panic, time seems to stretch and slow, but eventually he's able to leave the pair of waters on the table without spilling a single drop. The delivery is clunky, but thoughtful.

"This steak smells incredible." I set my soda on the table and lift the plate to my nose. I'm no culinary mastermind, but I know an expertly seasoned and perfectly cooked cut of meat when I see one. "Where'd you order from?"

Kade took the time to cut everything into bite-sized strips, so all I need is a fork.

"This is our official Seventy-Two South redo, since we never got around to ordering dinner." He angles his body slightly toward me, as though I'm more entertaining than anything that might light the television screen.

"You went all the way downtown to get us lunch?" The gesture is more significant than he realizes when held in comparison with my past. I place a hand on his leg and tilt my upper body to the right, hoping that he'll kiss me. "Thank you."

"Well, I also stopped by the lot to unfuck my office, but I was thinking of you the entire time." When he leans in to kiss me, my lips are pulled tight in laughter, and he winds up sharing a romantic smooch with my teeth.

Last night was amazing. Even the awkward moments were incredible. I can't thank Riley enough for asking me to meet his friends. When picking out an outfit and applying my best attempt at flirty makeup, I hadn't accounted for the improbable possibility of falling in love. And yet, here we are.

I owe Riley one last heartfelt apology that will likely come in the form of an email or a bottle of scotch. And to the other couples, I owe my gratitude. Without the cheerleading section, I might have bailed early in the evening or shrunk quietly into the background.

I'm still not convinced I was ever the rose between two thorns. At best, I was the shiny quarter, flipped to determine their fate. Or perhaps I was the paper the squares were written on.

I reach into the front pocket of my newly acquired hoodie and remove the stack of twenties I discovered shortly after driving home.

Setting the bills on the coffee table, I retract my hand without a word.

"If that's my payment for coming here to have sex with you, you can keep it." He delivers the line with a straight face, and I can't tell if he's joking or serious. "I'm not fully convinced you got off."

I didn't, but that doesn't mean I wasn't enjoying myself.

"Seriously, I think you're probably the only guy in a thirty-mile radius that cares about things like that."

Kade laughs around a mouthful of steak before swallowing. "Was that the distance setting on your dating profile?"

I roll my eyes and quirk a grin. "Maybe. But it's gone now. I can grab my phone and show you."

Mid-thirties Mingle sent an email to confirm my cancellation request and a short questionnaire about my experience. I was happy to report no longer being single, even if I hadn't technically met Kade through their service.

"You don't have to prove anything. I trust you. But I did want to ask about this boyfriend of yours." Kade overfills his fork with food before shoving it into his mouth. Given our size difference, I'm not sure how I'll properly implement the Heimlich maneuver when he eventually chokes.

His eating habits have me mildly concerned, but other than that…

"He's pretty great. What is it you wanna know?" This conversation might seem strange to some, considering Kade and my mystery boyfriend are one and the same, but it all makes sense to me.

"You made him sound dangerous. Are you sure you can trust him?"

Him being Kade.

Are you sure you can trust me?

That's what he's truly asking.

"I'm as sure as I can be, but only time will tell." I could fudge my answer and sing his praises, insisting there is no room for doubt, but neither of us can guarantee what happens in the future. So much of the path forward is outside of our control. "I trust he's a good person even if he does bad things."

"You know, I'm not as morally grey as you make me out to be. I'm starting to think you might be disappointed when you find out I actually pull cars out of ditches."

A laugh crinkles my nose. "No. I'm happy to hear that's the case."

Some things are better kept in books.

"I don't want you to be bored." He sets our plates on the table and pulls me onto his lap.

Kade thinking I could ever be bored with a man who's willing to wear a mask and pretend to break into my house for some afternoon sexy time is utterly laughable. If he brought fast-food tacos, knocked on the front door, and gave me a kiss, I'd still be over the moon. He could send me an afternoon text, talking about his day, or call to ask me about my latest project. We could curl up in bed, under a blanket, and watch a movie. Or simply sit beside each other in the front seat of my car, parked in a lot, no place special.

The who is what's important. Being with him is where my interest lies. What we do and where we go is relevant only because we're together.

"As fun as it is to have a night out on the town, this right here, having lunch together on the couch, is my favorite kind of date."

While I'm under no delusion that life will be perfect, I know I've found my person.

"I'm still not sure how we ended up here." The way Kade holds me in his arms tells me all I need to know.

I'm safe with him.

Safe enough to let my guard down. Safe enough to have a voice and share my thoughts. Safe enough to be myself. And safe enough to joke around.

"You won a bet, remember?" I snuggle into his embrace, happy to call this newfound, yet oddly familiar feeling home.

I'm not here for the money or the house or the lifetime supply of free towing. I don't want or need a prize package to sweeten the deal. I'm not only here for the good times or a short time or the time we spent rewriting our history. I'm here because it feels like where I'm meant to be. Like fate. Or destiny. With a little dash of luck.

"I consider those shared victories. And when *we* gamble, it's winner takes all."

The End

UNTIL
TIME
STANDS
STILL

MOSH PIT MEET CUTE

My hand tightens on the railing of the makeshift barricade as I glance over my shoulder, mentally preparing for the gothic brigades converging on my location. They file into the mosh pit one after the next, donning the same neon green wristband. I imagine the horror that vibrant hue must bring to their dark little souls and a sly smile lights my face.

I love music, but I've never invested enough of myself into one genre to make it my identity. Growing up in a home with parents still obsessed with 90's era rock music, my black t-shirts all came with a splash of color. Nirvana, Soundgarden, Nine Inch Nails, and Tool wrote the lullabies my mother sang to me. Those bands and a handful of others comprised every playlist, becoming the soundtrack of my youth.

The mummer of sixty thousand voices floods the arena as my unnoticed eyes move from one face to the next, catching each mid-conversation, until I'm the one who's caught.

A man.

No, strike that.

An absolutely gorgeous specimen of a man holds my gaze as a ragged breath stutters over my parted lips. He quirks a grin and winks. Actually winks. And I'm not sure if I should be embarrassed, annoyed, or tumbling head over heels in love, but goddamn, I'm ready for all of it.

I can't say how long we look at each other. It could be a fraction of a second or the collective length of several minutes. Time is relative. He holds me steady, stunned into silence, as the arena and its patrons fade into the foggy edges of my perceived notice. If it weren't for my hand gripping the rail, I fear I might float away, caught in a stiff breeze and carried off to sea like a runaway birthday balloon.

A guitar chord sings out on stage and the waiting crowd surges forward, filling in the minimal pockets of remaining space and breaking the spell. Soundcheck drum beats *tap tap tap. Boom boom boom.* "Check one. Check one." A heavily tattooed man barks into the mic at center stage before moving to his left. *Bow bum bumm bum bummm.* The bass guitar vibrates in my chest as the strings are struck in measured time.

I set my stance and tighten my grip on the metal bar, using both hands to lock in my position. This isn't my first concert and I'm well aware of the routine. The microphones and instruments all need to be tested. After which, a sustained moment of silence will stretch into what feels like forever as the anticipation builds to its maximum, sold-out capacity. And then the lights will drop into darkness. The waiting crowd will buzz with barely contained energy while the band readies themselves at the unseen edges of the stage.

Eternity exists within the span of a single moment.

Already, strangers begin to push and strain, all jockeying for a better position. The man behind me stuffs an arm into the narrow gap between my shoulder and the person next to me, touching my hand as he fumbles for the metal bar. I shudder at the unwelcome contact and he uses my recoil to his advantage, wedging himself in further.

Ratcheting up the pressure, his booted foot comes down on the thin canvas of my slip-on shoe and I have half a mind to elbow him in the face. Only, I'm here alone. And while I may be fully within my rights to defend myself, that's easier said than done.

The growing tension between us mounts as I attempt to remain firmly planted in place. My knuckles shine white under the strain, visible even in the dim light. I make the mistake of sucking in a deep breath, only to choke on the stench of beer, cigarettes, and male perspiration.

The first band hasn't even taken the stage and already the bully next to me is sweating like a pig on a hot summer day.

Oh, what I wouldn't give for a Dwane *The Rock* Johnson-sized boyfriend right about now. I doubt Mr. Pushy Pete Stinky Breath would be so bold if I had two hundred and sixty pounds of muscle wrapped around me.

I lean into the uninvited stranger, making it clear I

will not cave to his silent demands, and mumble under my breath, "Fucking asshole."

I'm not one of those women who garner any delusion about my strength, or lack thereof. I acknowledge this man's ability to overpower me and fully recognize my surroundings. Perhaps I am out of my depth, struggling to stay front-row in the mosh pit of the hottest ticket in town, but I don't care. I got here before he did and I'm determined to watch the show from this vantage point.

Normally, a venue would remain half-empty during the opening act, but the popularity of Miss Fortune has skyrocketed in recent months and nearly every seat is occupied. The all-girl pixie metal group has taken the internet by storm, and one might argue Orc Horde should be opening for them, instead of the other way around.

Seeing the fierce fairies take the stage bolsters my feminine ego. If these ladies can carve out a place for themselves in the testosterone-fueled world of heavy metal music, then surely, I can exude enough confidence to exist in this space.

The waiting masses cheer triumphantly as the stage

lights color the scene in blue and green, and a bold spotlight shines in white.

"Alright Cleveland, you know what to do. Let's fucking go!" The drummer shouts into her mic before smashing her sticks against a series of drum heads and cymbals. The rapid percussion sets the tone, as the bass and guitar follow suit.

Verses bellowed in sixteen bars light the fuse, but it's the chorus that nearly blows the stadium apart. The eruption of movement churns the bodies behind me as limbs flail and voices chant in unison.

I adjust my stance to counterbalance the thumping at my back while keeping pressure focused on my side. It's clear this mosh pit is not for the faint of heart, and we haven't even gotten through the first song. I do my best to ignore the asshole beside me but he makes no effort to reciprocate.

When his initial attempts to move me yield little success, he takes his abuse a step further and digs his elbow into my ribs. The steady increase of pressure has me questioning my choices, and wondering how far he's willing to take things. Is this guy prepared to crack a rib in order to conquer my territory?

I'm on the verge of tears, about to swallow my pride, admit defeat, and relocate to the back when the pain vanishes and Mr. Pushy Pete is dragged off the rail and swallowed by the pit.

Relief momentarily drowns my other senses, and I loosen my grip. I hadn't noticed, but now that I've relaxed, I realize I was fighting with every fiber of my being to preserve my slice of the rail. My toes were clenched, my muscles tight, and my forearms burning. It took everything in me to withstand the ebb and flow of the crowd while fending off one stupid boy.

I'm not sure I have it in me to endure another three hours of physical torture.

As if on cue, and perhaps sensing my weakness, muscular arms bracket my frame as tattooed hands rest on either side of mine. Another man has come to pillage my treasured location, and this one is even bigger. The song ends and I seize the seconds of silence to turn and issue my resignation. I know my limits, and even if I could hold onto my spot, I wouldn't be able to enjoy the show if I'm busy fighting for my life.

"I'm not gonna wrestle you for…" My submission dies away as my line of sight connects with his face.

"Well shit, I'm a little disappointed to hear you say that." He issues me a self-assured grin and tops it off with a wink. "Enjoy the show, princess. I've got you."

Never. Not once in my entire life has a man winked at me, and this sexy bastard has done it twice in the span of ten minutes. I scoff at his use of the word *princess* but do as I'm told and turn my attention toward the stage.

In preparation for the show, I downloaded the new album, printed out the lyrics, and researched the meaning of each song. I had thought the ladies of Miss Fortune were beautiful in their promotional photos, but in person, they're intensely dynamic and unquestionably stunning. Every woman in the place is probably feeling a little bi curious, and it's no wonder the men of the mosh pit are so desperate to increase their proximity.

The second song on their setlist is one of my favorites and I quickly lose myself in the vicious melody. "Faith, Trust, and Pixie Dust" is a three-minute *Peter Pan* retelling from Tinkerbell's point of view. It's bratty and vengeful and ultimately quite heartbreaking. I belt out each line, unconscious of the tears welling in my eyes.

When it's over, I blot the unfallen droplets with the collar of my t-shirt, careful to avoid smudging my makeup.

I've been single for the last two years, but prior to that I was hopelessly obsessed with my childhood best friend turned on-again-off-again boyfriend. For a long time, I thought our future was set in stone and guided by a love written in the stars, but it turned out to be nothing more than dust. More times than I care to count, I sat patiently waiting on the back burner while he prioritized the fleeting whims of girls he'd only recently met. Just once, I wanted to feel like the only woman in the room who mattered, but I was always a last resort.

Thankfully, the next song yanks me from the edge before I can slip into a downward spiral of regret. "A Penny for Your Sleep" is about the dangers of being a tooth fairy. Each song is paired with a mini-movie played on a series of televisions carefully arranged in predetermined locations. Currently, there's a night sky nymph cast in starlight, hovering over the drummer's left shoulder.

Before long, a classically trained string quartet accompanies the band on stage as they move seamlessly through what remains of their set. But of course, they save their most popular song for last.

The swarm of strangers surrounding me lose their minds once they register the first line. "Hallucinations" is a haunting tale of death spurred on by the green fairy. Every time I hear the lyrics I wonder if absinthe was really as dangerous as people claimed, or if it was simply a convenient excuse. Certainly, the wickedness of man has always existed.

It's so easy to get lost in music.

When the song ends and the set is over, I register how sore my legs are from dancing and how dry my throat feels after singing at the top of my lungs for forty-five minutes straight. I look down at the rail and notice the tattooed hands resting on either side of mine, have not moved an inch.

On the back of one hand is an old-fashioned clock face and the words *until time stands still*. My eyes trail along the cords of muscle comprising his thick forearm, over the defined bicep stretching the sleeve of his black cotton t-shirt, across the ridge of his hardened shoulder, until landing on the tattoo that grips his throat. I squint and intensify my gaze, taking in the intricate details of the black and gray mandala design I'm certain I've seen before.

Only when he dips his head to meet my eyes do I realize I've been staring.

"Hi." A single word is all I'm able to muster.

His undivided attention locks on me as seconds pass in unhurried silence.

It's funny the way the mind works. I'm conscious of the reality encasing me in a bubble of security, while the awareness of alternate scenarios play out at the edges of my thoughts.

I gently touch his shoulders, allowing my fingers to explore as my hands fall to his waist, before wrapping my arms around him and pressing my cheek to his chest. I pull back slightly. Just enough so I can look up and see him smiling. He leans in closer by bending his elbows until I'm trapped between his impressive physique and the unflinching metal railing. My lips part and my eyes close.

I want him to kiss me like he has a million times

before. I want to know he's mine and I'm his, and I want everyone else to know it too.

But his kiss never comes because he isn't pressing me snuggly against the rail. In fact, he hasn't moved. He's simply standing there, staring at me. A blue-eyed devil comes to claim my soul.

Fearful he might have seen the fantasy playing out behind my eyes, I open my mouth and allow the first thing that pops into my head to come tumbling out. "Thanks for saving my ass."

Although the words were unplanned, my appreciation is genuine. Not a single person touched me after he arrived, leaving me free to enjoy the band. Although, now that I think about it, not a single person touched me, including him. He locked his body around me like a steel cage but never grazed a single hair on my body.

I should be thankful he's not some creep looking for a cheap feel, but mostly I'm disappointed. He was merely being nice, and I mistakenly assumed he was flirting. What I took as genuine interest was no more than a one-sided attraction.

No wonder it felt familiar.

"You were doing pretty well on your own, but that guy crossed the line when he elbowed you and I couldn't let that stand." His eyes narrow as though he's trying to read my thoughts. "But I guess I sort of invaded your dance space without an invitation."

I huff out a small laugh before responding. "Considering you're the only reason I had space to dance, I'm willing to forgive the intrusion."

"I can leave if you'd like." His arms drop to his sides as panic tightens my chest.

"No!" I reach forward and catch his wrist as my false confidence disappears into the ether. "Wait."

He looks down at the point of contact and then back to my face, a playful smirk pulling his lips into a lopsided grin.

"You can stay." I release his wrist and nervously stuff my hands into my pockets. "I mean, obviously, you can do whatever you want, but… you're officially invited to stay. If you want to."

My awkward attempt at flirting reeks of desperation and the part of me who knows better curses my pitiful dating history.

The problem with slipping into a relationship with a guy you've known your whole life is that it's easy. Our mothers were best friends, so our future nuptials had been assumed since birth. Peter was always there. He was the first kid to arrive at my birthday parties and the last to leave. We'd spend holidays together and went on shared family vacations. He was even allowed to spend the night, which led to several *firsts*.

We dated all through high school and college. Or rather, I thought we did. In hindsight, the word *girlfriend* meant little more to him than *my friend who's a girl*. So, while I remained committed to the promises we made on summer days in my treehouse, he went off and did all the things a person is supposed to do in their twenties.

"Sorry." The embarrassment burns my cheeks as I turn away.

I've been to dozens of concerts alone and it's always the same. I start the evening on a high, excited to experience music in its purest form, only to wind up depressed. No matter the venue or genre I'm always the odd man out, surrounded by happy couples exchanging loving glances and affectionate embraces.

Being single sucks.

I plop my elbows down on the rail a bit too aggressively, causing a spike of pain to shoot through my arms as my face drops into my hands. I thought by this point in my life I'd be married, or at least in a committed relationship. It was all mapped out. I was supposed to count on my best friend. We were going to build a life together. But I'm twenty-five and single, and per his post on social media this morning, Peter is engaged to the love of his life.

"Fuck!" The word comes out with more force than necessary, but I can't be bothered to care. What does it matter? I don't even know why I'm still standing here. I should give up my spot and head home. I saw the band I came here to see, made an awkward fool of myself, and scared off the first guy who'd made any effort to notice me. I should call it a night.

"Can I get two of those?" An arm brushes past me and rests atop my shoulder.

I look out from behind my hands to see a man with the cooler exchange the twenty-dollar bill suspended in front of me for two bottles of ice-cold water. I'm so thirsty, their sudden appearance feels like a tease. Like a dangling carrot driving me forward. I want to dunk my head in the cooler full of ice and drown in refreshment. Anything to cool my cheeks, quench my thirst, and end my evening early.

In my rush to get here I forgot to stop for cash, and what I did have was barely enough to cover the parking fee. Now I'm doomed to die of dehydration.

The weight of the arm retracts and I watch in agony as the bottles disappear over my shoulder.

I should've stayed home, in bed, with a pint of ice cream… but ice cream in bed makes me think of Peter and the stupid sleepovers we had as kids.

"If you need something stronger, we can order from the bar and have it delivered. This venue has an app for that."

A single bottle of water reappears in front of me.

I hesitate for a split second, but my thirst gets the better of me. The bottle is cold against the heat of my palm, and I absorb the sensation as my fingers wrap around the container. Unfortunately, the thin plastic has the tensile strength of tissue paper, and my secure grip causes the sides to indent as water squirts out the top.

"Oh my god. I'm so sorry." I panic and fumble with the bottle as I turn to meet his face, fully prepared to apologize again. But I lose track of the words.

He slides the soaked hand through this dark hair with a laugh. "I've never made a girl squirt before. That was a first for me."

My free hand shoots to my face as I attempt to stifle a laugh, but it's no use. The vibration rattles my spine as the sound releases from my core. I snort and snicker. The muscles over my stomach tighten as I double over in a fit of unabashed giggles. The laughter comes with no end in sight until I'm clutching the stitch that cramps my side. If I'd taken a sip of water, I'm certain it would've come spraying out my nose.

I might not have many notches on my bedpost, but that's not to say I lack experience. During my time alone, I've amassed an impressive array of various toys and sexual accouterment. And when it comes to porn, I wouldn't claim to have seen it all, but I'm certain I've encountered my fair share. Squirting it's something I've searched for, but I'd be lying if I said I'd never stumbled across it.

"I think I'm dead," The sentiment gets tacked on to what remains of a laugh as I try to regain my composure.

This perfect man cannot be real.

"It's so hot here. Does that mean we're in hell?" He looks around, as though considering the possibility.

"If we are, so be it. I'm sure I've done plenty to deserve it." Two dresser drawers stuffed full of glass dildoes and latex monster cocks will have certainly bought me a ticket, and if that's not enough, I'm sure my deleted browser history would seal my fate. "At least the company is good."

"And there's ice water." He raises his bottle in the form of a toast. "Cheers, to a well-deserved eternity together."

I tap the bottom of my plastic bottle to his and finally take a swig. The chilled liquid turns my insides to ice.

"Thanks for this." I dry the corner of my mouth with my thumb and watch his eyes track the movement. "And for everything else. Not to be weird, but… you have no idea how badly I needed this."

I motion back and forth between us.

"Is that jerk from earlier still weighing on your mind, or something else? If he hurt you…" His forehead creases as his eyebrows knit together, and it's as though he can't bring himself to complete the thought.

"No, I'm fine. It's not that. But you're certainly welcome to avenge me in the mosh pit, should you accidentally bump into him." I'm joking, of course. I hope he knows that.

"Oh, that's a given." He glances over his shoulder and scans the crowd as though he's locating his target. "Come on, tell me. You might as well get it off your chest so we can enjoy what remains of our eternity. Is it boyfriend troubles?"

I let out a long breath and debate my next move. Talking about an ex seems like a surefire way to ruin any interaction with the opposite sex. Anyone who's ever watched a rom-com or read a romance book knows that. But I don't want to make something up and get caught in a lie. No matter how bad the truth sounds, lying is always worse. And I have a sneaking suspicion he won't let this drop until I make a full confession.

"If you have a boyfriend or a husband…" He nearly chokes on the word as he glances at my left hand. "You can tell me, and I'll be on my best behavior."

"I don't have a boyfriend," I say, shaking my head. "Or a husband. I have a childhood friend turned boyfriend turned cheating ex who got engaged this morning. And I know it's stupid, but it pisses me off that I had to find out from a post online. Like I'm nobody. And it's not that I want him back, because I don't. We haven't been together in a long time and I don't miss that part… I just wish we'd never dated so I wouldn't have to lose my best friend."

I drop my eyes, shocked by my outburst and afraid of what his reaction might be. Maybe I should've lied. I could've said my dog was sick and left it at that.

"Do you need a hug?"

I nod my head as he steps closer.

"Come here." He brackets his arms around my shoulders in a loose embrace. "Is this okay?"

Initially, it's the sort of hug that feels half-hearted and I'm tempted to pull away, but the greater part of me pushes forward. What the hell? I've come this far. I might as well go all the way. Bringing my arms around his waist, I press the side of my face into his chest. The second I commit, he matches my energy and pulls me closer.

Turns out, hugs are a lot like therapy. It's easier to bare your soul to a stranger, knowing you won't have to see them again tomorrow.

I don't let go, and neither does he. And after a while, I sink in deeper as he slowly backs me against the metal railing. The hand cupping the back of my head twists into my hair as a slight tug angles my face upward. When I open my eyes, his lips are dangerously close to mine.

"Are you going to kiss me?" The question is barely audible over the booming drumbeat of my heart, but somehow, he hears me.

"Definitely." He smiles and readjusts the angle of my face before planting a kiss on the top of my head.

My cheeks flush with embarrassment and I push back against him. It's bad enough that I jump to conclusions and ask stupid questions. The last thing I need is him teasing me. I give his arm a playful smack in mock annoyance and attempt to play off my awkward blushing.

This is silly. The guy is literally a stranger and I'm over here staring into his eyes with lust-fueled longing and practically begging him to kiss me. As if he would want to.

I swallow the lump in my throat with a sip of water and turn toward the stage, suddenly fascinated by the second band's stage crew.

"Does your ex still follow you on social media?" He slips into position behind me, only this time he presses himself firmly against my back and grips the railing so his hands are flush with mine.

"Yeah. But I meant what I said. I'm not trying to get back with him. I've been single for a long time." Maybe he thinks I'm still in love with my ex and that's why he didn't kiss me. "Can't we just have fun together and forget he exists?"

"This will be fun."

I look over my shoulder in an effort to read his expression, but in doing so I miss what's happening directly in front of me. His focus is on something else, or someone.

"Do you trust me?" He glances down at me with a cocky grin.

Whatever he's got in mind, it's bound to be interesting, but the question remains. Do I trust him?

"I trust you until you give me a reason not to." I smile and shake my head, having no idea what I've agreed to.

"That's my girl."

His words send an electric charge surging through my limbs and buzzing in my core. Without even knowing it, he set me ablaze. With three little words, he did the one thing I've always wanted and never experienced. Even if he didn't mean it, it doesn't matter. I'm willing to take what I can get.

As much as I love the view from my feminist high horse, I should probably relinquish the reins.

There's something so unbelievably sexy about being claimed by a man who looks like he could fuck the ability to walk straight out of me. My breath hitches at the thought and I bite my bottom lip.

His gaze lingers on the movement until his eyes shift to something behind me. "Would you mind taking a picture of us? It's kind of an important night."

I turn to see who he's talking to and find a woman standing in the narrow passage reserved for security. A moment ago, I saw her on stage taking photos of the crowd. I guess I'm not the only one drawn in by his charm and good looks.

He types a four-digit password into his phone and clicks on the camera icon.

I wasn't mentally prepared for an impromptu photo shoot with a would-be dark romance cover model, but here I am. And I did agree to trust him. I also agreed to have fun, and I suppose there's no time like the present to start paying up.

I fluff my hair and tilt my head before remembering the tears flooding my eyes during the first set. "Oh shit. Does my makeup look okay?"

She looks around the phone to give me an encouraging thumbs up and a smile.

"You look beautiful." He brushes my hair to one side and kisses my neck. "Now relax, and pretend you like me."

The edges of my vision blur and the arena falls into silence as his fingers settle against my neck and his thumb brushes across my bottom lip. "I do like you."

He leans in closer and I feel his breath as it passes between us. "I like you too."

"Well, goddamn. You two are fucking hot. If you post any of these online make sure you tag the show. These photos are fire." She hands me the phone before using a black-painted box to hop back on stage. I follow her fluid movement, impressed by the gymnast-like quality of her vault.

Before I can look down and see anything, he snatches the phone from me and holds out his empty hand.

"What the hell? You aren't even going to let me see them?" My faux exasperation lacks bite and my smile gives me away.

"You can see them tomorrow. For now, I need your phone." He dips his fingers into my back pocket and retrieves the cell phone I recognize. "What platforms does your ex follow you on?"

And with that, the pieces fall into place.

"I don't know. All of them, I guess. Are you seriously doing this? The guy couldn't be bothered to give a shit while we were together. Why would he care now?"

"He'll care because you're mine." His words snap like a rubber band. "You're no longer the little girl sitting home, waiting for him to text. Your ex is finally going to come face to face with the fact he fucked up and you moved on."

He holds the phone out to me. "Unless you haven't moved on?"

I tap the home button to light the screen and press it a second time to allow access to my phone. It never occurred to me that a strange man might someday want full, unrestricted access to my phone, so I never thought to password-protect my device.

"Okay, but…" I momentarily rethink my willingness to play along and stretch onto my tiptoes, hoping to see my screen. "Don't make it a pregnancy announcement. That's not a joke to some people, and I don't want to give my mother a heart attack."

He laughs and holds the phone higher. "If I posted that, my mom would be planning our wedding."

"Jokes on her. Who needs a wedding when we've already committed to an eternity?" I cheers the air with my bottle and take a small sip. I'm trying to drink it slowly so I don't end up having to pee half a dozen times before the end of the show.

"Good point. Although I do like the idea of putting a baby in you."

His comment makes me cough and sputter as I pull in a sharp breath and droplets of ten-dollar water are sucked into my lungs. One hand reflexively covers my mouth while the other makes the universal sign for *I'm gonna need a minute*. Twenty minutes ago I was suffering the effects of thirst and now I'm on the verge of drowning. Maybe this really is hell.

Unfortunately, there's no time for dying. The waiting crowd shifts as bodies heave forward indicating the second band is about to take the stage. I grip the rail knowing better than to be caught ill-prepared, and watch as the blue and green stage lights shift into vibrant red and yellow.

I don't know much about the next group other than they dress in costume and classify their style as brutal orc metal. Whatever that means.

"I turned it off so you aren't tempted to peek." He brushes the back of his hand parallel to my spine before depositing the phone into my pocket. "I want you here with me."

Again, his words let loose an electrical storm of Mothra-sized butterflies in the vast cavern of my insides. I've never had a man want me, whether for a night or an eternity.

"Tell me what you did and I promise I won't peek." I sound like I'm trying to be cute, but the effect is unintentional. This man has me ready to beg, and I'm not even sure he realizes.

"I didn't lie, if that's what you're worried about. I simply made sure we were mutuals and then posted the photos from my page. You, being the dear you are, shared them."

"So, we're friends now! Oh goodie." I clasp my hands together, and bat my eyelashes, doing my best impression of a fairy-tale princess.

"Well, technically we're followers, and I may or may not have revised your profile to reflect your updated relationship status." His arms wrap around my waist as he pulls me closer.

"I thought you said you didn't lie." There's a slight hint of longing in my voice and a pinch of optimism but it's overshadowed by nervousness and a desperate need for him to kiss me.

"I didn't." He looks at me, seeming both hungry and tentative as if waiting for me to play long and fearful I won't. Or maybe I'm projecting my feelings onto him. He maintains a level of distance even in his nearness that's impossible to ignore.

I want to lose myself in these moments with him, but it's hard to let down my walls when he still feels like a stranger. Albeit a stranger I've known my whole life, but a stranger nonetheless.

"If we're doing this, will you at least tell me your name?" I want to add a playful jab about his refusal to kiss me but I'm afraid it might be too much.

As he holds me in his arms all traces of his self-assured cockiness melt away and I can almost hear his thoughts as they take shape behind his eyes. *Can I trust you?*

"You don't have to tell me if…" Initially, I didn't think I was asking for much, but maybe it's more than he wants to give. After all, what's more personal than a name?

"Cole," he says, cutting me off as I backpedal.

"Like Nate King or 'Ol King?" I joke without thinking and I want to smack myself for being stupid, but he only laughs.

"Oddly enough, King Cole was my nickname in high school." He releases his grip on my waist and grabs the bar behind me.

"Prom or Homecoming?" I venture a guess.

"Both, actually. I was annoyingly popular." He smiles, and I can almost see the outline of his crown.

"Why am I not the least bit surprised?"

In school I was a bit of a floater, drifting between cliques, never standing out as part of one or another. Peter was the annoyingly popular guy in our high school and I always felt invisible standing next to him, like his light didn't extend to the dark corner where he kept our relationship hidden.

The crowd pushes in around us as the band takes the stage, but Cole's attention remains. The way he looks at me, I can't imagine he's ever allowed anyone to feel invisible in his presence. He leans forward and presses his lips to my neck before loudly whispering in my ear, "You're the queen I waited for."

I shake my head and roll my eyes because it's a cheesy line designed to make me melt. But I also eat it up.

"I thought I was your princess?" I'm not sure how he's doing it, but this man's got me straightening my tiara.

"You are." He lifts one hand to cup my face and I lean into his touch. "Now trust me to protect you and watch the show."

I see myself lifting on tip-toes to kiss him, but my feet remain flat on the floor. This eternity with him will only last a couple more hours, and I don't want to ruin it.

I turn toward the stage and find the rhythm as he presses himself against me. The thumb of his left hand brushes over mine, before the tips of his fingers sweep up and down my arm. It tickles at first, but it also feels incredible.

How the hell am I going to let him go?

Cole sings along with the chorus as waves of churning bodies crash against him. I feel the vibrations as they pass through his core, and I wonder how he can remain steady while braced only by one hand. Surely, he'd rather be out there, mixing it up in the pit. Not sidelined here with me as a human shield.

After a few songs, I glance up and catch him scanning the mass of people behind us. "If you want to get in there, you should go."

He looks at me with furrowed brows as though he's working through his options and questioning whether or not this is a test.

"I'll be fine," I reassure him, in case my safety was the concern keeping him locked in place.

He empties his pockets and begins stuffing their contents into mine. His phone, wallet, and keys test the limit of my belt, and I'm afraid if I try to move my weighted pants will drop around my ankles. He then finishes what remains of his water and crushes the bottle.

"Are you sure you'll be okay without me?" He means it as a simple question but it's become more complicated with every lingering touch.

I don't want to lie or say too much, so I bite my bottom lip and nod my head. I don't know anymore if I'll be okay without him. Not merely right now, but later when he finally says goodbye for good. I know it's an impossible ask, but I don't want this concert to end.

Why must this eternity exist in the span of only one night?

Cole kisses the top of my head before turning me away from him and securing my hands to the railing. The stage lights burn like fire as the band of orcs bellow growling lines of death metal chorus. "I'll be close by if you need me."

He brushes his hand along my arm and kisses my shoulder before disappearing into the maelstrom of swirling bodies.

I glance over my shoulder to watch him, and my anxiety feels slightly silly. He's only going into a mosh pit, not departing for battle. And, clearly, he intends to come back after leaving me with his personal effects. But still, I can't help but worry.

His phone buzzes wildly in my pocket, and I'm half-tempted to check it, but it isn't my place to be nosey.

I catch a glimpse of him helping someone who's fallen and my heart flutters. Cole is adorably tough and I'm lucky to have met him. In the few short hours we've known each other, he's shown me that not everyone is an asshole, and I appreciate him for that.

For not knowing any of the songs, I'm surprised by how quickly I'm caught in the rhythm. It's only when strong hands appear at my waist and light kisses pepper my neck and shoulder that I remember how long it's been since he was last near. Cole checks in between each track but doesn't stay until the last.

He tucks himself in behind me, sticky and shirtless, as he belts out the lyrics to the final song.

After the band exits the stage, I take one last sip of my water and hand him what's left of the bottle. It's not exactly cold, but it's better than nothing.

He swallows half of what remains in a single gulp and pours the rest over his head.

"You're the best," He crows while lifting me off my feet and crushing me against his chest.

I squeal in a mix of delight and horror. "Oh my god, you're so sweaty!" But my cries only encourage him.

My next words are chosen more carefully and seem to have the desired effect. "Stop! You're getting me wet."

Cole sets me on the ground but holds me until I find my footing. The lust burning in his eyes is unmistakable, even to a novice like me, and I'm certain this is the time when his lips will meet mine, but he only holds me deep in his gaze.

What is he waiting for, a gold-engraved invitation?

We stand frozen like statues, solidified in an extended moment until the phone buzzing in my pocket shatters the effect. I take a minute to retrieve his belongings and I hand him the items one by one, careful to return each in the same condition in which I received it. I feel lighter once they're gone but I miss the heaviness of their certainty.

"This was going off pretty much non-stop, but I promise I didn't look at it." Even as I hand him the phone the screen lights with an incoming message.

"Sorry about that. I should've turned it off." He slips it into his pocket without so much as a glance and takes my hand. "I was supposed to meet with my buddies an hour ago so I'm sure they've been blowing up my phone."

"Oh." The bulk of my response sticks in my throat and I stand in muted silence, unable to process everything I'm feeling.

"You should come with me." He lays the offer on the table, but I politely decline.

"I wouldn't want to intrude on your evening any more than I already have. I'm sorry I kept you from your friends. I didn't realize..." Tears sting the back of my eyes but I force a smile. "Thank you for keeping me company and indulging my mood swings. I'm sure it's not how you wanted to spend your time."

"Don't say that." He cups my face and wipes away a single tear as it rolls down my cheek.

I lean into his caress and bring my hands up to wrap around his wrist. It's selfish for me to want him to stay, and I won't make him choose.

For years I cried and pleaded with Peter, begging him to pick me, but his boys were always more important. The older we got, the less I meant to him, until eventually he started dating and I became the other woman.

"I'll always come back to you, Tinkerbell." I can still hear Peter's lies in my head. The memory of all the times I believed him makes me sick.

I pull back from Cole's touch as I push him away. "I'm sorry, this isn't because of you. It's been one of those days, you know? You should go. I'll be *fine* without you."

The sharp point of the lie lodges in my chest, and I'm certain the overwhelming pain makes my previous heartbreak pale in comparison. I try to tell myself that everything will be okay, but the compounding lies only exacerbate my torture.

"If you really won't come with me, I promise I'll come back." His continued kindness threatens to leave me broken, but only because I know I'll miss him. "It's just that I gave them my word and they're counting on me."

I dry my face and straighten my spine, recalling my ability to stand on my own. It's nice that he cares, but it isn't Cole's job to protect me. Sure. Maybe I wasn't prepared for his abrupt departure, but there would always come a point in the night when goodbye was inevitable.

"It was nice meeting you," I say with a smile, and extend my hand into the growing space between us.

He merely glowers at my offered gesture and shakes his head. "You need to quit with that shit. Not to sound like an asshole, but there's no way I'm ending this night with a fucking handshake."

"Alright." I drop my hand and lean casually against the rail, hoping to slow my racing heart and appear nonchalant. "So then, you're coming back for a proper goodbye?" I say with a wink.

Cole grips the railing on either side of me and leans close enough to turn my legs to jello. "I've wanted to kiss you all evening, but if I do it now, I know you'll leave, and I'm not ready for that to happen. If you stay right here, I promise you'll see me again. I'll come back and we'll watch the end of the show together."

"You don't have to promise me anything." I let my head drop to the side but he catches my chin.

"It's a little late for that, don't you think?" He lets out a heavy breath, as though the air in his lungs is weighted. "I hadn't planned for this."

His admission makes me smile because I understand the feeling. Leading up to tonight I thought I had played out every hypothetical scenario and constructed a contingency plan for each variation. I was certain that my overthinking had prepared me for anything, but I never saw him coming.

"Please don't leave. I'll be back as soon as possible." He kisses my forehead but doesn't pull away.

"Go meet your friends." I try to push him back but he's a wall of muscle and bone. "I promise I won't lose our spot. And if for some reason you can't make it…"

"Hey, look at me. I'll always come back to you." He crushes me against his chest as we sway to the sounds of the cheering crowd. We've danced around this non-goodbye for so long the headlining band is about to take the stage.

I dip my fingers into Cole's pocket, where his phone continues its tantrum, like a spoiled child pleading for attention. I'm tempted to give his ass a squeeze but think better of it. He hasn't been inappropriate with me, and while I desperately want him to touch me, I appreciate the respect he's shown.

"Text your friends and tell them you're on your way. I'll wait here for you..." I press the phone into his hand before bringing it to my lips. Maybe it's weird for a girl to kiss the back of a guy's hand. I'm certain it is, but if I can't have his lips, I at least need this. "Until security kicks me out."

I wait for him to say something, to respond in some way, but he doesn't. We simply stand there holding on to each other, neither one of us wanting to be the first to let go. It's only when the crowd drives forward that he turns me toward the stage, kisses the top of my head, and disappears.

I'll always come back to you.

Those words replay in my head as they have so many times before, only now it's Cole's voice that I hear.

To the passive observer, I probably look like the biggest Troll Hammer fan in history. My eyes brimming with tears as the band takes the stage. If the photographer notices, I'm likely to end up on the band's website for all the world to see. Reminiscent of the days when women fainted at the sight of skinny, shaggy-haired boys named The Beatles.

The absurdity of the idea makes me laugh.

While I may not be the band's number-one fan, I do know a lot of their songs, and I'm excited when they open with one of my favorites. "Bridges" has a catchy downbeat that picks up quickly and I'm instantly swept away in the fervor. It's heavy metal music with a jaunty undertone that reminds me of pirate sea shanties.

At the conclusion of the first song, I glance behind me, half expecting to feel Cole's hand on my hip and his kiss lingering on my shoulder, but the only people I see are strangers. Disappointed, I turn back and I catch the eye of a venue security guard who's taken up residence against the stage directly in front of me. He smiles and regards me with a nod, and I'm oddly thankful that he missed the part when I was crying.

The band sounds great and their stage show is amazing, but I miss having someone to share it with. I know that wherever Cole went, it's going to take him a while to get back, but time is a luxury we no longer have. Each song feels like a countdown to the end when I'll be forced to leave with ringing ears and a shattered heart.

Lost in regret, I nearly miss the announcement.

"Welcome to the stage, straight from the sweltering depths of the forgotten realm… The Dark Goblin King!" The troll's voice rumbles in my chest, as sixty thousand people lose their minds.

The goblin king takes the stage clad in leather, armor, and a veneer custom-made to fit his face. The sight makes my skin heat, causing my hands to feel clammy. Maybe it's just the warmth from the surrounding bodies closing in on me and not my racing heart, but I feel like I'm on fire.

I follow him online, and I remember seeing videos that featured the condensed thirty-hour process it takes to complete each mask. He's never posted a photograph of his actual face, but his body is the stuff of legend. And don't even get me started on his voice. In one video, he asked his dog if she'd *been a bad girl*, after coming home to find a pillow torn open, and I nearly melted into my chair. When I tell you that this man has made me climax more times than I can count while simply existing in a pixelated two-dimensional form, it's no exaggeration.

Jareth and Troll Hammer have only collaborated on three songs, so far as I know, and I wonder if they'll play them all. I pull my eyes from the stage and scan the pit, searching the crowd for a familiar face. I can't believe he's missing this. Maybe there's still a chance, though he'll have a hell of a time making it to the front row now that the dark goblin king himself, Jareth Cole is on the stage.

I close my eyes as the instruments construct the soundtrack to the best night of my life, and imagine strong arms encasing me in a shield of personal protection. I wish I had been clever enough to embed my phone number into his contact list while he was busy mixing it up in the mosh pit. Or confident enough to let go of my past and own what I was feeling. Or maybe all I needed to be was daring enough to go with him.

Too often, I get stuck in my head, thinking I'll always be the stupid girl who wasted her time waiting for a lost boy who was never coming back to the treehouse. But enough is enough. I need to stop allowing teenage heartbreak and the poor choices of others to define who I am.

Peter Pan never deserved Tinkerbell. She would've been better off with the croc.

Fueled by heavy metal music and a burning need to nail the coffin shut, I remove the phone from my pocket and turn it on. I intend to unfollow my ex and block his number, but the sight of several thousand notifications knocks me off course.

What the hell happened?

For a moment I assume I must have been hacked, but then I see it. The source of the uproar. I swipe past the missed calls and messages from Peter, no longer interested in what he has to say. There's a series of photos capturing the image of a handsome man and a girl who looks like me, and the caption *When this eternity ends, I'll find you in the next, and every infinity thereafter. Cheers to sharing ice water in hell.*

I'm tagged in the photos and they were shared by my account, but the original post came from Jareth Cole.

My eyes shift between the face illuminated on my screen and the man on stage until once again I am caught.

The deep timbre of his voice mirrors my beating heart as Jareth leans forward and I can hear what he's saying without saying it. Beneath the lines of the refrain, on a stage in front of sixty thousand screaming fans, he's telling me *Get off your phone. I want you here with me.*

Mouthing the words *I'm sorry,* I deposit the phone back into my pocket.

In hindsight, the connection seems obvious. The tattoos, the nickname, the unflinching conviction that my ex would be jealous. "He'll care because you're mine," he'd said. I was so focused on the idea of being claimed that I never stopped to wonder about the specifics of his statement.

I sing along with the lyrics I recognize, as tingling currents of electrical energy crackle beneath my skin. The moment is surreal. My feelings from the last few hours mix with lustful fantasies from the past and the profound realization of what Jareth has done.

He's always gone to great lengths to conceal his identity. But with one post he pulled off the mask and revealed himself for all to see, and he did it for me. I look on in a mix of disbelief and awe, still unable to comprehend the blinding reality. Jareth didn't simply claim me for the night in a post that could be taken down tomorrow, and forgotten just as quickly.

He linked the two of us together and then flipped on a spotlight whose power rivaled the sun.

By the third song, people begin crowd surfing, and I momentarily see stars when a booted foot connects with the side of my head. I press my hand firmly against my temple, but the damage is done. It takes several seconds for my vision to clear, but before it does I feel strong arms around me. They are arms that feel sturdy and self-assured, but they don't feel like home.

The security guard lifts me over the fence and deposits me in the open space between the fans and the stage as crowd surfers run past, eager for an opportunity to get back out there.

"Are you okay?" He projects his voice like a megaphone and uses his bear paws to angle my face toward the stage lights, checking for signs of injury. "Your boyfriend won't be happy if I let you get hurt."

Between the band and the mass of people enthusiastically singing along, the noise in the arena is deafening, and yet I'm certain I heard him correctly.

Another security guard ushers several bodies along, pushing them in the direction of the exit, and I suppose I'm meant to follow suit. After all, this area isn't meant for fans or girls with not-so-secret crushes. I take a final glance at the stage, painfully aware that I've broken my end of the agreement. I'll never be able to get back into the spot on the rail where I promised to wait for him, and there's no way he'll find me once I'm swallowed by the crowd.

I should've said goodbye when I had the chance.

The problem with waiting for the perfect moment is that you don't recognize it until it's past.

I'm not sure where I'm headed or where I'm meant to be. The life my parents mapped out for me was little more than a quest for fool's gold, but that isn't their fault. Or mine. It isn't even my ex's fault, despite my will to blame him. We were only kids in a treehouse defending each other from invisible pirates. I loved him and he loved me the way best friends were always meant to. But unlike the characters we embodied, Peter and I grew up.

After college, he landed a job as an engineer and a position as the assistant coach for our high school football team. Peter carved out a path for himself, and now he's engaged to an elementary school teacher and in the process of buying a new home.

As for me, I took a job at the county helping families in need of assistance, joined a book club at the local library, and fell in love with a dark goblin king.

I attempt to swallow the lump in my throat as tears blur my vision, and I take a step toward the exit. But my retreat is halted.

"Where ya off to, princess?" The question ripples through the building, amplified by the arena's sound system, causing me to look toward the nearest monitor. The image of the goblin king jumping off stage plays out on the jumbotron as the music fades and the crowd falls silent.

His hands encircle my waist and I nearly collapse into his touch.

I don't know how to do this.

As much as I've craved the glow of acknowledgment, I've always shied away from the spotlight, not looking to be the center of everyone's attention. But now that I'm here on display for all to see, I'm wondering how anyone withstands the scrutiny.

The weight of his touch disappears and the onlooking crowd collectively reacts, but I don't need to glance at the monitor to know what's happened. The voices of the people next to me who recognize him from earlier in the evening call out as their hands reach forward, but security reinforces the boundary with their bodies.

I turn to meet the formidable entity behind me as time slows to a stop and I find Cole's smiling face.

"I meant what I said." His voice is no longer playing over the speaker but I catch every note. "I'll always come back to you. But next time, just come with me, okay? I fucking missed you."

I nod my head and reflect his smile, not allowing myself the space to overthink it. "I missed you too."

If hell is an eternity and eternity is a moment, let this be the hell I burn in.

He cups my face with one hand and I melt into his touch. "Now that you know who I am, do you still want to do this with me?"

"That depends..." My response seems to shake him, as though he's worried he might lose me, so I hurry to set his mind at ease. "Are you willing to wear the mask for me later, when we're alone?"

The glow of the stage light reflects in his eyes as a devilish grin rearranges his features. "Definitely."

"That's what you said about the kiss," I tease.

"Yeah, about that…" He leans in closer. "Are you with me? Like, really with me? I need to know because once I kiss you there's no going back."

Maybe I should take a moment to think about what that means, but time is a luxury my heart is unwilling to afford my brain.

I know that I want him. I want to feel protected by the certainty of his embrace. I want to bathe in the glow of his spotlight. I want to know that he's mine and I am his, and I want everyone else to know it too. I want him to kiss me for the first time like he has in every infinity, and I never want him to stop.

"I'm with you…" My arms come around his waist as I pull him closer. "Until time stands still."

I know it's a lot to promise after only a few hours, but when it's right your whole body knows.

His lips meet mine as the waiting crowd erupts, and Troll Hammer continues their set.

OTHER BOOKS BY THIS AUTHOR

Locked Away

(book one in the locked away series)

Between The Holidays

(a spicy why choose romance)

Drifting Apart

(book two in the locked away series)

Mosh Pit Meet Cute

(a short story)

CONNECT WITH ME ON SOCIAL MEDIA

If you enjoyed this book, please consider leaving a review. Word of mouth is worth its weight in gold for any indie author.

But more importantly, thank you for being a part of my story.

For information on upcoming titles and a schedule of in-person events, follow me on:

instagram.com/author_amanda_bryk

facebook.com/LockedAwaySeries

threads.net/author_amanda_bryk

goodreads.com/Amanda_Bryk

tiktok.com/author_amanda_bryk

www.ingramcontent.com/pod-product-compliance
Lightning Source LLC
Chambersburg PA
CBHW070306310726
48976CB00005B/1598